SAVAGE TRAITOR

THE SAVAGES SERIES

STELLA BRIE

Cover Design by Moonstruck Cover Design & Photography, moonstruckcoverdesign.com

Editing: Kaye Kemp Book Polishing

Proofreading: Bookish Dreams Editing

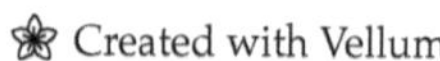 Created with Vellum

AUTHOR'S NOTE

AUTHOR'S NOTE

This book is a Reverse Harem romance, and it ends on a cliffhanger. The heroine does not have to choose between male interests. Recommended for 18+ due to mature content.

This book contains references to abuse and stalking that may be difficult for some readers. It also contains death, violence, and cursing. Please take care of yourself and read at your own discretion.

PLAYLIST

"I Ran (So Far Away)" - Hidden Citizens

"Fight Back "- NEFFEX

"Dynamite" - Native 51

"Enemies - The Score

"Twilight Zone" - Golden Earring

"Even the Score" - Native 51

"Melhor Sozinha" - Luísa Sonza

"Flowers" - Svrcina

"Get Up" (feat. Brock Monroe) - Molly Kate Kestner

"Savages" - Royal Deluxe

INSPIRATION

I'm a geek—inspired and fascinated by what is happening within our constantly evolving digital and virtual worlds. Web 3.0, the metaverse, NFTs, cryptocurrency, and things yet to come are full of endless possibilities. I feel lucky to have a front-row seat. This is my small attempt to pull a glimpse of it into our everyday lives. (Just a glimpse - the series is not pure tech or sci-fi).

This story is fiction and <u>takes liberties</u> with the current state or boundaries of technology. Some of the technology exists today, some *might* exist in the future, and the rest is *likely* pure fiction meaning it's probably made up. ;-) Enjoy!

CHAPTER 1

<u>HENLEY</u>

The alarm screams into the night, jolting me from my dreams. *Intruder.* Terror instantly floods my body. I open my eyes, but I'm unable to move. The rest of me is frozen. Fear is in control, every muscle locked down without thought or rationality. Past alarms blur with the present but they all carry the same warning. My mind fills with thoughts of him, and the shrieking alarms fade until I hear none of them. All I hear is him, whispering to me.

Is he here? My breath rushes in and out, releasing me from fear's hold. My eyes dart frantically around the tiny space, trying to locate him, but find nothing. Relief rushes over me. With his absence, the real world including the noise, filters back, eclipsing the whispers. The pounding of my heart echoes loudly in my ears, actively competing with the alarm. Struggling to think, I push against the memories and reach for the present. *Intruder. Plan. First step? Phone.*

The phone lies beside me on the bed, and I snatch it up. *Done.* Gripping my lifeline tightly in my hand, I take deep breaths in and out while my eyes sweep the bedroom again. The night light

1

plugged into the outlet casts a golden glow on the reassuringly empty room, and with my mattress and box springs sitting directly on the floor, I've eliminated the possibility of any monsters hiding under my bed. I breathe out slowly, until the fog of the past lifts.

I cautiously roll to my side and peer down into the cavernous room below. With my bed raised above the rest of the loft, I'm able to view the entire length of my home. From the kitchen to my desk, the soft lighting placed strategically throughout the open concept illuminates almost every inch of the space, and I see nothing out of the ordinary. I lie there for a few minutes, barely breathing, waiting, but nothing moves.

The empty loft, while reassuring, still doesn't explain the alarm. I slide from the soft mattress to the cold platform floor. Keeping my eyes glued to the living area below, I open the drawer of my night-stand and reach for the gun inside. My forefinger trails up the butt and around the grip until it rests alongside the trigger guard, while my thumb eases underneath. Once the two are in place, I curl the rest of my fingers around the front of the grip and slide my palm across the rough surface until I find the hold taught by my instruc-tor. Gripping it firmly, I lift it out of the drawer and bring it to my side with the muzzle pointed away.

Check the cameras. Raising the phone in my left hand, I tap on an app and bring up my security cameras. The cameras give me visuals on areas I can't see—my bathroom, the hallway in front of my entry door, and anything outside the building. My home is an industrial loft in what was once a small hat factory, but it's still a decent size building and it takes a couple of minutes to view each area.

Flicking through all the cameras, I find… nothing. Not a shadow or hint of movement. Puzzled, I slowly go through them again, scru-tinizing every millimeter of each frame, and yet, it's all clear. I rewind the cameras back thirty minutes to review the past, but no one approaches the building.

My mind sifts through the possibilities wondering if someone could have found a way to evade my cameras or if it could be a malfunction. The security system came highly recommended, and it's supposed to be the best on the market, but as I know all too well, technology isn't foolproof. I tested it extensively to make sure it would perform to my exceptionally high standards, and it passed with flying colors, but even I can't predict every scenario. This is the first time I've had an issue in four years, though, which seems odd, and "odd" is a loose thread waiting for someone to pull it.

Setting the gun and phone on the floor, I grab the leggings from the foot of the bed, pull them on, then shove my phone into the side pocket. Picking up the gun, I point it away from me and crawl over to the edge of the loft area. Aiming the gun down the ladder first, I quickly slide forward and peek over the edge. The empty rungs of the ladder stare back at me. I pull myself forward a few more inches, until I'm hanging over the ledge, to peer under the platform to the area below. My green velvet couch sits alone with only my dark grey furry throw for company.

Pushing back, I spin around and throw my leg over the ladder and place my foot on the second rung. Keeping the gun pointed away, I quickly swing my other leg over and scurry down the ladder. It only takes a few seconds, but my anxiety spikes every second my back is to the room. I hadn't factored in how vulnerable I'd be climbing down, and I make a mental note to replace the ladder with stairs.

My foot touches the cold wood below, and I scramble to drop the remaining foot beside it. Widening my stance, I bring the gun up, place my left hand under the butt for support, and quickly scan the condo again. When I find nothing, I take in a deep breath and slowly let it out. And another. After the third one, I think I've got my nerves under control again, although my hands are still trembling.

The bathroom is the only area inside the condo I can't see, and while the cameras didn't show anyone in there, I know how easily they can be hacked. Stepping quietly, I make my way over to the doorframe and stop. With the gun out in front of me, I square up behind it and step around the doorframe. An empty green tiled shower, small vanity, and bare toilet greet me. I roll my shoulders and blow out a huge sigh of relief.

Slumping against the door, I lower the gun until it's back by my side and pointing toward the floor. My arm shakes with the need to put it on the counter, but I refuse to let my guard down until I know why the alarm is going off. The mirror over the sink catches a ghost in its reflection.

Dark blue eyes filled with fear stare back at me from a face almost absent of color. Even my lips are white from being pressed tightly together. The only other color is the bold pink of my hair. I hate this look. It pisses me off to see the fear again. I tighten my jaw.

Shoving away from the bathroom door, I stalk over to my desk and tap the button to shut off the alarm. Nothing happens. I tap it a few more times. It refuses to turn off. Glancing behind me one last time, I carefully set the gun on the desk and drop into the chair.

My fingers are stiff from gripping the gun, so I flex them a few times to get the blood circulating again. Once they're limber, I fire off a sequence of keystrokes until the log file from the security system pops up on the screen. Reading through the list of recent actions, everything seems normal. It ran through its regularly scheduled built-in systems check and everything passed, which means it's not likely to be a malfunction. Biting my lip, I keep reading until I find something interesting.

A half hour ago, this computer sent my security system a series of commands, but it ignored them because they were out-of-the-box, default commands programmed by the manufacturer. My system wouldn't recognize them because I'd replaced them with custom commands of my own to add another layer of security. My precautions paid off. The system didn't respond to any of the defaults except for one—fire.

Someone hacked my alarm by making it believe there was a fire in my condo. Fire is the only default setting I didn't change because I wanted to automatically trigger the sprinkler system and send an alert, with my address, to the fire department. I frown. None of which happened.

Examining the inputs, I see the executing command for fire was rapidly followed by a confirm-command instructing the system to request user confirmation before executing the next step. They triggered the alarm but halted any further action by the system. I was hacked.

I cancel the command, turn off the alarm, and reset the system. When the noise stops, the silence is almost as deafening as the alarm.

Clever, but what's the point? I think silently. *To scare me? Show off their skills?*

The protection I've built into my computer is too sophisticated to be hacked in thirty minutes. *This isn't the first time they've been in my computer.*

A click of my mouse and a program designed to capture all computer activity opens. Hitting *Run*, it compiles a log with the most recent events, keystrokes, logins, and history. A hacker friend developed the program for a client, but I'd modified it to fit my needs.

When I was hacking for a living, I ran it twice a day to catch potential threats, but after switching almost exclusively to product design four years ago, I stopped running it as frequently. It works quickly and efficiently, and ten minutes later, a list of all computer activity from the last week is displayed on the screen.

The list is huge, which isn't surprising. I live on this computer. I don't even own a TV. Work or play, this is the only constant in my life. With a combination of the mouse and a few control keys, I highlight and delete my activity from the last week. It takes about twenty minutes, and when I'm done, I'm still staring at a surprisingly large list of activity. Someone else has been very busy on my computer. Stunned at how often they'd accessed my computer in the last week, I sift through the information.

Not surprisingly, the hacker focused on personal files—bank records, property files, health information, and browser history.

They spent the most amount of time in my banking and property files.

Shit. Please tell me they didn't take everything.

I scramble over to the back-up computer on my left and pull up my bank accounts and cryptocurrency wallets. This computer is on an entirely different network that's not even remotely associated with me or my location and only used for emergencies to limit its exposure to the web. This certainly qualifies. I review each account and wallet and check the balance. It's all there. Relief makes me dizzy. A hacker, but apparently, not a thief. Prior to logging off, I systematically change the password on each one. It won't stop a truly talented hacker, but hopefully, it will give me enough time to move everything.

I bring up the substantial list of property files, including the places I rent. It's a mix of dummy locations, safe houses—including the one I live in now—and a few income properties.

I swivel back to my main computer and the log file. The hacker swept through my most recent communications, my old hacking jobs, and my special products folder. Anger wars with fear. Someone has been digging into every inch of my life. When I get close to the end of the week, two lines change everything. My address. They pulled my address from the security system... three days ago.

Bile rushes up, burning my throat, and I tip my chair over in a rush to grab the trash can beside my desk. I slam to my knees, get my head over the lid, and throw up, over and over, until I reach the dry heaves state. Good thing I only had grilled chicken and rice for dinner instead of the pasta I'd originally planned. I wipe my mouth with my sleeve.

When my stomach stops cramping, I shove the can away from me but remain on the floor. I need a few minutes to think. The cold sweeps up through my knees until it reaches my body. Shivering, I cross my arms and stare down at the old wood, visually tracing the lines and scuff marks made by my rolling desk chair and years of factory workers.

Given my considerable hacking capabilities, it means I'm facing someone with skills at least equal, if not better, to mine. There are quite a few talented hackers out there, but the odds of a random stranger hacking my system and not taking anything but my address would be astronomical. I personally know two people who could hack my computer for a week without me knowing about it. One is my mentor, and the other is my stalker. Only one cares where I live. Only one likes to visit me in the middle of the night.

I want to laugh so badly. I feel the wild, hysterical laughter bubbling up inside me, wanting to be free. The thought of him obliterating every piece of my life and shattering the safety I'd fought so hard for the last few years makes me feel completely unhinged.

Is he going to stalk me forever? I throw my silent question out in the universe. A wave rises from the depths of me, and my throat tightens, aching to let it all out, but I can't. It doesn't help, and I don't have the time to waste. He's had my address for two days now, and I can either fall apart or get moving. If I don't, any chance of freedom will be lost.

I've come up with a lot of escape plans over the last ten years. Elaborate, complicated plans with millions of details paired with equally impressive contingency options for when things go wrong—and they always do. He's a formidably clever foe who thinks a hundred steps ahead of me, and it's uncanny how accurate he is at guessing the plan I'll execute to escape him. Most of my success has been due to sheer luck, but sometimes I surprise him... and myself.

My eyes shift from the floor to the large canvas hanging on the wall beside my desk. Behind the beautiful abstract art is a tunnel. It was originally used as a fire escape for the employees of the factory. When I bought the run-down building and designed my loft, I made the contractor fully encase and extend the tunnel into the drainage system beneath the building. My escape tunnel is crude, but I've tested it and it works. More importantly, there's no record of it anywhere, not anymore.

Once I reach the drainage system, it's only a half mile to the garage down the street, where I have two vehicles with go bags stashed. From the garage, I'm able to drive to one of the safe houses not listed in my property file.

If I hurry, I can be gone within thirty minutes.

Yet I can't make myself move.

My eyes sweep over the space I affectionately call industrial luxury chic. All the building materials are the usual combination of brick, exposed metal pipes, wood floors, and large windows encased in black metal. In contrast, my furnishings are all luxurious fabrics—velvets, rich linens, silks, cashmere, and of course, fake fur. Every inch of this place was carefully planned and decorated, and it reflects the love I poured into it. My home for the last four years and the longest I've lived anywhere since childhood.

I was giddy when I found the abandoned factory for an incredibly cheap price. Nobody wanted to live or raise a family in this part of town. Since I spent most of my time hiding inside anyway, it suited me perfectly. I spent months designing my home to fit me. It's mine. And... I don't want to give it up.

He went to a lot of effort to get my address. Maybe I should let him come here. I turn my head to stare at the gun on my desk. I'm more prepared this time, and he wouldn't expect me to defend myself. Flashbacks threaten to flood my mind, but I refuse to let them in. Only one of us would walk away this time, and if it's not me, I'm okay with that scenario. At least it would be over.

Run... or stay and fight? For the first time in years, I contemplate staying.

CHAPTER 2

HENLEY

I stagger up from the floor twenty minutes later with my brain firing rapidly. The sun rises in an hour, and I need to get moving. Staying and fighting could cost me everything, but the only thing I lose by running is my home. It sucks, but I've got the resources to rebuild. In the past, I'd run because of fear. Today, I'll run because of purpose. My purpose. More specifically, the projects I'm working on now will make a real difference in the world. What's a home compared to saving someone's life?

If my stalker follows past patterns, he won't be here until around midnight. I will be long gone before then, but it gives me some precious time this morning to wrap things up here. It's imperative he finds nothing he can use against me.

With the safety on and gun in hand, I complete the first few tasks on my to-do list, then sit down at my desk. Securing my money is a huge priority. I already have another set of bank accounts and wallets established under a different alias, so I carefully transfer everything into them. It pays to have multiple back-ups of everything—a lesson learned the hard way.

When I first went on the run, I was desperate for money and completely uninformed about the dark web and illegal hacking and naïvely left my computer open to unscrupulous hackers, as well as my stalker. The former stole almost every cent I'd made over the course of a year, and the latter tracked down my location and broke into my home.

At a local coffee shop using the free Wi-Fi, my makeshift alarm sent me an alert to tell me someone had entered my crappy, rundown apartment. I didn't have the funds for anything sophisticated, but I'd left my spare smartphone in the room. When I'd activated its microphone, it picked up a soft voice singing "Little Brain, Little Brain, where are you?"

Terrified, I bolted, leaving everything behind. With only some emergency cash and my computer, I got in my car and didn't stop driving for three days. With no back-up account or contingency plan, I had to live out of my car for a couple months until I could save up enough money to rent a cheap, by the week motel room. Then, I lived on scraps for another four months, until I had money stashed in multiple accounts, extra clothes and go bags hidden in various locations, and a rental booked under a different alias in another city. I refused to start from scratch the next time I had to run.

It wasn't the only close call. No matter where I went or how diligently I covered my tracks, he always found me. Until I met MarcoPolo.

Finishing the transactions, I close my back-up computer and turn to the main computer to wipe the hard drive. All essential files are backed up nightly, so I won't lose anything important, but it won't be safe to use until it's completely clean.

A notification pops up on a private messaging app.

A live stream is connected to the lab.

I waver for a second, tempted to open it with this computer, but it's compromised. I click *start* to erase the hard drive.

While it's running, I grab the back-up computer, download the apps I need, and put on my virtual reality, or VR, headset. After authenticating myself, I enter the virtual lab I share with MarcoPolo. MarcoPolo is his screen name, or handle, but it's the only name I know. The name drove me crazy for the longest time because all I wanted to do was sing Marco—and answer, Polo—every time I spoke to him. I begged to call him Marco, but for the longest time, he refused. Two years ago, he finally relented, but I had to agree to only use it in his presence. All communications still had to include his full handle. To him, I was Nyx, because I love the night.

The lab is where Marco and I meet to discuss or create our latest brainchild. I gaze around the high-tech room, marveling at the dynamic space we created in the metaverse. We chose to design our lab using a myriad of purple hues to represent wisdom. It's calming but vibrant at the same time.

It's sparsely furnished, with a few tables and chairs, but the primary focus are the numerous glass walls we utilize like monitors to display our code to each other. We simply type in the real world, and it appears here. It's manic-looking with code lining the walls. It fits us, though, as we tend to work on multiple projects until one nears its finished state.

When we became virtual friends, we discovered a mutual passion for using technology to solve real-world problems and help people. Most of our products are software- or application-driven, but over the last two years, we've branched out into wearable tech —devices used or worn by individuals with technology embedded within them to bridge the virtual and physical worlds. We build the ideas by hand in the physical world, and once built, we scan them into the virtual world so we can work on them together. The lab is littered with our various prototypes.

We've been working together for five years but have only had this virtual space for the last two and a half years. It's a million times easier working in this lab than the private chat room we used when we first started developing tech together.

A play button displays on one of the glass walls, so I walk over and tap it. The live stream started one minute and thirty-seven seconds ago. I rewind it to the beginning. A large, unfamiliar room appears first. Grey cinder block walls encase a room filled with tables cluttered with parts—computers, monitors, and other mechanical pieces. A man sits at a desk directly in front of the camera, with another man standing before him.

The man closest to me darts a glance at the camera. He's handsome, with a dark complexion, strong jawline, and thick, almost black wavy hair peppered with a little grey at the temples. He appears to be in his late forties, but it's hard to tell. The only signs of age are the deep crow's feet around his dark brown eyes. A lifetime is carved into those grooves, and they alone tell a story.

My stomach churns. Marco and I use avatars to hide our identities from each other. It's a safety precaution we established when we first started working together, and we never felt the urge to change the status quo.

I've never seen his face, but I'd bet my life this is him. I stare at the screen, trying to take in all the details of my friend—suddenly wishing I'd found the courage to suggest we meet in real life. His vitality leaps off the screen. Paired with his brilliant mind, he's a man who could easily command armies.

I turn up the volume and lean forward. My well-honed instincts are screaming, but it seems I've been relegated to the role of bystander. Nothing I do allows me to break into the feed nor trace it back to its origin. I can only watch.

Something like regret flashes across Marco's expressive eyes before they harden and turn to the man standing in front of him.

"I have to admit, I never expected it to be you, and I'm rarely surprised," he hurls angrily at the man in front of him. "You were untouchable, but I guess everybody has a price, eh? I take great satisfaction in knowing they'll kill you slowly and painfully."

Muscles strain the sleeves of his button-up shirt when the man shrugs in reply. Mid-thirties, I'd guess. Dark hair and eyes. His face is distinctive, but not attractive. I tilt my head. The expression "face like a prizefighter" comes to mind. Broad forehead, topped with close cropped hair, a wide, crooked nose likely broken several times, and thick lips. He glances to his left and raises an eyebrow.

I jerk when I hear another man's voice. I search the room but see no one. Based on the angle of the first man's stare, he must be standing in view of the camera, but the screen only shows a few lines of distortion. He must be using some type of disruptor—top of the line one too, or I'd see more lines on the screen. Instead, he's practically invisible.

"It appears the AR technology we purchased is locked and needs a key. Since you ignored my polite requests for the information, I thought we'd pay you a visit and get it ourselves. You wouldn't happen to have it on you, would you?"

Marco gives a derisive laugh. "'Purchased' would indicate you paid for it, but we received no payment. You're also not the buyer I chose, so how did you get the software?"

I blink. There's only one augmented reality, or AR, technology project we've been working on that's ready for the market. We packaged it up for the broker a month ago, but this is the first I've heard about a buyer. It's revolutionary. It also has the potential for a huge payout. While we absolutely want the money, our priority is finding the right buyer for it, preferably a technology giant who could integrate the tech into an existing device or operating system so it can be easily accessed by thousands of doctors and other medical professionals. Now I'm learning it sold and the money has disappeared, along with the software.

Silence reigns. Then the disembodied voice chuckles. "It seems my employer is more ruthless than I realized. I promise I submitted a bid. The highest one, in fact. With Diego's help, I made sure of it. No matter. Free means more money for me in the long run. It does complicate today's… negotiation, per se. Why don't you save us some trouble and give us the key, and we'll be on our way?"

Marco jerks his head to indicate the man in front of him. "Having seen his face, I doubt it." He runs a hand through his thick hair.

"When you contacted me directly, it raised a red flag. Very few individuals know who I am or what I do. I'm guessing Diego told you?"

"He did," the voice confirms. "For years, I'd wondered who was behind JF Technologies. You so cleverly hid yourself from the spotlight, and even with my talents, I couldn't find a trace of your identity. When I heard JF Technologies was accepting bids for AR technology that would revolutionize the medical industry, I could practically see the money rolling into my account. I informed my employer, who was immediately keen to acquire it, and lucky for us, we already had Diego on the payroll. The rest is history."

Marco's jaw tightens, and he glares over at Diego. "Desgraçado! What else have you sold them?"

Diego sneers. "Does it matter? It's not like you missed the money, and I deserve my cut."

"You have been more than amply compensated over the years. Greed will be your downfall," Marco says with disgust before turning to the other man. He waves to the computer behind him. "The software will be shared with the world, not owned and controlled by one individual," Marco informs him.

"So self-righteous. Weren't you set to gain from the sale of this technology? If you're so noble, why didn't you release it to the world, hmmm? Could this mysterious partner of yours, CJ Tech, have insisted on a fat paycheck?"

I tense. "Give him the key, Marco. Who gives a shit about the money? Your life is worth more," I say urgently, as if he can hear me. Guilt washes over me. I insisted we get paid for this invention.

"Besides," the invisible man continues, "you're only delaying the inevitable. I know perfectly well the key is a cryptographic algorithm. I certainly have the skills to break it, but it will take time, and my employer's not the patient type. Why don't you save me a considerable amount of effort and give me the key? Or I could hunt down this partner of yours."

I shiver. The confidence in his voice is unnerving.

Marco lifts his hand and gives a careless wave. "I'm an old man, and I forgot the key." He smirks. "You *might* be able to break it, but can you do it in time? Tick-tock."

Silence reigns for a few seconds, until the man gives a forced laugh in return. "Clever. You added an expiration date. If the key isn't entered within a specific time frame, the data will be lost. Touché. I love a good challenge, and it's been a while since I had one. I'm curious about this colleague of yours. They must be talented to work side by side with you. Who knows, maybe they'll be more willing to share their copy of the software or give me the key."

Marco's hand clenches on the arm of his chair.

"Don't like that idea, huh? Unfortunately, you've put me in a tight spot, and I'll do anything to stay in my employer's good graces," he tells him. "Too bad you won't be here to see it. I truly wish we didn't have to say goodbye. You're a remarkable foe, and quite possibly a match for my brilliance. Take care of him." Footsteps echo in the room, indicating his departure.

Marco pivots to sneer at the tough-looking man in front of him, who's now gripping a silencer, and holds up a finger. "Juliana, meu anjo, I'm coming." He grunts and looks down at his chest. A second later, blood spreads rapidly across the white fabric of his shirt. He lays his head back on the chair and turns toward the video camera. He winks. "I'll miss them… and you." Sadness covers his face before it falls slack.

I stare unblinking at the man frozen in death on the screen. A loud noise fills the air, but it's nothing close to human, and I strangle it into silence. My chest feels tight, like a band is squeezing across it, and I take deep breaths to ease the pressure.

This man saved my life and gave it purpose. He took me under his wing and taught me more than I could ever learn on my own. My mentor and only friend, I owe him so much. My hand drifts up to touch the screen.

"I'll miss you, too. Meu amigo." My throat tightens, and tears fill my eyes. He taught me how to call him *my friend* in his native language. The lab wavers in my vision.

Someone shouts, "What the fuck?" I blink rapidly to clear my vision.

The man who shot Marco curses again and walks closer to the desk. He shoves everything aside to find where Marco was looking when he spoke his last words. His brutish face appears up close to the camera. Raising his phone, he calls someone.

"We've got a problem. He recorded the whole thing. You need to get back in here and see if he sent it to anyone." He hangs up and steps out of view.

Tears stream down my face, but I laugh. He did exactly what Marco planned. He stepped into the camera. *Gotcha.* I rewind, capture his image, and immediately start running facial recognition software against it. It shouldn't be too hard to find Diego.

Reeling, I send copies of the video to several different locations. I don't know how good this hacker is, but he sounded pretty confident in his ability to decipher the key. Finding a video won't be too hard for him.

I run around the lab, saving copies of all our projects to my laptop, while also forwarding them to a second secure location. I don't even know what to do with Marco's projects. I know he has a family, but he never said where or who. I didn't even know his real name. A sob bursts out, the walls begin to waver, and I quickly finish what I'm doing.

I rip the headset off, and our virtual world disappears. Grief tears through me, destroying everything in its path, and I wrap my arms tightly around my body to keep all the shattered pieces from escaping. Marco was my mentor, but more importantly, my friend. The only one I've allowed myself to have in years.

Incredibly brilliant and one-of-a-kind, he's the only smart person I've ever met who cared more for others than himself, often empathizing with those in poor or tough situations. He dedicated his life to anonymously rescuing them.

I was one of those people. Alone and terrified, I was desperately looking for a way to disappear—impossible to do until I met Marco. Somehow, he did what I couldn't and hid me from my stalker. For five years, I've had peace. I didn't dare hope it was permanent, but I treasured every moment of freedom.

It was the beginning of our friendship. When we started working together, it became a dream I never had the courage to envision until him.

For the first time in five years, I'm utterly alone again. No family. No friends. No safety.

HENLEY

The chime of the doorbell startles me. I swipe at the tears on my face, then reach for my gun and phone. Tapping the app to bring up the camera by the front door, I check to see who's knocking. A young man stands by the door holding an envelope. He looks like a typical bike courier, with his helmet, jacket, backpack, and gloves. I switch to the outside camera and see a bike chained to the pole that I know wasn't there earlier today.

"Can I help you?" I ask via the app.

The guy peers around and spots the doorbell camera I'd set up as a decoy. He holds the envelope up to it, so I can see my name and address on it. Unfortunately, the camera's fake, and I can't immediately read it. With the real camera, I zoom in until I can read the address.

Nyx, 742 Carnival Drive, Dallas, TX 12414

I freeze. There's only one person who calls me Nyx.

The courier tilts his head. "Hello? Are you there? This package requires a signature."

"Coming, just a sec," I tell him before shoving my phone in my back pocket. Unwilling to give up the gun, I transfer it to my left hand and stride over to open the door. I hold the gun behind the door and smile at the young man, who flashes me an impatient smile in return.

"Sign here," he says, thrusting his phone toward me.

I scrawl a couple of lines across the screen with my finger.

He nods, taps the phone, and hands me the envelope. He's already turning away as I shut the door and reset the locks.

Putting the envelope under my arm, I pull up the cameras and watch him leave. When he's on gone, I hurry over to the desk, set the gun down, and open the envelope.

I pull out two letters, a key, and a piece of paper with eight numbers on it.

Nyx,

I'm resorting to old-fashioned methods to send you this information, because my system's been compromised and I'm being followed.

After we delivered the software, our broker, Savage Enterprises, Inc. (SEI) accepted bids, then filtered them based on the criteria you and I discussed. None of the initial buyers met our requirements, so we agreed to close the event. We then reached out directly to the individuals you and I liked best to discuss the software and gauge their interest. Interest peaked; we re-opened the bidding.

As soon as the bidding started, my computer was hacked and a couple key files from our project were stolen. Thankfully, I didn't have a copy of the final software on my computer, so they only got bits and pieces.

Unable to trace the hacker, it raised a red flag, and I decided to safeguard the software. Deleting all but three copies, I secretly encrypted them with a symmetric cryptographic key.

SEI brokered a deal with one of our approved buyers and we delivered a copy of the software to them, but before I could send them the key to un-encrypt it, the buyer turned up dead and the purchase money disappeared. Not just the money, but the financial transaction itself was wiped from existence.

Given your hacking background and past experience with the banking system, I thought it might be you. Furious, I hacked into your computer and searched through every file. I also reached out to my sources on the dark web. Based on what I found, I realized it wasn't you.

My sources tell me the last hacking job you took was right before we sold our first software application. Our projects must mean a lot to you if you're willing to give up the exorbitant money you can make from other activities. You live modestly and only spend money on two things—food delivery (fast food is bad for you!) and real estate, but you go nowhere and do nothing but work. Life isn't all work, Henley. Yes, I know your real name, and have for a long time. It's a good name for a strong person like yourself and suits you better than Nyx. But I digress.

The person who stole the software and killed the buyer needs the key to unlock the files. I'm the only one with the key and, therefore, their next target.

My name has never been associated with JF Technologies. The only individuals who know about my connection to it are either family or they work at the highest levels in SEI. I trust my family, which means SEI has a mole.

Someone has been following me closely the last couple of days, and I'm worried their patience is running out. I'll try to get the key to you, but if the worst happens and you don't hear from me, you'll need the two remaining copies of the software to figure out the key.

The first copy is hidden on SEI's in-house servers. To get access, give Mateo Santos the other letter and the following code word—JulianaFrancisca. As you know, Juliana was my wife. Francisca was my sister, and they died together a long time ago, which is why I honored them with the name of my company. More importantly, only those in my family know their names.

Once you're in the servers, search for the name of my favorite watering hole. You're the <u>only one</u> who knows it, so the file should be safe until you can get to it. Don't trust anyone with the information.

The second copy is on a physical drive in my office. You'll need the eight-digit code to enter. I thought you'd appreciate the irony of having a virtual and physical copy. Look for something that reminds you of me, and you'll find it. The third copy is in the hands of the thieves. If the key isn't entered in the next three weeks, the data on all three copies will be rendered undecipherable. It's the only way I could be sure our software would stay out of unscrupulous hands.

I'm ashamed I suspected you, but I hope with your history (and mine), you'll understand and forgive me. It's my greatest wish to apologize to you in person, but if that doesn't happen, please know I'm sorry. I value our friendship and partnership more than I can ever explain.

In fact, I've come to realize how selfish I've been to keep you so busy with work. I should have insisted you find a life a long time ago. A smart young woman such as yourself shouldn't be in hiding. All you need is a little faith. You're a different person than the scared young girl I met five years ago. You're strong and capable now, a fighter. Don't let him take your life and leave you with nothing but ashes. The best revenge is to live and live well. Trust me, I know this to be true.

Until I see you again,

> *MarcoPolo, but you can call me Marcos (my real name)*

The letter was sent two days ago. His instincts were spot on, and he'd been right to encrypt the software, but I wish he'd destroyed it. We could have rebuilt it now that we know how the technology works. It would have taken time, but at least he'd be alive.

I don't fault him for believing it was me, but it makes me sad. Because of the past, neither Marco-err, Marcos or I could ever fully trust each other. We were both hiding from the world. But I'm glad he realized my innocence before he died, or he wouldn't have set up the video and I wouldn't have captured the face of his killer.

And without the letter, I wouldn't know Marcos is the one who's been hacking my computer, not my stalker. The sheer relief makes me tear up. I'm still safe, and my address, my home, remains hidden from the psycho in my past.

I glance at the other letter. It's addressed to Mateo Santos, but there are no words, only rows of numbers. Another encrypted message, but I'm assuming Mateo has the cypher to decode that one.

SEI's headquarters are in Miami, Florida. I'm going there first. But where is Marcos' office located? I drop the paper on the desk and pick up the envelope to see if it has his address on it, but it's gibberish and clearly fake. I check the letter to see if there's an address at the top or on the back.

When I turn it over, the light reflects off something faint toward the bottom. I squint, trying to see if my eyes are playing tricks on me, but I can't tell until I run the pads of my fingers over the area and feel tiny indentations. Something *is* imprinted on the bottom of the letter. I grab a pencil out of the cup and shade the area. It's an address in Miami, Florida.

DALLAS TO MIAMI is about twenty hours of drive time. Longer if I need to spend the night somewhere. I wish I could fly, but the sheer number of cameras makes it impossible for me. Driving is the only safe way to stay off the radar, plus it gives me transportation if I need to escape quickly.

It takes fifteen minutes to pack the few clothes I own—mainly jeans, leggings, and a few shirts. As Marcos so kindly pointed out, I don't go anywhere, so I don't see the need for a closet full of clothes. After adding a couple pairs of tennis shoes, a pair of flip-flops, and some basic items, I'm done.

I'm heading to the kitchen to grab a cooler for drinks and snacks when I hear a ding. Walking over to my computer, I see a message from the lab, stating a match has been found. I sit and bring up the file.

Diego Gutierrez, with an address in Miami, Florida—no surprise there. Same face. Hair is a bit longer in the pic, but it's definitely the shooter. Thirty-five years old, Bachelor of Business Administration from the University of Florida. Siblings and parents still alive and living in Miami. Not married. Employed as chief of security at... Savage Enterprises. *Fuck me.* Diego joined the company in 2007 right out of college, along with Thiago Santos, CEO. Bastards. I'm glad Marcos knew who betrayed him in the end, but this just got a hell of a lot more complicated.

CHAPTER 4

HENLEY

Exhaustion beats at me when I stop for the night. This has got to be the longest Monday of my life. Who could have guessed my day would start with a blaring alarm in the wee hours of the morning and end at around midnight in Tallahassee, Florida? I'm past the halfway point, but construction delays on I-10 meant my twelve-hour drive turned into fourteen.

My shoulder twinges when I reach for the wig in the passenger seat, but I ignore it and pull the medium length, mid-brown hair over my pink strands. I learned a long time ago a good nondescript wig can make you invisible. This one is the perfect example. The hair is substandard and kind of dull, the cut is boringly straight with bangs, and the length hits a little past my shoulders. I plop on a pair of gradient yellow-tinted glasses, and my blue eyes shift toward green. Perfect disguise.

The hotel clerk barely looks at me when she checks me in, and I get to my room quickly. It's a standard queen room, nothing fancy, although it smells a bit musty, so I turn on the window unit to circulate the air. After setting my bags down, I tap on a food delivery app and order a pizza.

While I wait, I open the file I compiled on Savage Enterprises, Inc and sift through it to see if I missed any red flags.

Marcos had been using SEI as a middleman to sell his tech for years. When he suggested we use them to broker our latest project, I completed an initial investigation into the company. SEI was started in 1999 by a group of inventors who needed an umbrella company to sell their tech. The original company was named Angel Consultancy. Based on a paper written by a Microsoft developer on Peer-to-Peer Tunneling Protocol, the group used the information to build one of the first virtual private networks, or VPNs, and sold it six months later. The large transaction seeded the investment for the company and established it as a leader in the tech industry. When the investor group sold the company to Thiago Santos and the Santos family in 2007, it was a large company, but nothing near the powerhouse it is today.

Fifteen years later, SEI is synonymous with innovative tech and security. The massive conglomerate is divided into three main divisions—security systems both physical and virtual, financial services, and technology research and development, or R&D. Each division is run by a member of the Santos family. Thiago Santos, CEO, thirty-five, from Miami, oversees the company and the security division. Grayson Santos, thirty-two, CFO, leads everything financial, and Mateo Santos, thirty-two, CTO, heads up all tech, including the R&D division.

The company's phenomenal reputation and solid financials were reason enough to contract with them, but what sold me was their rigorous acceptance process and seal of approval. They test and guarantee every piece of tech they broker. If it doesn't pass, they don't sell it. Their reputation is pure gold.

What did I miss?

The phone ringing interrupts my thoughts. After confirming my pizza is at the front desk, I head down. A young girl is standing in the lobby, pizza in hand, scrolling through her phone. Taking the box, I tip her, get a Diet Dr. Pepper from the vending machine, and return to my room.

When I open the box, the aroma of oregano, cheese, and pepperoni hits me, and I take a deep breath to savor the smell before grabbing a piece. I'm so hungry, I burn my mouth, inhaling the first slice of hot, cheesy goodness. Quickly finishing that one, I grab a second slice and pace back and forth, thinking about SEI and Marcos.

The safest option would be to get the copies and head back to Dallas. If the killers or SEI want to find CJ Tech, they'll search forever. It doesn't exist.

When Marcos asked me five years ago for the name of my company, I picked the initials from my mother and father's first names—Catherine and James. CJ Tech. But I never registered the company. The only conceivable way to connect me to technology Marcos brokered in the past is when he paid CJ Tech my percentage of the profits. With my "creative banking" skills, I immediately routed the payments through various institutions and accounts before it reached its final destination. And now the account doesn't exist at all because I closed it this morning when I moved my money to the back-up. The money is traceable, but it would take quite some time, and the killers seem to be in a hurry. I only need a couple of days to bounce the money around and make every past payment to CJ Tech disappear forever.

Marcos' face flashes before my eyes, making me grit my teeth. As for Diego, I could release the video of him killing Marcos to the FBI or the public and put him behind bars. It would also put SEI in the spotlight, and hopefully, under investigation, without revealing myself to them. I stop pacing and nod my head. It's a good plan. It means justice for my friend while I remain safely out of the crosshairs and hidden from my stalker.

I finish my dinner and grab a shower. Not bothering to dry my hair, I fall into bed and I'm out. Three hours later, I wake, tossing and turning, Marcos' sad face swirling around and around in my brain.

———

THE SEVEN-HOUR DRIVE on Tuesday feels like a blip in time compared to yesterday's marathon. I pass exit signs for Disney and sigh wistfully. I've always wanted to go, but my mom thought it was a frivolous waste of time for her "gifted" child. I crane my neck when I pass by the exit, but it's too far from the entrance to get a glimpse of anything. Probably a good thing. Safety trumps mouse ears and thrilling rides, right?

Marcos' words about getting a life pop into my head. I chew my lip. Maybe I shouldn't be so quick to dismiss the idea. With a good disguise, I could figure out a way to minimize the risk. The parks are crowded, and I doubt anyone would be searching for me there. I could stay close to groups. It would be a blast. I grin. I wonder if twenty-seven is too old for Disney.

A couple hours later, the ocean appears on my left. The green and blue hues of the water beckon to me, while the white caps of the waves promise endless fun. It's magnificent, and I can barely keep my eyes on the busy road in front of me. With a tap, the window rolls down and the salty air flows into the car, making me smile. The beach is such a happy place. My stomach growls loudly, interrupting my thoughts, and I glance around for a place to eat. A sign for Boston's on the Beach promises oceanfront views and good food, and without thinking, I pull into the parking lot.

I sit in the car for fifteen minutes debating the safety of eating in a restaurant, but I can't talk myself out of it. My hands tremble as I pull on the brown wig and glasses, but I'm not sure if it's excitement or fear. Maybe both. Eating in public isn't something I've allowed myself to do in... forever, and I'm shocked by my actions. Marcos' death or his words seem to be igniting a rebellion within me. With a deep breath, I open the door and get out of the car. The tangy, salty breeze hits me first, followed by the roar of the ocean waves, and I slam the door shut.

At my request, the hostess seats me outside in the sunshine and warmth with a clear view of the sand and ocean in front of me. I try to remember the last time I was at the beach, and David's perfect white smile pops into my head. Sophomore year. We skipped our last class in summer school to take the train from MIT to Revere Beach to go to the Sandcastle Sculpting tournament. It was a day filled with laughter, sunshine, and steamy kisses on the boardwalk with the roar of the ocean behind us. My fingers trace my lips, aching to capture the feel of another time and place.

"Can I take your order?"

I jump and drop my hand to my lap. Heat crawls up my neck, and I know my face is going to be bright red in about twenty seconds. Turning toward him, I quickly order the shrimp tacos and a beer. The waiter asks for my ID, and I hand him the fake one in my purse. He barely glances at it before nodding and handing it back to me.

"I'll be back in a second with your beer," he informs me, then takes off.

The ocean draws my eyes back to it while I wait for the waiter to return. I hadn't thought of David in years, not since he dumped me for cheating on him. I'd been devastated... and innocent, but no matter how hard I tried to tell him the truth, he refused to believe me.

I snort. If only he knew how lucky he was to get off so easy. He was the first casualty of my stalker's obsession, but he certainly wasn't the last.

The waiter returns with my beer and tacos, and I scarf them down. The sunshine dims beneath the clouds of the past, but I savor the moment as much as possible. I'm safe, healthy, and having lunch in public for the first time in five years. Maybe this is Marcos' gift to me.

CHAPTER 5

HENLEY

The apartment I rented in South Beach is a basic one-room studio a couple blocks from the beach. For a hundred and six dollars a night, I get privacy and the ability to blend into the population. After I check in, I gather a few things and head out to find a clothing store nearby. I can't exactly wear jeans or leggings to SEI tomorrow, but I've never been to the headquarters of any company, so I'm not sure what would be appropriate. I'm hoping I'll know it when I see it.

Two hours later, all I've found is teeny tiny fabric for exorbitant prices. I hold up the hanger with a scrap for a top and an equally sized bandeau skirt hanging off it. All for four hundred and ninety-five dollars. A quick glance at my watch shows me time is running out. I need to find something. I guess I could order from my favorite massive online store with next day delivery, but if it doesn't fit, I'll be out of luck.

Down the street, the shirts in the display window of a boutique called French Kiss catch my eye. They're dressy, button-down, and more importantly, not sheer. Should I take a chance? I peer into the store, but I can't tell if they have what I need.

"Can I help you?" a dry voice drawls beside me.

I jump and jerk my head to the right. A young man, flamboyantly dressed in various shades of orange with bright pink hair, stands by the door of the shop with a hand on his hip and an eyebrow raised as high as a skyscraper.

"Umm, maybe? I have a meeting at SEI tomorrow, and I'm not sure what to wear. I've been searching for a couple of hours, but I haven't found anything. Everything seems a little bit… skimpy… for a business appointment. Should I call it quits and wear jeans or order something from Ama—" I stop talking when I see the horrified expression on his face.

He gives a big sigh. "Oh, honey, you need serious help," he says dramatically, pausing to look me up and down. "It must be your lucky day. I don't usually take on charity cases, but the pink hair shows a splash of personality, even with those drab clothes, so… what the hell?" He waves a hand wildly toward the interior of the shop.

I ignore the comment about my clothes and practically run into the shop. If he can help me, I'll take it.

"Seriously? I'd be truly, truly grateful. I mostly, umm, work from home, so my clothes are a bit on the casual side," I offer as an excuse. When I see mannequins clothed in elegant colors and luxurious fabrics, I breathe a quiet sigh of relief.

He gives an elegant snort. "Casual doesn't mean you have to abandon all style. SEI, you said? Very nice. Are you going for an interview?" He taps his chin and glances around the shop for a minute before he starts pulling several things.

"A meeting with one of the executives," I reply, although "meeting" might be a stretch because the executive doesn't know I'm coming. I figured it was best to surprise Mateo Santos. "Do you have something that will work?"

A tilt of his head and a raise of that remarkable eyebrow tell me what he thought of my question. "When I'm done, you won't even recognize yourself. Okay, I've pulled a few outfits for you. I wasn't sure if you wanted to tone down your pink hair or enhance it, so I grabbed both."

I bite my lip. "I didn't realize the color of my hair mattered. I'll be blonde for the meeting, with brown eyes," I throw out there casually, hoping he doesn't ask me why I'm changing my appearance.

He stops and glares at me, then shoves the clothes into my arms. "Hold these for a second," he says curtly, his bright pink platform shoe tapping wildly on the floor. He takes a deep breath and holds it for a second, then releases it. "We're starting over. To find you the best outfit, hair and eye color are crucial details. What color blonde are you going to be?"

I try to think of a good example. "Like Reese Witherspoon in *Sweet Home Alabama*?" I love that movie. "My eyes will be medium brown."

"Okay," he begins, then continues, "now that I have an idea of the foundation I'm working with, we can get you into the perfect outfit." He glances around the shop. "Hold on." In two steps, he grabs a box from a rack nearby. "This just arrived, and I think it will work." Motioning to the changing room on my right, he shepherds me into the small space and places the box on the ground.

I stand there for a second, waiting for him to sort through the clothes in my arms. Silk slides against my skin, and I smile. All the clothes feel luxurious, like the fabrics in my loft, and I'm excited about wearing something so beautiful.

He hangs a few of them on the right and the rest on the left until my arms are empty. Opening the box, he pulls out a beautiful blonde wig and carefully places it over my pink hair. "There. This temporary fix will help us find the right outfit," he states with satisfaction. "Although I don't believe you should change yourself for anyone, not even an employer, I know sometimes you have to conform to the norm."

I shrug. "It's an important meeting," I state quietly, as if it's the reason I'm putting on a disguise.

"Aren't they all?" he retorts. With a flick of his hand, he hands me an outfit and closes the curtain. "I guessed at the size, so we might need to adjust a little. Although I'm good at what I do, if I do say so myself."

I laugh, strip down to my boring beige underwear, and slide into the first outfit. When I gaze in the mirror, my smile fades, along with the gangly girl I'm used to seeing. In her place is someone new. I raise my hand and wiggle my fingers, and the mirror does the same. It's me.

Milestones define the passage of time, but those are missing from my life. One minute, I'm a young scholarship student at MIT with the world at my fingertips. The next, I'm an object of obsession constantly on the run, searching for safety and anonymity.

Visually, the college-aged hacker is gone, replaced with an accomplished adult woman. More than the clothes, there's a maturity in my face that wasn't noticeable before, or it's been so long since I truly looked in the mirror, I missed the subtle changes. In my mind, time stopped while I hid in the shadows, but now I see it never did. It slipped by at the same speed, but unnoticed without those important markers.

I finish tucking the pearl pink blouse into the elegant cream pants. Everything fits like a dream, and I swallow before opening the curtain to get his opinion.

He eyes me for a second. "Size is perfect," he muses. "I'm not sure I like this outfit for a meeting. It's too sweet, like cotton candy." He hands me the next outfit. "What are you doing for shoes?"

I step back into the changing room. "I'm not sure," I reply tentatively, as if I hadn't thought about ordering a pair online tonight. I don't want to give him heart failure. I pull off the first outfit and dress in the second.

The pants are black, with a wide belt and full legs that fall in a straight line to the ground. Topped with the shimmery, light green button-down blouse, it feels professional and elegant. This is the outfit.

"Hello?" he queries impatiently. "Are you going to show me?"

I pull back the curtain. He straightens but doesn't say a word. I smooth my hands down the pants, then check to make sure the shirt is tucked in as it should be.

Motioning for me to twirl, he tilts his head and examines every inch of the outfit. His brown eyes light up. "Stop fidgeting. You look amazing. From waif to powerhouse with a swath of silk and the finest of wools and a fairy godfather, of course," he declares dramatically, then takes a bow when I clap.

A pair of black shoes appear, accompanied by an order to try them on. They're a little big, but the pumps coordinate well with the outfit. I smile.

He frowns and hands me a slightly different black pair with a peep toe.

I switch the shoes and find the second pair fits better but wait until I get his approval to squeal with happiness. Not only do I have an outfit for tomorrow, but it's gorgeous and screams successful woman.

With a twirl, I laugh and dance back into the changing room to take it all off. I slip back into my comfortable jeans and T-shirt and ignore the twinge of disappointment. With a lopsided smile, I pull back the curtain. "Do you think I could take the cream pants and pink blouse too?"

He hesitates. "Why don't I ring up the first outfit, then you can decide if you want the second?"

I noticed the price tags in the dressing room, and the one outfit alone is three times what I'd usually spend on clothes in a year, but it's not as if I don't have the money. "I'll take both outfits and the shoes," I insist with a smile. "My name's Henley."

A sparkle appears in his eyes. "Peyton. If you want the second outfit, you'll need a different pair of shoes for it," he cautions. "Black would be too harsh against the cream and pink." When I agree, he heads to the back and comes out with a tan version of the black peep toe shoes and rings me up.

"Peyton, I can't thank you enough. You've been a lifesaver," I state firmly. I'm not sure how I'll be able to repay him, but with one outfit, he restored a piece of me I'd been missing for a long time.

<u>HENLEY</u>

The large glass building stands tall and rigid in the midday sun, but I refuse to let the imposing structure intimidate me. SEI headquarters. This is it. With a deep breath, I enter and head to one of the beautiful receptionists sitting at the front desk. She sweeps a critical eye over me, then smiles. I've passed the first hurdle.

Thank you, Peyton, I send silently into the air.

"Hello, I'd like to see Mateo Santos please," I inform her quietly.

She clicks on the keyboard. "Do you have an appointment?"

"No, but I'm positive he'll see me," I state confidently, while I mentally cross all my fingers and toes. "Please tell him Marcos sent me."

She gives me a hesitant look but motions to the sleek white leather couches nearby. "I'll give him a call. Please make yourself comfortable."

I nod and head over to sit down. With my black purse in my lap, I watch as she picks up the phone and speaks into it. Surprise flits across her face.

She hangs up and glances over at me. "He'll be here in a couple of minutes." Her gaze is curious, but I smile to indicate I heard her.

The lobby is packed with professionals coming and going from all directions. The women are dressed with flair, and I can't help but admire their outfits and wonder what it would be like to dress so beautifully for work every day. My leggings are comfortable, but they get old after a while.

I'm so glad I didn't wear jeans. Although, they look good on the tall, dark-haired man striding through the crowd, his long, lean legs encased in dark blue denim. Heads swivel in his direction, but it's obvious they couldn't care less about his lack of business attire.

Entranced at the sight of such flagrant disregard for convention, I continue to watch him. He appears completely oblivious to the people around him as he types furiously into his phone, yet somehow manages to navigate expertly through the busy crowd.

He occasionally stops typing to shove the mass of wavy dark brown hair back from his forehead, but within seconds, it falls haphazardly around his face again. He reaches the reception desk and leans over to say something to one of the women.

The receptionist I spoke to earlier smiles at him, then points to me.

Is he Mateo Santos? I wonder silently.

When he turns toward me, I automatically smooth a hand down my pants and stand to greet him. With his dark complexion and black-rimmed glasses, he reminds me of an Italian professor I had in college, although he's certainly more... Is it wrong to say a man is beautiful instead of handsome? I smile at him.

Instead of returning my smile, his face is blank, and his dark brown eyes flick down to my feet and almost immediately back up. Yet I doubt he missed one detail of my appearance.

Without taking his eyes from mine, he walks over and gazes down at me but says nothing.

At five foot nine, I'm not exactly short, and with three-inch heels on, we're close in height. From a distance, his eyes seemed cold and unforgiving, but up close, little gold flecks change their dark reflection into something deliciously warm and friendly. Well, it would be friendly if he weren't practically frowning at me.

"Who are you?" he bluntly asks, with little regard for polite introductions.

I swallow hard and debate how to answer him. With Diego still in position as chief of security, I don't want any of them to know who I am, but I need to give Mateo enough information he'll trust me.

"Are you Mateo Santos?" I inquire politely to confirm I'm speaking to the correct person. Although I briefly researched him last night, the article only had a side profile picture of him and I was too tired to find more. When he nods, I continue, "Do you mind showing me your ID?" I can feel the heat crawling across my face, but I stand my ground. I glance at the ID he shows me and almost laugh when I see the impatient expression the DMV captured on his face.

"I work for CJ Tech. Our partner, JF Technologies, left a copy of our software on your servers. I've been sent to retrieve it."

A tiny flicker of surprise makes his eyes widen, but other than the small tell, he remains stoic. "Do you have proof of your identity and employment with CJ Tech?"

I open my purse, and using the tips of my press-on nails, I carefully grab the letter Marcos sent to me and hold it out for Mateo to take. "I was instructed to give this letter to you, along with the code word JulianaFrancisca." I don't say anything else because I don't know what's in the letter.

Mateo narrows his eyes but says nothing, only takes the letter from me. When he opens it, he gives me a startled look, but says nothing, only takes out his phone and snaps a picture of the letter. He folds the letter and puts it into his pocket, then proceeds to tap on his phone.

Interesting, a decoding app certainly makes things easier. I wonder how secure it is. If the message dissolves after it's read, it might be decently secure, or at least enough to send messages. If it retains any of the initial image or message, though, even in temporary cache, it wouldn't be hard to break the code, given the cipher and message are in the same location. I wonder—

A throat clears, and I glance up at Mateo, but he's still staring at his phone.

While Mateo was reading the letter and I was off in la-la-land, someone else walked up. Embarrassed, I swivel my attention to the left.

This is business attire at a whole new level, I muse.

Incredibly good-looking, the man is wearing a navy pinstriped suit with a lavender button-down shirt and a navy and lavender tie. Similar in height to Mateo, but different everywhere else. Light complected, but tan, like he spends a lot of time outdoors. Unlike Mateo's rebellious hair, every strand of this man's caramel brown hair is tamed and styled perfectly. Longer on top, with a consistent wave from front to back, and short on the sides—it suits him. Flashing a blinding white smile, he chuckles, but I notice the humor doesn't reach his cold, deep blue eyes. The epitome of polished marble. High style and cold.

He holds out his hand. "Hello, beautiful, I'm Grayson. You are?"

Grayson Santos. I'm standing with two of the three power-houses who run SEI. Me, a hacker. Well, product designer now, but a peon all the same.

"I'm with CJ Tech," I reply with same answer I gave Mateo. Unfortunately, Grayson is more persistent.

"Hmm, so you say. Do you have a name I can call you by?" He slips a bit of doubt into the conversation, and I narrow my eyes.

His thumb caresses my hand, and a shiver of pleasure runs down my spine. He smiles knowingly. Irritated, I jerk my hand from his and stick it in my pocket for a second to let it recover. Grayson's smooth flirting screams big leagues, but with my awkwardness and lack of dating, I'm not even on the little league roster.

Luscious red flowers on the receptionist's desk catch my eye.

"Rose," I state, using my sweetest tone. "Rose Davis."

He steps in close, gives me a kiss on one cheek, then switches and gives me a kiss on the other. The expensive cologne he wears wraps around us both, and I freeze.

"Hmm, you smell as divinely as you look, beautiful Rose," he rasps huskily before stepping back.

While his smile is charming, his eyes watch me like a cat playing with a mouse. I deliberately wipe my face on each side.

"Do you greet all your business colleagues the same way?" I ask to cover up the nerves flaring inside me. It's been a while since anyone has given me even the slightest of kisses, but to use them as a tactic to rattle me is low.

Mateo chuckles, and Grayson levels a hard stare at him.

"Well, Rose, I'd like to verify this message with the head of JF Technologies first. I hope you understand," Mateo states matter-of-factly.

Confused, I stare at him. Either he's stalling or he doesn't know Marcos is dead. Which is it? If he's stalling, it could mean he knows Diego killed him and he's trying to work out how to get the key. If he doesn't know Marcos is dead, does that mean *nobody* knows? Marcos said his circle was small, consisting only of family, a couple of friends, and SEI. I don't know whether to tell him or not. I debate it for the briefest of seconds, but Marcos' letter said not to trust anyone, so I say nothing.

My voice squeaks a bit when I reply. "Marcos told me to give you the code word and letter, and you would give me access so I could grab the file," I explain to him. "I promise, I'll be in and out in less than five minutes."

He hesitates. "Why don't you give me the name of the file and I'll pull it up for you? Then I can make sure it's the correct software before I hand it over."

I bite my bottom lip. "I can't. I'm sorry. Marcos didn't want anyone outside of CJ Tech to know the file name," I tell him.

He looks shocked for a second. "Marcos would never—"

His words are interrupted by a loud voice calling his name behind him. When he turns to the side, I see Diego's angry face and my heart starts racing in triple time.

He doesn't know you know. He doesn't know you have the video.

Mateo glances at Grayson and turns to face Diego.

"Diego, I need a few minutes to finish my conversation. Please wait for me in my office," he states firmly.

Diego completely ignores him and slides between Mateo and Grayson to face me directly. "I'm Diego Gutierrez, Chief of Security at SEI. Did I hear you say CJ Tech? Is that your company?"

From 2D to 3D, video to flesh, he's even more brutish up close. *I know what you did… traitor*, reverberates in my mind while I stare at the man who murdered my friend in cold blood. His small, almost black eyes, the perfect mirror for the absolute blackness of his soul. My stomach twists like it's going to hurl my lunch all over his ill-fitting black suit, and I step back. He follows like a predator about to pounce on his prey.

Surprisingly, a blue pinstripe suit checks his step forward, and he jerks to a stop. My eyes dart to Grayson's face, but he's staring at Diego. Not a word is exchanged, but Diego stumbles back a couple of steps. Mateo snorts, which earns him a hateful glare from Diego and an amused chuckle from Grayson.

He might be physically blocked, but it doesn't stop Diego. After all, it would be a hell of a coup to bring his employer someone from CJ Tech and possibly the key.

"I'm waiting," he reminds me curtly.

I bring my hand up and twirl a piece of hair by my ear. "Sorry, lost my train of thought," I reply in my sweetest voice. "Oh, right, CJ Tech. Sort of. I mean, I'm a part-time virtual assistant, but I hope to come on full-time in the future. Why? Are you guys hiring?" I smile at all three and open my purse. "I think I have a card in here." I pretend to dig around. "No, I'm sorry. Maybe I could drop one off at the receptionist's desk later this week?"

I can feel Mateo and Grayson staring at me, but I continue to gaze at Diego with a smile on my face.

Surprisingly, his lips twist into a mockery of a smile and his voice softens. "Why don't you give me your name and number, and we can try to get you an interview with SEI? In the meantime, we've been trying to get in touch with your boss to discuss some software we sold for him. If you give me his name and contact information, I'll contact him directly." He raises his hand to get his phone out of his inside jacket pocket, and I flinch.

Flashbacks of him raising the gun and shooting Marcos point-blank in the chest fill my mind. I blink rapidly to clear the vision and try to focus on answering him. Name. What is my name? My mind blanks. *Shit.* What did I just tell Grayson? This is what happens when you lie. I start sweating. The sun slips through the window behind me, striking the gold pin on Grayson's tie.

"Goldie. My name's Goldie," I blurt out, apparently at the end of my limited acting ability. "My boss sent me to SEI to request a file, but I forgot the name. I'll call back with the information as well as my contact info." I thrust a hand toward Mateo but drop it when he doesn't raise his. "Mr. Gutierrez is right. I've taken up too much of your time. Thanks so much. We'll talk soon."

Grayson puts his hand out to grab me, but I slip past him. I inhale, once, twice, but there doesn't seem to be enough air for me. I need to get out of here right now. My instincts are screaming for me to run, but I clamp down on the fear. Reciting the Fibonacci sequence to distract myself, I maintain a steady pace out the door.

Once outside, I turn in the direction of the parking garage. When I get past the garage entrance, I start running toward the street behind it, where I've parked my car. I'm clammy by the time I get there, but my only focus is on getting away.

I drive for several blocks, making sure to frequently check my rearview mirror for any followers. When it's all clear, I swing over to the curb, open the door, and let the fear and tears pour out of me. After rinsing my mouth out, I close the door and lean my head against the seat.

That didn't go well, and I don't know how to get the file now. I'm sure hacking SEI would be like hacking the CIA. With time, I might be able to do it, but I have less than three weeks to enter the key before the data is rendered unrecoverable. If they hadn't killed Marcos, I'd let it play out, but I refuse to let his killers go free.

Diego's a huge problem. I know he's a murderer, and he knows someone from CJ Tech is in Miami. I'd taken some precautions before I went to SEI, but whether they will be enough, I don't know. He'll be searching for a tall, buxom blonde, not a gangly young woman with pink hair. And thanks to a YouTube video, I used extensive highlighting and contouring to alter the shape of my face.

I also erased my earlier fingerprints from Mateo's letter using art gum, which is why I was careful not to touch it today. The last thing I want is someone to find Henley Davis. I peel off the fake nails and toss them into the empty cup in my console.

Mateo and Grayson Santos. Powerful, brilliant, and, of course, good-looking—but whose side are they on? I don't know, but I'll keep digging.

But first, I'm going to concentrate on getting the drive from Marcos' office and let things die down at SEI.

CHAPTER 7

<u>THIAGO</u>

Mateo's distracted "hello" tells me he's in his lab and likely down the latest tech rabbit hole. He wouldn't even answer the phone if I didn't force him to abide by my rules.

"Updates?" I demand, needing to know how our last deal went off the rails.

"I haven't had time to investigate further," he replies with a huff. "We've been countering cyberattacks since yesterday, and it's been a race to get everything locked down before they can slip through our firewalls."

I stop in the middle of the sidewalk. A man curses behind me, and I level a hard stare at him. He raises his hands in exasperation but says nothing else when he walks by. I flick a hand toward Diego, and he moves behind me to act as a barrier.

"Is someone flooding the system?" I ask, referring to a common cyberattack tactic used against large corporations like ours.

"No, the hacker's using a combination of tactics to get into the system. So far, the new security system we installed a few weeks ago is doing its job and blocking each attack with the appropriate response, but the attacker is persistent and focused on finding information. As a precaution, I've shuttered most of our on-site servers until the attack is over," Mateo informs me in his usual controlled tone, although I detect the strain he's trying to hide. "Before you ask, it started with a phishing email sent to one of our employees, but instead of it bringing back a single type of malware, it returned with a host of them."

"Fuck! We hold training every month to prevent this sort of thing. Who was it?" I ask through clenched teeth to hold in the roar that is threatening to escape. Mateo doesn't deserve my rage.

He pauses, and I tense. Mateo's pragmatic and not one to hold back when delivering bad news, which means I'm not going to like the answer. "It was a new employee I hired for the IT department," he admits slowly, then continues. "But I don't think it's her fault. Something strange is going on."

"What?" I demand, doubly worried by Mateo's choice of word. He deals in absolutes, not speculation.

"An admin for CJ Tech came to see me yesterday. She provided me with Marcos' code word, along with an encoded letter. The letter demanded I give her exclusive access to all his files," he states slowly, his voice full of disbelief. "He's never given access to an outsider, and I can't believe he would do so now. Thankfully, she left before I could decide whether to trust her."

What the…? Shock renders me speechless. Marcos gave an *outsider* access to his files? What the hell was he thinking? I pinch the bridge of my nose.

"Don't give anyone access until after we speak to Marcos," I order him. "Do you think CJ Tech is behind the attacks? Also, what's happening with the IT employee?"

Mateo blows out a breath. "Grayson's questioning her while I manage our defenses. As for CJ Tech, I don't have any facts yet. All I know is our attacker is exceptionally good. It's taking everything I know to block them."

I stare at the blue sky and contemplate Mateo's words. I can consider this incident separately or in conjunction with the deal that went sideways last week. My gut says they're related, especially with the recent visit from CJ Tech, but Mateo doesn't like to assume because it influences results. He'll investigate the two separately and only connect them if he discovers a correlation, but we need to speed this along before someone finds out about the death of the buyer and calls our reputation into question.

I drop my head down and gaze across the busy plaza. "Get Marcos into the office to help, and ask him about CJ Tech," I order.

"I tried calling him earlier, but he didn't answer," Mateo informs me.

I hear the furious tapping on the keyboard while he speaks to me, so I force myself to remain calm. "When was the last time he checked in? Can you see if he's in his office?" The typing stops while Mateo brings up an app on his phone. The app logs every entry into Marcos' office.

"Three entries this week. Two on Monday and one last night," he returns. The typing starts up again. "He might have fallen asleep."

Marcos is the one person who refuses to abide by my rules, hence the tracker on the keypad. "I'll have Diego send someone over there to check on him. In the meantime, I'll call Grayson and get an update on the employee. Do you need me to cancel this meeting and head back to Miami?" I offer, although I know his answer will be no. It took months to set up this meeting in New York.

"I've taken care of the attack. I want to start my investigation, and you'll get in my way. Is there anything else?" he asks abruptly, impatient to get off the phone and dive in. There's nothing more enticing to Mateo than facts that don't line up.

"No, thanks," I return, hanging up. Gesturing to Diego, I tell him to get someone over to Marcos' office and wake him up. We need him to go into SEI and assist Mateo with the investigation of the attack.

Diego frowns. "We had an attack. Why didn't Mateo notify me?" he demands angrily.

As chief of security for SEI, he's right—he should have been notified immediately. I curse silently, knowing Mateo deliberately didn't tell Diego. The two can't stand each other. Diego thinks Mateo is an intellectual snob, and he's right. Mateo is dismissive of any suggestion Diego makes to improve the security of the company, as well as our personal security, because his data shows we should be focused on virtual, not physical, attacks.

They're both right, but I can't get them to see it. We have enough brains in the company to handle anything virtual, but we need someone with muscle and street smarts to manage the physical security. I don't have enough time to oversee it all. Diego's IQ might fall within the normal range, but he's good at his job. Criminals don't always use a virtual door when they attack.

"I'll have a talk with Mateo," I assure him. "Can you get someone over to wake up Marcos? We need his assistance with the attack, and he's not answering his phone."

Diego stiffens. "Why don't I return to Miami and get Marcos and bring him to SEI? Peter can manage everything here. I've trained him well."

I shake my head. "No, I want you with me today. Send Jason to get him," I order him. Diego tilts his chin and picks up his cell. I dial Grayson.

"I thought you'd be calling sooner," he says, answering my call.

"If I'd known what was happening, I would have," I retort.

Silence. "Sorry, man, it's been a long day. Let me step out," he returns apologetically. A muffled conversation happens in the background, then he's back. "Cecilia Martinez, thirty, single, solid financials, clean background check. Hell, we just hired her, so she was thoroughly vetted two weeks ago." He pauses. "She insists she knows better and hasn't opened any suspicious emails since she started working here. If she had, she would have reported it immediately."

I frown and ask, "What do you think?" Grayson's ability to spot a liar is uncanny. His past was the perfect training ground, after all.

"She's pretty and smart, but naïve. Easily charmed. Honest too. She's likely innocent. I investigated her desk and computer. She sits in the middle of the IT room with her back to everyone. It wouldn't be too hard for someone to capture her password," he returns with confidence. "I assume Mateo told you about our visitor yesterday. Remarkable blend of truth and lies coming out of her delectable mouth."

"He did, and it's highly suspicious, but until we speak to Marcos, we are not giving her access to his files," I reply curtly. "For the employee, give her two weeks' severance and cut her loose. We have a zero-tolerance policy, and this is too big to sweep under the rug. Plus, if CJ Tech is behind it, I want to eliminate any potential allies or entry points."

He doesn't respond for a second. "Will do," he replies, his voice short.

I know he hates firing people, but it can't be helped. "Jason is going to retrieve Marcos. Can you text me when Marcos arrives?"

"Have Mateo do it," he fires back and hangs up.

Rolling my head to ease the tension in my neck, I send a quick text to Mateo with Grayson's updates and my request for a text when Marcos arrives. Three dots appear and disappear, and I grunt impatiently.

A thumbs up emoji finally appears.

Both are pissed now, but they can get over it. I don't have time to run the company, investigate the attack, and soothe their feelings. I motion to Diego and head into the building for the meeting I'm already late in attending.

CHAPTER 8

HENLEY

The meeting at SEI yesterday didn't go well, but I'm determined today is going to be different. After grabbing a late lunch from the deli around the corner, I head toward Marcos' office. Twenty minutes later, I'm parked down the street from a ten-story brown brick office building. For two hours, I watch all the people coming and going. Nobody looks suspicious or appears to be watching the building, but I can't afford to be careless.

I jam the bike helmet over my favorite nondescript brown wig and grab the overnight envelope from the front seat. I'd written JF Technologies on the front, along with the building's address, but with pencil, so it's barely noticeable. I don't know what I'll find, but a blank envelope would stand out. With my glasses, jacket, and gloves, I'm hoping to pass for a courier.

The lobby is busy when I walk into the building, but instead of going to the security desk, I head toward the directory on the wall. The list of businesses varies but includes five doctor offices, a dentist, three attorneys, an accounting firm, and about eight miscellaneous companies, but JF Technologies isn't listed. Any of them could be a front for his office, so I guess I'll check each one.

I'm headed toward the elevators when the security guard stops me. "Not so fast. We need you to sign in at the front desk and get a badge, please."

I shrug and follow him over to the desk. With a flourish, I sign my name and hand him an ID, and he scans into the system. It spits out a sticker with the picture of me, my name, and VISITOR in bold letters. I slap it on my shirt and turn toward the elevators.

"Miss…" he calls out. "We need the name of the company, too." He taps the clipboard where I signed my name.

I pretend to glance at the envelope in my hand and state, "Frank and Associates." It's one of the attorneys listed on the directory.

He writes down the info and waves his hand to let me go.

It takes an hour and a half, but I check every single office in the building, even the three attorneys. Marcos had a weird sense of humor, and I could picture him using a lawyer's name as a front for his office. They're all busy offices full of people, but no JF Technologies.

Frustrated, I get into the elevator and push my way to the very back. It stops and starts, with people getting on and off, but I need time to think, so I keep riding it. Could I have been mistaken? Maybe the gibberish he wrote on the envelope for the return address are directions or some type of code? I sigh. I'll have to examine it when I get back to the rental.

The door opens, the final two people in the elevator get out, but instead of the marble lobby, I'm staring at grey concrete pillars. Startled, I step out and find myself in an underground parking garage, with cars parked in neat little rows like soldiers.

I swivel around to hit the button on the elevator, but the grey cinder block walls next to the door make me pause. They're remarkably similar to the ones in Marcos' video. Could he have hidden his office in the basement?

Leaving the elevator, I walk the perimeter of the garage until I see a door in the corner. I insert the key he sent me, but it doesn't work. I continue my search around the perimeter but have no luck with the second door either. I spot a third door, insert the key… and strike gold. It opens, and I dart inside, turn on the light, and discover a small utility room filled with green electrical panels. And walls. That's it.

The nape of my neck is clammy, and I fan myself with the envelope. Nerves. *It's not breaking the law when you have a key*, I remind myself.

Marcos sent me an eight-digit code, which means I'm looking for an entry panel. I open each of the green metal doors and find switches, circuits, and wires. Next, I scour the walls, but they're blank. I glance up, but there's only a ceiling. I groan in frustration. Maybe I'm supposed to flip circuits to enter the code. I open the panels again to check if there are numbers on them, but they're plain white and blank. I'm tempted to slam it shut, but I refrain. Legal or not, no need to tell everyone I'm here.

Think through the problem, I tell myself.

I back up to the door and start over. The room is encased in three walls. The electrical panel on my left covers one entire wall. It only leaves the wall in front of me and the wall on my right. I've ruled out the electrical panel. Stepping in front of the wall in the rear, I push on each cinder block. They're all solid. I move to the wall on my right and do the same. Solid.

I'm sweating profusely now, and my head is itching like crazy under the wig and helmet. I stretch a finger under the edge and scratch, but it does very little. I blow out a huge breath. It feels late, and I glance at the time on my phone. Five o'clock. People are going to be leaving work soon, and I can't risk getting caught in the building, much less in an electrical room. I'm going to have to come back tomorrow.

Before I open the door, I shut off the light, not wanting its brightness to alert anyone in the garage to my presence. And that's when I see it. A glow in the corner on the floor. A keypad, flat to the surface, grey keys barely glowing on the grey concrete. Utterly unobtrusive and brilliant.

I turn the light back on, whip out the piece of paper with the numerical digits, and hurry over to the pad. When the final number is entered, the back wall swings silently open, and I'm staring at a hallway. I'd whistle at his ingenuity, but I'm in awe of the resources it took to have this built. It must have been done when the building itself was being developed. If that's the case, it might mean Marcos owned the building. Thankfully, the lights are on, and I walk down the hall into a large room identical to the one in the video. I've found it. Marcos' office.

I immediately look to the end of the room, expecting to see him dead in his chair, but he's not there. The video cut off shortly after his death, so I'm not sure if his killers moved him or if someone else has been here. A large, reddish-brown stain covers the floor under his rolling desk chair. Footprints and streaks from the wheels line the surface, but I can't tell anything from the marks.

Mentally comparing the video with the room, I find one other item missing. A small scanner. It's another AR project we were working on for the medical community. It maps a person's veins and displays them on the surface of the skin. It's a small project, but it will impact the lives of everyone who gets their blood drawn. It's ready for the market. We'd hoped to sell it to the same people who bought our larger project. I guess the killers thought the same.

It's hard to imagine Marcos working and creating in this space. The only pop of personality are the posters and pictures on the wall. The rest is bland and kind of dark. It doesn't suit his creative and flamboyant personality at all. I walk over to the desk and glance at the shelves around the computer.

A couple of pics are taped to the shelves, and I get closer. In one photograph, two women in bikinis stand on a beach, posing with a small, dark-haired little boy between them. I flip it over. "Silva 1993." I snap a pic with my phone of the front and back. The second photo is of three young boys on Ocean Drive in Miami. Nothing is written on the back of this one. I snap another pic.

To the right of the pic, the shelves have been stripped bare. A cord dangles out of the wall. I glance behind me and angle my body to see if I'm right. Yep. This is where the camera that recorded his death was located.

Shivering, I carefully move the chair back and place a large book on the floor in front of his desk. I stand on the book, then tap on the mouse to waken the computer. It's on. I type c-m-d and run the same compiler on his computer that I ran on my own. It's the program he developed, so I'm hoping it works. It does, and a log file appears.

All the activity is from three days ago—the day he died. Everything else must have been erased. The first command jumps out at me. "Run Nyx." Opening a separate window, I run Nyx, and an image of a colorful neon bar pops up. I frown. Does he want me to go to his bar? Is that where he hid a copy of the key? I snap a pic in case I'm missing something.

The rest of the activity is split between a search to find the video file and a query for any AR code located on the computer. It nets a big fat zero, which is a relief. It means the killer couldn't trace the video's destination, and he failed to get any more of our tech. I delete the log file and the compiler program.

I need to get the copy of our software and get out of here. A clock on the wall says six o'clock. I've already been in this room for an hour. I scan the rest of the desk area, but there's nothing. Moving over to the tables littered with tech prototypes, I sift through everything, opening drawers, peering into pockets, but I don't find a drive.

A mannequin standing beside the table is wearing a shimmering silver vest. Intrigued, I finger the material and find a network of tiny wires. It's wearable tech and a new project Marcos must have been working on separately. I wonder where he was going with it. I flip the edges open and see sensors lining the inside. *Hmmm.* My mind immediately sparks with ideas, but I rein it in. *Focus.*

I glance around the room. Brazilian posters line the wall, along with framed pieces of art. Marcos was from Rio and would often reminiscence about food, dancing, or his favorite places. I recognize a few of the places he mentioned in the posters.

A striking painting of a tequila bottle and some limes stands out to me. With a wry smile, I rush over and pull it down to check behind it. There's nothing on the wall or taped to the back. I glide my fingers around the edge of the frame and discover a raised area in the bottom corner, covered by tape. *I knew it.* I pull the tape off and find the drive. Marcos loved tequila. He could wax poetically for hours about the assorted flavors, colors, and types of his favorite liquor.

My eyes water, and I blink. *Damn it.* What am I supposed to do without him? I feel like half my brain's missing. I grip the drive in my fist. He went to all this trouble to safeguard our technology. Why? He hated "the bad guys," as he used to put it. I'd joke that hacking wasn't exactly legal and we were also the bad guys at one point in time. He told me true bad guys lack a conscience. We still had ours, and we might not be entirely good, but we will be once we save the world, one piece of tech at a time. I believed him, counted on it, in fact.

I hang the picture back on the wall and head toward the door. Something makes me grab the vest on my way out, and I stuff it in my jacket and zip it back up. I leave everything else the way I found it. I don't know if he has anyone who will come looking for him or if the killers will return, but I don't want to alert anyone to my presence. I walk through the hallway into the utility room and the office door automatically closes behind me. I open the exterior door and peek out. It's empty. Instead of heading to the elevators, I decide to sneak out of the garage and follow the ramp to the entrance.

And of course, there's a guard on duty here too. He frowns and stops me. Before he can say a word, I hold up the overnight envelope.

"Got off on the wrong floor. I tried to hop back on the elevator, but it was taking forever. I have one more delivery to make tonight and need to hustle to get there in time, so I followed the ramp. Hope that's okay, man," I explain to the guard, with a worried expression on my face.

He eyes the envelope, then sighs and jerks his hand toward the street. "I'm supposed to take you upstairs to the security office, but I'll let you go this time. Don't exit this way in the future. Go on."

"Thanks, I appreciate it," I say loudly, my voice filled with genuine gratitude. "Have a good night!"

When I reach my car, I get in and floor it back to the apartment. Stepping in, I slam the door closed, turn the deadbolt, and rip off the helmet and wig. My knees give out, and I slide down into a puddle on the floor. I'm not sure I'm cut out for this espionage stuff. The anonymity of computer hacking doesn't faze me, but physically being there in person makes me want to throw up. I give a shaky laugh.

The vest tumbles out when I lower the zipper, but I leave it lying on my lap. I grab the drive from the right pocket, pull off the sweaty nylon jacket, and toss it in the direction of the sofa. It misses by a mile and lands in a pile on the floor.

I let my head fall back against the door and stare down at the drive. Worth more than the GDP of a small country, it lies useless and tiny in my hand. In the right device, though, this software will save thousands of lives every single day.

CHAPTER 9

<u>THIAGO</u>

The meeting was a complete waste of my fucking time. I storm out of the building and into the SUV waiting at the curb. We'd been hoping to partner with the large medical device company on an innovative technology we were developing in-house, but they only wanted to discuss SEI's financial solvency. After going round and round for two hours, I coolly informed them SEI wasn't for sale and we'd find a partner worthy of our consideration, but it wouldn't be them.

Tugging at the tie around my thick neck, I ease it off and throw it down on the seat beside me. Diego glances at me in the rearview mirror.

"Airport. We're not staying," I practically snarl at him.

He raises an eyebrow but stomps on the gas without a word.

I check my phone for the twentieth time. Not one text from Mateo, Marcos, or Grayson. I call Mateo.

"We're in the middle of another attack. They appear to be adapting and returning in waves," Mateo spits out and hangs up.

Grayson doesn't answer.

"Have you heard from Jason? Did he find Marcos?" Thoroughly frustrated at the lack of response from everyone else, I turn to Diego to give me some damn answers.

I watch him bow up, hackles clearly raised, before he remembers who's asking the questions. "Jason arrived about thirty minutes ago. Marcos wasn't in his office. So Jason is waiting in the parking garage to see if he returns."

My gut is churning. *What the hell is going on?* I wonder. "Post someone at his condo too." Diego nods and picks up his phone. "Have my car waiting for me when we land. Take the SUV to the office and watch over Mateo and Grayson." I throw out a hand when he starts to protest. "I can handle myself. I'm going to hunt down Marcos and have a little chat."

Diego is pissed, but he knows when to argue and when to follow orders, and he swallows his protest.

We board the jet, and minutes later, I watch while the lights of the city rapidly fall away. Something is wrong. I feel it in my gut.

We land at a private airport near downtown Miami two hours later, and I step off the plane with Diego. After giving him a few last-minute orders, I fold my body into the dark green roadster waiting on the tarmac and put the top down. While I usually savor the fine metal design and luxury of the Aston Martin DBS, I rarely push it to the limits. Tonight, I use every bit of its seven hundred and fifteen horsepower to get me across town in mere minutes.

A boom rips the air, and startled, I let off the gas for a second to search for the source of the noise. A large plume of fire shoots into the night sky not far from me, and I stomp on the gas. It's coming from the same direction as Marcos' office.

Rounding the corner, I screech to a halt outside the entrance to the underground parking garage. Fire streams through the wide opening and blocks me from entering. I spin the car around and head to the front entrance. It's the same. The entire building is engulfed in fire. Frantically, I throw open the car door to get out, but a fire truck lays on its horn behind me. I slam the door shut and move my car down the street.

Running back, I walk the perimeter, trying to find another way inside, but a police officer stops me.

"I have employees in this building!" I shout to be heard over the roar of the fire and the mini explosions still happening on the upper floors.

"At this time of night? How many?" The police officer grabs the radio on his shoulder while he waits for me to respond.

I shove a hand through my hair. "Two security guards, and potentially two employees. I'm not sure, though. Security guards would either be at the front desk or making rounds through the building. The employees would be in the basement. One could be in the underground parking garage in a black SUV or in a nearby office." I watch the man raise an eyebrow at my answer, but I don't fucking answer to him, and I glare back.

"What about cleaning crews? Do you know their schedule?"

I glance at my watch and shake my head in relief. "It's eight-fifteen. They don't start until nine p.m. There could be individuals in the other offices, though."

"We found one security guard," he informs me, pointing to the covered body on the ground. "They're checking the upper floors now."

He grabs the radio on his shoulder and speaks into it. "Fire Chief, this is MPD. Two probable occupants in the basement. Check the underground parking for a black SUV. There's also a nearby office..." He pauses and glances at me.

I grimace. "It's hard to explain, but the entrance is through a door marked 'Utility Room.' Once inside, the entry panel is in the right corner on the floor. The code is 11322549. The door that can only be opened with the code," I tell him, gritting my teeth the entire time, knowing how this appears. "It's not what you're thinking. We don't have a meth lab down there. We develop highly classified technology which requires a secure, hidden location."

He relays the information to the firefighters.

"Are you fucking serious?" a voice returns on the radio. "Rodriguez, get a team and head down into the garage. Search for a black SUV with a possible occupant. I'll give you further instructions once you can assess the situation. Fucking drug dealers."

The police officer smirks at me before speaking into the radio again. "Copy that." He laughs when the voice on the other end says "Shit!" before the radio goes silent. "Do you have any ID on you?"

I raise an eyebrow and pull out my wallet. Handing him the ID, I pace while he walks away to call it in. Dismissing him, I try to call Marcos again, but it goes straight to voicemail. I debate calling Mateo or Grayson. Or Diego. It's his man in there too. I pick up the phone, but a shout from the police officer makes me pause.

"They found a man in the SUV. They're bringing him out now," he informs me, motioning toward the left side of the building.

I see a firefighter laying someone on the ground near the ambulance, and I race over and drop to my knees. Most of the body is heavily burned, but I clench my jaw and force myself to lean in closer. Blue eyes stare dully back at me.

Guilt wars with relief. "Jason, it's Thiago. We're going to get you some help, okay? Hang in there," I state firmly. "Did you see Marcos?"

He looks at me helplessly.

The paramedics shove me away, and I allow myself to fall back until I'm sitting on the ground, watching them work frantically on Jason. In less than a minute, he's gone. Signing the cross, I hang my head and say a prayer. He was a good man. Thirty-three years old, married, with a young daughter. He'd previously been in the Army, but eagerly accepted our offer of employment. Working as part of SEI's security team allowed him to be home and not thousands of miles away from "his girls," as he called them. Now, he's dead. On my watch. I shudder.

The camera crews arrive, and I get to my feet. Turning my back on them, I walk over to the police officer and stand at his side.

He hands me my ID. "Sorry about your man," he offers quietly.

I nod wearily. "A good man," I reply without going into further details. "Any news?"

"They found the door you mentioned. It had been blown off its hinges and was lying about thirty feet away. They can't get into the office, though. Fire is too intense," he explains before turning to face me. "Based on their experience, they think the fire originated from that office. Possibly even an explosion. If anyone was in there..." He doesn't finish the sentence, only claps me on the shoulder after delivering the devastating news. He walks away to redirect the camera crew away from me and back to their van.

I knew something was wrong, but I didn't realize we were at war.

———

WEARY, I pull up to the valet at the office. The idea of parking in the underground garage is abhorrent right now. I hand the young man my keys, and his eyes widen before he breaks out in a huge smile. I stand there until he looks at me.

"M-Mr. Santos," he stammers. "Good morning, sir. I'll take good care of her."

"I know you will, Brian," I state firmly, reassured now he knows whose car he's driving. Walking through the glass doors, I nod to everyone I see, and they stare anxiously back at me. Who the hell knows what I even look like right now? I didn't think to check before coming here.

I'd waited all night, but they didn't find Marcos' body. They confirmed the blast originated from his office, though. If he had been in there, they wouldn't find any evidence until the fire was completely out and they could comb through the ashes. All we can do is wait for them to get back to us, although I did put in a call to the mayor to ask for his assistance in speeding up the process. I'm sure that will piss off more than a few people, but I'll use every resource at my disposal to start getting some answers.

Unfortunately, they found bodies in several other offices. Besides Jason and the security guard, six other people died in the explosion or from the fire. I called our corporate attorney on the way to the office to get them started on finding out the names. SEI owns the building, and this has all the hallmarks of a fucking PR disaster, especially since the blast originated from our secret office in the basement. The speculation and lawsuits are going to hit hard and fast.

When I walk into my office a few minutes later, Mateo and Grayson are waiting for me. Mateo stops typing to glance at me in shock, but Grayson jumps up and strides over to me.

"What the fuck happened? You look like hell ran you over and backed up to do it again," he says, reaching for me, but I wave him off. He leaves the room for a second and returns with a wet cloth and a mirror. "Here. Wash your face, asshole."

I smile at the flood of cuss words streaming out of his mouth. He only does it when he's really upset. The rest of the time, he's the epitome of carefully cultivated sophistication.

"I didn't know you cared," I remark dryly, knowing it will piss him off further.

He stomps over to the bar cart and pours two bourbons neat. He hands one to me, then downs the other. I must look bad if he's not taking the bait.

Glancing in the mirror, the fine layer of dirt and ash covering my face is sobering. I clean a bit of it off, but the rest can wait until I shower. The bourbon calls to me like a siren, and I swallow the contents, hoping it will chase the numbness away.

"There was an explosion at Marcos' office last night," I begin quietly, taking my time to explain every minute and detail from the night.

"So we don't know if Marcos was in the building at the time?" Grayson confirms. He sinks into the chair.

I shrug. "We won't know for sure until they can comb through the… rubble," I slowly reply.

I wait for Mateo to say something, but he's typing away on his laptop. I give him a few minutes, but he says nothing. Furious, I throw my crystal glass at the wall, but I don't watch it shatter. My eyes never leave Mateo. He surges to his feet.

Stomping over to me, he shoves the laptop into my gut.

"Marcos entered his office Monday morning around three-thirty a.m. and again at six a.m. Cameras show him leaving around seven a.m.," he informs me, pointing to the laptop.

Grayson stands next to me, and we both peer at the image frozen on the screen. It's a grainy picture of Marcos' car leaving the underground garage with the timestamp of seven-thirteen a.m. along with Monday's date.

"Wednesday evening, my app reports him entering his office again, but the cameras in the building don't show him entering or exiting. Not one of the twenty-two cameras we placed in the building caught a glimpse of him. I don't have an explanation for it." He stops and swallows a few times.

"It happened again yesterday. The app reported someone entering around five-thirty. He always parked in the garage. So, why aren't the cameras showing his car entering or exiting the last two times? My theory is it wasn't him, but I can't prove it. If we were to use your preferred method and *assume* he only went to the office on Monday, then where has he been this week? He goes to four places on a regular basis. His office, SEI, the condo, or home. He's not been to any of them."

"If it wasn't him on Wednesday or Thursday, do you think it was someone he sent?" Grayson asks Mateo.

Mateo shakes his head. "I do. There are two explanations—he either trusted someone enough to give them access, or he was forced to give access, but we all know he'd rather... He would never give in. Someone he trusted is the only logical answer."

"Who does he know, and more importantly, trust, besides us?" I ask in disbelief.

"Given the code word and encrypted letter, possibly CJ Tech, which I don't understand. Marcos trusts very few people, and he's only worked with CJ Tech on one project," Mateo speculates. "The trust is there, though. The letter clearly ordered me to give her access. If she hadn't run off, I probably would have tried to stall and get a hold of Marcos, but at the end of the day, I would have had to let her look at Marcos' files."

He opens his mouth to say something else, but Diego walks into the office.

"How could you not tell me Jason was dead?" he shouts, furiously shaking his fist at me. "Do I have no respect around here?"

Grayson steps to the side. In two steps, I grab his thick neck and slam him against the wall.

"Don't you ever shout at me again. Do you hear me?" I rasp quietly, waiting for him to answer, but he simply narrows his eyes. "I was headed to your office next to inform you of our loss. Once I've had a shower, I'll stop by Jason's house and speak to his wife."

He snorts in disgust, and I jerk his head forward and slam it back again harder. "Watch yourself, Diego. I'm way past the limits of my patience this morning,"

He jerks his head. "She knows. Who do you think called me in hysterics? That idiot Jason told her he was waiting in the SUV until Marcos showed up. I'll stop by their house to smooth things over." He glances at Mateo and smirks. "Heard you were up all last night fielding attacks. Did they get in?"

I still. "Weren't you here to see for yourself? I ordered you to come straight here and set up security for Grayson and Mateo. Are you telling me you didn't follow my orders?" I wait for him to answer my question.

He swallows. "I've been here in the building the whole time, but they were busy and I didn't want to bother them. Besides, I could easily watch them from the cameras. Two of my men also walked the hallways."

Furious at his insolence, my fingers flex on his windpipe, and I relish in the sound of air whistling from his throat. Fear crosses his face. Already on edge, my control wavers, but I rein it in.

"First of all, I'll go to Jason's house alone. You can drop by later if you wish. Two, the next time you half-ass comply with one of my orders will be the last time. Understood? Three, did you post someone at the condo?" I watch his face drain of color when I get to the last question. "Go do your job. Earn my respect. I'll speak to you later." I open my hand and let him fall against the wall.

He jerks upright and strides angrily out of the office.

"He's been overstepping his bounds a lot lately," Grayson reminds me. "Maybe it's time we restructured our security team."

"Losing Jason was a gut punch, but I'll keep an eye on him," I reluctantly acknowledge. "Right now, we need to start figuring out who's gunning for us and what the hell is going on." My brain sifts quickly through the threads and prioritizes our next steps. "Mateo, keep searching for Marcos. Also, let me know what you find on those cyberattacks. The timing is too coincidental." He nods. "Grayson, investigate CJ Tech. I want to know everything there is to know about them." He nods once.

I head to the bathroom in my office. "After I shower and visit Jason's family, I'm going to investigate the death of Marcos' buyer. The initial report stated accidental death, but I'm skeptical." I stop at the doorway and face them both. "If it was murder, were we collateral damage or the target? Getting that answer will determine how hard we hit back. Regardless, we're at war and we surrender to no one. Agreed?"

They each agree, but it's not necessary. We have never given anyone quarter, and we don't intend to start now.

CHAPTER 10

HENLEY

I feel like there should be a ritual before I hack. When I flex my fingers to limber them up, the *Rocky* theme starts playing in my head, and I can't help but throw a few mock punches before I dive into the computer. Anticipation and adrenaline fill me with a euphoric high, and I laugh. I love creating new software and products, but occasionally, it feels good to do something bad, and hacking is the ultimate adrenaline rush.

If I'm going to stick around Miami for a while, I need more info on SEI and the men who run it, and not just the stuff they're willing to share with the shareholders or public. When I investigated them previously, I ran each of them through a background check and they were clean. Which probably should have been a red flag, but with Marcos' backing, I didn't worry too much.

Using a program from my hacking days, I tap into the global banking system and track down all the accounts for SEI. Then I run the program. It collates all the data first, then searches for patterns and anomalies, like multiple transactions for the same set of funds, manipulation of depreciation values, money or assets that simply disappear, mixing of personal and company funds, offshore accounts, and various other creative accounting methods. It takes days to get the results, but it saves months of manual effort on my part.

I sweep through their personal accounts. I don't expect to find anything remotely criminal, but you can glean a lot of information from someone's daily transactions. For example, mine informed Marcos of my serious food delivery habit. If he'd wanted to come in and kill me, all he had to do was deliver my food. I shiver. Kind of a scary thought.

When I review the bank statement for each of the Santos men, I see the usual tycoon purchases, consisting of expensive meals, luxury cars, custom tailored clothing, jewelry, and flowers every Sunday. *Every Sunday?* A mother or grandmother, perhaps? They only differ in their hobbies. Thiago likes expensive gym equipment and cars. Mateo spends an exorbitant amount on education, which sort of makes the nerd in me giddy, and Grayson likes yachts. I whistle. Expensive hobby.

I google Thiago Santos. Dozens and dozens of pictures pop up. He's big, muscular, and surprisingly, quite tall, with a strong, slightly harsh face. He easily dominates every image. Dark complected with straight, jet-black hair swept back from a broad forehead. Intense, obsidian brown eyes stare arrogantly into the camera. He's a beautiful statue carved from the hardest of stone.

Often pictured with a beautiful woman at his side, but never the same one. Just the same type—glamorous, curvaceous Amazons. I eye the diamond bracelet on one woman's arm. He may not be fond of commitment, but with the amount he spends regularly at the jewelry store, I don't think they mind.

Bachelor's degree in electrical engineering from the University of Florida. MBA from Wharton's School of Business. Bought SEI when he was twenty and named himself CEO. Launched the first SEI security system at twenty-one.

I grab my notebook and jot down a note to find out where he

got the money to buy a large corporation at the age of twenty. I add a note about the flowers on Sunday.

Needing to escape Thiago's intensity, I switch to Mateo Santos. With wavy hair, a little longer than expected, glasses, and full lips, he's certainly every bit as good-looking as Thiago but without the overwhelming dominance.

He seems to live a quieter life, given the few pictures of him. And unlike Thiago, he's rarely photographed with a woman, but when he is, they appear with him at every event for a short period of time, indicating some type of dating scenario. He prefers smart, accomplished women. His most recent dates include a lawyer, a cellist, the CEO of a pharmaceutical company, and a surgeon. I raise my eyebrows. Impressive.

I straighten when I read his credentials. Double major from MIT. Graduated a couple of years before I stepped foot on campus. Bachelor's degrees in applied physics and computer engineering. Master's degree in computer engineering from Stanford. *Genius* level IQ. Joined SEI three years after Thiago at the age of twenty, appointed as CTO, but remained in California until he was twenty-five. He continuously adds to his knowledge base with a myriad of super advanced classes in various subjects.

Mmm, brainy intelligence wrapped in an extremely attractive package—the epitome of a sexy professor, I muse.

There's a knock at the door, and I reach for my phone out of habit before remembering I'm in a rental. *Nobody knows you're here,* I remind myself, and hurry to open it. A beautiful brown package lies on the doorstep. It's truly wonderful when you can order something and get it the next day. The logistics boggle the mind, though.

I set the box down on the coffee table and use my pen to score the tape and open it. There are several listening devices, voice-activated recorders, and wireless spy cameras inside the box. And three tiny receivers. The best way to truly know someone is to spy on them.

I'd found Thiago's downtown condo last night when I did a quick property search, and I'd attempted to hack into the camera network. But my usual hacking methods didn't work. Not surprising. Thiago upgraded the security system at his condo, and it's the best I've ever seen for a home system. I could *probably* hack it if I had spare time, but it's easier to plant a few bugs the old-fashioned way. After I finish my research, I'm heading over to see if I can get inside.

Setting the materials aside, I quickly search for Grayson Santos. A bold headline catches my attention. *"The Savages' youngest seen jet setting with a bevy of beauties around the Mediterranean."* The Savages? I click on the article.

THE SANTOS FAMILY controls Savage Enterprises, Inc., one of the world's largest conglomerates in the world of security and tech, but they're shrouded in mystery. Nicknamed The Savages in the early days, the moniker represented the ruthless tactics deployed against their competitors—often running them out of business entirely. A competitor who'd lost everything bitterly commented on the name of their company on TV, noting it was only fitting a company named Savage Enterprises would be run by a bunch of savages. The nickname stuck. Women especially seem to love it. This week, Grayson Santos displays a staggering sign of wealth with the purchase of his new yacht...

A PICTURE of Grayson standing on the deck of a large white yacht is followed by several pics of him surrounded by a group of tanned, gorgeous women wearing short, silky dresses and dripping in diamonds. I recognize a few heiresses and a couple of popular female actors. He certainly plays in the upper echelons of society.

Instead of one woman, Grayson is always accompanied by at least two—but usually three or four—women. Every article speaks ad nauseum about his playboy ways, making me roll my eyes.

If it weren't for the serious expression in his eyes and the impeccable credentials I uncovered, I'd think he was good for nothing but flirting and spending money. His MBA from Wharton and position as CFO at SEI tells me he's not all play and no work.

I leave the laptop open to allow the banking program to keep running and open the big red tote I "borrowed" from the grocery store this morning. Unzipping a makeup case filled with tampons, I shove a few of the tiny spy gadgets into the bottom, zip it up, and toss it into the tote. I throw a stack of red Foodie delivery flyers and a few pens I'd grabbed from the same grocery store on top of the case.

I move to the mirror by the door and pull a ball cap over my short, wavy blue hair. This wig gives the illusion of youth, especially when paired with my oversized sunglasses. With a deep breath, I head out to bug Thiago's condo.

CHAPTER 11

HENLEY

The bell rings above me when I step into the restaurant. I head straight to the counter and explain I'm a delivery driver for Foodie and I'm here to pick up an order for a... I glance at my phone and pretend to get the name... Mr. Santos.

The lady scrutinizes me, and my heart starts racing.

What now?

"Is the order not ready?" I ask casually, frantically replaying the last three minutes in my head to see if I said or did anything suspicious.

She breaks out in a wide smile. "No, it's fine. I added extra hot sauce and a few of the sopapillas he likes for dessert. He probably forgot. A busy man."

Stunned, I stare at her for a second or five, then force my shoulders to move in what I hope resembles a shrug.

"Sorry, I haven't delivered food to this customer before today, so I don't know what he usually orders. I can find his last order if you want?" I hold up my phone like I could magically find his past orders.

I guess I could, but I'd need about twenty minutes to hack into the system. Maybe I could explain I'm new to buy some time? She doesn't say anything, so I tap on the screen.

"Don't be silly," she admonishes me. "We always take good care of our regular customers. You tell him Juanita says hello and be sure to mention how much we appreciate his business." She shoves a large brown paper bag full of food into my hands.

The smell of Mexican food drifts up, and I moan.

"It smells delicious," I state with utter conviction. Plus, if Santos is a regular customer, it's got to be good. He doesn't strike me as a man who would settle for less than the best. "Thanks!"

I turn to head toward the door, and she grabs my arm. I freeze.

"Here," she says, shoving a warm aluminum foil wrapped log into my hand. "You're too skinny. Eat." She waves me on and moves over to the next customer.

I grin to show my appreciation. "Thank you!" I hurry out the door before she can say or do anything else. What are the odds I'd pick a restaurant frequented by Thiago Santos himself?! With a gusty sigh, I drop into the front seat of my car and place "his" food in the passenger seat.

Unable to resist its siren lure, I unwrap it and discover a massive burrito. I take a huge bite, and an explosion of flavors burst like fireworks in my mouth. Guacamole, black beans, rice, shredded fajita chicken, and pico de gallo have been combined with avocado crema and delicious seasonings to create the best burrito I've ever had in my entire life. Granted, I'm only twenty-seven and I have plenty of time to put this bold statement to the test, but to date, I declare it the unequivocal winner.

I pull out into traffic and head toward the condo three blocks over.

Stuffing the last bite into my mouth just as I reach his building, I park the car in the visitor's spot out front. Mmm, so freaking good. I'll have to order my own food from there.

Yanking the large brown bag toward me, I sift through the order to snag the sopapillas and honey. It's one of my favorite desserts, and since this is an entirely fictitious order that I paid for, I feel justified in taking them. If I could take it all, I would, but I want to make sure there's food in there in case the security desk checks. I leave my contraband on the seat and take a deep breath. Showtime.

———

"I DON'T HAVE any notice from Mr. Santos about an order," the burly security guard gruffly informs me. He finishes checking the clipboard and stares at me suspiciously.

I give him a worried frown in return. "This is my first week delivering food, and I don't know what to tell you. The order appears on my phone, along with the address of the restaurant. I pick it up, check to make sure it's correct, then deliver it to the customer." I try to explain it as if I'm new to the process. Letting my eyes water, I glance quickly at my phone and hunch my shoulders.

He sighs. "Give me the food," he demands with his hand out.

I bite my lip like I'm worried he's going to throw it away but hand it over. The pained expression on his face makes me want to laugh, so I stare down at the black tennis shoes on my feet. When I hear ruffling, I watch while he opens every container to make sure there's nothing but food in it.

He nods in satisfaction and sets it aside, then beckons for my bag. This time, I'm biting my lip for real while I pray he doesn't dig too deep into the makeup case. He pulls out the flyers and sets them aside before he pulls out the makeup case. One bushy eyebrow raises, and I give a half shrug like I don't know what to say. He opens it and stops for a second when he notices the tampons. Pushing a few aside, he peers down in it for a second before closing it.

"I'll have to pat you down too."

"Seriously? Is this guy famous or something?" I joke and put my arms out to the sides. He's quick and efficient and doesn't linger, which is a relief.

"Just a businessman who values his privacy," he sternly informs me. "All right. The elevator will take you directly to his suite. Put the food in the kitchen and come straight down."

He returns everything to me, and I walk quickly to the elevator.

"Thanks, I'll hurry," I assure him with a smile. When the doors close, I maintain the role of a young delivery driver for the cameras and bop my head like I'm listening to music.

When the doors glide open, I'm standing at the entrance of an immaculate and exceedingly modern penthouse. White marble floors gleam against the black and gold patterned art deco wallpaper on the foyer's walls. The excessive gold chandelier on the ceiling casts shards of light onto every available surface until they sparkle. The gold metal foyer table and mirror on my right offers more than pretty design, it's also functional. I plop the food down.

Hurrying farther into the condo, I yank on a pair of plastic gloves and place my spy gadgets in three areas—the living room, primary bedroom, and office. One more item. I pull out my keys, select the one to my mailbox, and peel a tiny square from its back. This microscopic receiver will allow me to access his network from the comfort of my laptop. My eyes dart around the room. I need to find a good place for it.

A bead of sweat rolls down my forehead, and I swipe my forearm across to catch it. When I spot the perfect place in the corner, I hurry over the retro radio sitting on the bookshelves. It might have the appearance of a regular old-fashioned radio and it plays AM/FM, but it also integrates with Bluetooth to play digital. It's the perfect hiding place for my receiver because bug detectors won't be able to distinguish between its receivers and mine. I stick it on the back. The only other place would have been a TV box, but I didn't see one in the condo. I automatically glance at the books on the shelves, but instead of boring engineering tomes, I see a shelf full of spy thrillers. I chuckle. Oh, the irony.

I hurry to the elevator and push the button for the ground floor. I stick a hand in my jeans pocket and use the abrasion of the fabric to carefully peel off one glove, then the other. When I step out, the security guard is busy, so I wave and saunter to the front door.

"Miss, excuse me," the security guard calls out.

Pretending to listen to my music, I keep walking.

An old lady stops in front of me and taps me on the arm. She waves to the desk behind me. "The security guard is calling for you, dear."

Damn it. I pull an earbud out of my ear. "Did you say something, ma'am?" I feel bad for making her repeat herself, but in for a penny and all that.

This time, I turn around after she tells me and glance back at the security guard. He's waving a… phone. *Fuck me.*

Saying a little prayer it's the restaurant calling to tell me they forgot something, I grudgingly return and take the phone.

"Hello?" I say breathlessly.

"This is Thiago Santos, and I want to know what you're doing in my condo," a hard voice on the phone states with almost exaggerated politeness.

"Yes, sir, I delivered the order," I reply, unable to say anything else with the security guard glaring at me suspiciously. "If that's all, I have another delivery to make."

"If you hang up this phone, I'll have you arrested," he coolly informs me. "Tell me, what did you do while you were in there?"

I pause. Would he have me arrested? The food order is real. I'm registered as a driver on the app—under one of my fake names, of course—so I kind of shrug for the benefit of the security guard. "I placed the food in the kitchen," I state firmly. "Sir, I'm sorry, but my other order is getting cold, and I need to go."

At my continued charade, he goes silent for a second. "It's a good thing I don't hunt children. Did someone pay you to deliver the food?"

Child? He thinks I'm a child. I glance down at my torn jeans, Converse and almost laugh. Paid me? Wait. He's watching me from the security cameras. "I'm paid by Foodie, but I'd love a tip," I jokingly add while I pull my hat down tighter.

"Why don't you tell me what you did while you were in my condo for… four minutes and thirty-two seconds?"

Someone lays on their horn, and I hear him muffling the phone while he speaks to someone. He's stalling. Shit. "Sir, thank you so much for all the kind words. I'll be sure to let my boss know. Bye." I hang up. The security guard seems relieved by the end of the call. "Sorry, I've got to go. So late." I take off running.

Jumping into the car, I don't even bother with the seatbelt, just reverse and floor it out of there. I'm about a half mile down the road when a glance in the rearview mirror shows two black SUVs flying into the condo parking lot. Freaking A, that was close. I press my foot down harder on the pedal to get some distance between us. It might be time to switch cars.

The adrenaline races through my body, causing my hands to shake and my heart to pound wildly in my chest. Fear intertwines with the false high, and I feel my mind slipping into a panic attack. Control, gain control. Using a technique my therapist taught me, I recite Albert Einstein's "Wonders of Science" speech, and my mind switches from panic to the constructive miracle of invention.

Unlike the high I get from hacking, the threat of getting physically caught reminds me too much of my years running from my stalker and barely escaping him.

When I get back to the apartment, I flop down on the couch with a sopapilla and think about the call. Thiago's good, calling and speaking to me so sweetly while he sends his goons after me. He started out angry, but somewhere in the conversation, the tone changed. I frown. He was… amused.

With a lick of each finger, I get the last taste of honey off my fingers. I'm positive he'll find the bugs, but they're mostly decoys, anyway. The real gadget is the receiver. It's a door, an open invitation for me to walk inside. From this cozy spot on the couch, I can connect to his network.

One down, two more to go. I chew the inside of my cheek. The problem is, I hadn't found any other properties in the name of Santos or Savage Enterprises, nor did their banks list any lease or mortgage payments. I'm going to have to think of another way to find out where Mateo and Grayson live. Tomorrow, though. I've had enough excitement today.

CHAPTER 12

MATEO

Music slowly trickles in, replacing patterns with beats until I can no longer focus, and I pull myself out of the rabbit hole to shut off the alarm. I take off my glasses and rub my eyes. My brow creases as I mentally examine the information I uncovered. At first, the cyberattacks seemed equally dispersed throughout the company, but two programs were singularly focused on files located only on the R&D servers. My department.

A Trojan was deployed in an attempt to create a backdoor for the hacker to slip behind our firewalls. It had a spyware program piggybacked on top, which was set to search for information on three specific computers—Marcos', mine, and Cecilia's. I frown. Cecilia's is the anomaly in any pattern I try to establish between the three of us. The one thing I know connects us all is SEI, but it's too much of a common denominator to mean anything. If I can figure out another connection, I'll know *what* the hacker was searching for in our files.

The rest of the attacks were simply annoyances—viruses and malware designed to shift our focus away from the real purpose of the attack. If we hadn't installed the new security system to beta test it on our own corporation, they'd have gotten whatever it was they were after and caused untold havoc. On the bright side, we now have real performance data on the new system to show potential clients. Thiago will be happy.

The alarm goes off a second time, and this time, I hear the song and not vague musical notes. "Twilight Zone" by Golden Earring's opening line makes me grimace. It's closer to midnight, not two a.m. I don't have to wonder which one chose this song. It's almost as entertaining to guess whether Grayson or Thiago chose the song as it is to be surprised by it.

Grayson started it when we were kids, although it was a record, not a phone back then. Any time I'd lose myself in a computational problem, he'd play a song to bring the real world into focus. It was a gentler way to pull me out of the dark holes I'd fall into.

The song changes frequently, but not on any specific schedule, so I'm constantly surprised. I don't know how they do it because I swear my phone is always with me, yet it always appears. Honestly, I don't want to know how they do it. One of the few things I'm able to leave as a mystery.

Tonight… Grayson chose this song. It's full of his dark humor and sense of irony. An old but good one. I shoot off a text to him.

Standing, I stretch out my tight muscles. My custom designed ergonomic chair helps, but I'm still stiff. It cost a fortune, but if I calculate use per minute, it probably pays for itself in a month. Hmm… I slip my glasses on and grab a sticky to write the thought down. Couldn't hurt to know. I wonder if Grayson could use the data to calculate depreciation value. I add the additional notation.

The alarm goes off for a third and final time. I put the sticky down on the desk and walk out the door and into the elevator. If I don't leave by the third alarm, they'll come and drag me home. If it's Grayson, we usually find a nearby late-night bar and grab an incognito drink and some unhealthy food. Thiago… I wince. He gets up around four a.m. to work out, so he gets a little… irritated.

The elevator opens, and I flinch. Ever since the fire, the underground garage makes me uneasy. We haven't heard anything yet about the cause of the explosion or if they've found anything in the rubble, but I'm worried sick. I keep reminding myself Marcos is likely on one of his "special" trips. He disappears for a week or two on a regular basis to go on his rescue missions, but he usually finds a way to send us an encrypted message to let us know he's okay. It seems longer, but I guess it's only been a week since I saw him last.

When I get in my car, it clicks but doesn't start. Puzzled, I glance at the dash and the battery displays zero percent. It's completely out of charge. I frown. I charged it yesterday. Or maybe it was the day before? I groan. The days are blurring together this week. Ever since the cyberattacks, I've been running on three or four hours of sleep a night.

I'm not getting home this way, but I add garage superchargers to my mental to-do list. Being able to charge electric vehicles at the office would be a huge help for several individuals, not just me.

Opening the door, I get out and head back to the elevator. A squeak sounds to my left, and I jerk my head, expecting to see someone, but nobody is there. I run a hand through my hair. I need sleep.

I tap the app and request a rideshare. Miami never sleeps, so I shouldn't have any issues getting a car quickly, especially on a Saturday night. With a wave to the security guard on my way out, I pass through the doors and immediately get a notice telling me my driver, Cassie, is here, in a dark grey Nissan Rogue. At least it isn't one of the small vehicles where I have to scrunch into the backseat.

"Name?" I ask, opening the door.

A husky yet somehow familiar voice greets me. "Cassie, that's me. And you?"

My brow furrows. Where have I heard that voice?

"Mateo," I say absentmindedly.

A combination of oranges, jasmine, and other tropical fragrances wraps around me as I slide into the backseat, and I inwardly groan. It's been a while since I've gone on a date and the smell is all woman.

"Great, where are we headed tonight?" Cassie asks after putting the car in gear. She adjusts the phone on the dash, and it blinks for a second. "Okay, I have the address now. I think I might have to get a new phone."

I catch her blue eyes in the rearview mirror. "Have we met before?" I'm good with voices. Must be all those years of listening to songs.

She shrugs. "I've been doing this for a few years," she replies with a wave of her hand, like she's heard the same comment a million times. "How's your night?"

She might have been my driver before, but I don't think that's it. Her voice is bugging for me some reason. My phone buzzes, and I answer. "I'm on my way home. Had a bit of a mishap with my car, but I grabbed a rideshare."

Thiago shuffles around for a minute. "What happened with your car?"

I groan. "No charge. I must have forgotten with everything going on the past few days," I admit sheepishly. A huge yawn catches me, and I pause for a second. "Sorry for the yawn. I need sleep. But it was worth it. The cyberattacks were deliberate, set off to divert our focus while it attempted to establish a backdoor to the R&D servers. It's a breakthrough."

"If they're connected to the buyer, maybe they're looking for more tech to steal," he says with a frustrated groan. Silent for a few minutes, I can almost hear his brain sifting through the possibilities. "Prior to tonight, has your car ever run out of charge?"

Of course he wouldn't let that go. He's suspicious of everything these days. "Once," I admit with a roll of my eyes. The rear window shatters, and glass showers down on top of me.

Cassie screams. She whirls around to gape at me, her blue eyes wide with terror.

"It wasn't me," I assure her. The car swerves wildly back and forth. "What is it? A rock? A flat tire?" I grip the seat in front of me until the car levels out. I can hear Thiago yelling from my lap where I dropped the phone, and I pick it up to reassure him but pause when she yells.

"Get down!"

I drop immediately. It's a good thing. The windows on both sides of me shatter. "Fuck!"

"Someone's… oh God… shooting at us." She taps frantically on the phone in front of her until a map of streets is laid out. A litany of curse words continues to roll out of her mouth while she drives erratically to evade our pursuers.

I raise the phone. "Thiago—my gun's in the car." I hear heavy breathing and a litany of cuss words. He's pissed I broke one of his cardinal rules. Gun or bodyguard, our choice, but alone and without protection is not an option.

Two minutes later, she turns right at the last minute. We barely make the turn, but the car behind shoots past, gaining us a reprieve.

"What in the hell? Is someone trying to kill you too?"

Too?

My head feels like it's going to explode. I raise my hand to massage my temples, but it's wet. With a frown, I tap the flash on and take a picture of myself. Turning it off, I inform Thiago.

"My head's bleeding heavily too. Maybe a shard of glass hit me. I don't know." The blood flows down my face, so I take off my glasses and slip them into my pocket. Tearing off a large chunk of my shirt, I press it to the wound. "Fuck!" It hurts like hell.

"What?!" Cassie shouts. She types "hospital" into the map on the phone. It displays results almost instantly. "We're ten minutes from the nearest hospital. Hang on, okay? Shit, shit, shit." She turns left at the light.

Why does she need a map? Didn't she tell me she's been a rideshare driver for a while?

A black sedan passing in the opposite lane brakes hard, and the screech from the tires tells me they're our attackers. A loud squeal rends the air, reminiscent of a car doing a hard U-turn. I squint out the shattered rear window. *Pzzt.*

"Are you crazy? Get down!" she screams.

The car swerves wildly, and I push myself up to see the road. "Take the next right. If you can gain some distance, take another immediate right, then pull into the parking garage on the left, in the middle, and shut off your lights."

She nods.

I raise the phone to let Thiago know what we're planning. "Tell me you have someone on the way to help," I demand, pain making me hoarse. "We're heading toward the Old Bay parking garages to try to lose them."

"I heard," he states in a clipped voice. "I'm tracking you, and we're on our way. ETA in twelve minutes."

She makes the first right turn at the last second, but the car chasing us also makes the turn. Both cars are flying down the street, one behind the other. The right turn on to Old Bay is getting closer and closer, but we're in the left lane. Some other car is in the right lane.

I hear her whisper a prayer over and over. Mashing her foot down to the floor, she pulls ahead of the car on the right, and at the last second, makes the right turn directly in front of their car.

I close my eyes and brace myself for them to T-bone us on my side of the vehicle, but with a long blare of the horn, they somehow miss us. Maybe we had enough distance or maybe they slowed down, but we avoided collision by a whisper and a prayer. And gained a few precious seconds.

Old Bay Street is full of parking garages because it's near a huge apartment complex covering several city blocks. She turns left into the middle garage.

"We're parking in the middle garage off of Old Bay," I explain to Thiago. "Hurry. I doubt we have twelve minutes." I hear Grayson cussing beside him and smile. "Hey, man, glad to know you care. Nice song tonight."

A loud groan fills the air. "It was until it came true," he retorts. "Fuck, man. Hang in there. Thiago's driving, so we should be able to cut down the ETA." I hear Thiago asking what song he picked, and I laugh. That's going to be an uncomfortable conversation.

Cassie parks on the third floor with the blown out rear window toward the wall. She turns off the car and peels her shaking hands off the steering wheel. Grabbing her bag from the floor, she slips it over her shoulder, then grabs her phone and gets out.

That's good. She can hide before they get here. She doesn't need to become a target for SEI's enemies. The door beside me opens, and I cautiously lean away from it.

A slim arm slides around me, and I turn to find her lips right in front of me. "You smell sweet, so… seet. Why do you smell like para… para… dise?" Why am I slurring? A small hand slaps my cheek a couple of times. I jerk my head back and scowl at her.

"I need you to get out of the car, Mateo. Right now. I'll help, but when I pull, you need to stand at the same time," she instructs me. "I'll even give you the name of my body wash since you seem to like it so much, although I think you should stick with yours."

When she heaves, I move forward clumsily, causing her to stumble back into the car behind her. I slide up against her. Mmm, she fits so well.

"Sorry, let me straighten us," she says breathlessly before shifting me to her right side. "Let's go." She closes the car door, and with her propping me up, we head toward the elevator. Lights bounce around the garage, and she swivels her head wildly.

"Go," I order her. "Hide or leave. They want me, not you."

She rolls her eyes at me. "Don't be stupid." Heading over to the corner, she hides us behind a large white van. She pulls off her jacket, then her T-shirt, until she's squatting in front of me wearing a plain beige bra.

I raise my eyebrows. "What are you doing?" My eyes automatically glance down at the creamy tops of her breasts.

She pulls her jacket back on, and I sigh in disappointment.

She laughs.

"You would deny a dying man such a beautiful sight?" I jokingly question.

She balls up the shirt and swaps it for the blood soaked rag in my hand, then places my hand on it and presses down hard.

The pain makes my head swim, and I drop my head between my knees.

"You must keep pressure on this. How close are your... friends?"

What's it been? How long since I spoke to Thiago? I ease up. "Still six or seven minutes out," I inform her. "Got any ideas?"

"Maybe," she returns vaguely. "Hold tight." She grabs her phone and starts tapping furiously at various apps until she finds the right one.

Her fingers move fast when she starts typing, even faster than mine. "You're good in a crisis. Who are you texting?"

"You'd be surprised at how resourceful you can be when you're backed into a corner. Not texting. Trying to see if there's anything nearby that can help us," she says without looking up from her phone.

A car screeches to a halt at the end of the third row, and I hear shouting and doors slamming. They've found us. Six minutes until the calvary gets here. An eternity. For someone who usually sees time as a variable to factor into a computation, I'm acutely aware of it right now. The voices and footsteps get louder and closer.

I put my hand on her shoulder. "Please, go," I whisper. "You can make it out of here. Slide behind that pillar to the stairs on the left and make your way down." I'd been mapping out a route while she typed, but with the way the world is blurring, I won't make it. She can, though.

She shrugs off my hand but doesn't move.

Gritting my teeth from the pain, I set down the cloth, grip her hips and pull her back until she's farther behind me and more protected by the van. She never even stops typing. When I peer under the van, I see a black shoe about three cars away. When blood drips on the concrete floor, I ease up and place her shirt back on the wound.

"There. Cross your fingers," she whispers.

When I look over, her head is cocked to the side like she's waiting for something.

An ear-piercing siren shatters the silence. Then a second, and a third. Shrill and continuous, someone's bound to get pissed and call 911. Footsteps pound on the concrete, doors slam, and we hear the roar of their car heading out of the garage.

"What did you do?"

She shrugs and helps me stand. "Set off a few alarms. We need to get you out of here," she says urgently, which tells me I'm not looking too good.

Her slim body is taut against mine as she braces herself to take more of my weight. I focus on the delicious smell surrounding her and the feel of her against me, which gives me the motivation to place one foot in front of the other. Step by step, we make our way to her car. The strength in my legs slowly leaves me until I can't walk any farther.

"Here." I point to the ground.

A squeal of tires sounds below.

She props me up and gently sweeps my hair back from my forehead so I can see. "I think your friends are here. I'll go check."

I grab her hand and squeeze. "Obrigado. Be careful."

The garage blurs, then disappears.

CHAPTER 13

<u>THIAGO</u>

G rayson glares at me when I start shouting, so I step out into the hospital hallway. Diego is silent on the other end of the phone, and I force myself to pause and take a deep breath in and out to calm down. Maybe if I switch tactics, I'll get some movement.

"Diego, we've been friends a long time, correct? Since we were kids. I know if it were your family who'd been shot, you would tear this city inside out to find who did it. And I'd be right by your side, using all my resources to help you," I state firmly. He sighs. "I'm asking you to put aside your feelings about Mateo and help me find who shot him. I can't protect my family against a ghost."

"Pulling out the violins, huh?" He chuckles. "Someone hacked the cameras and erased them. I'll keep banging on doors, but we're hitting brick walls right and left. As soon as I have anything, I'll call you back." He hangs up.

Furious, I grip the phone tightly, barely refraining from throwing it against the wall. Someone might have been able to take out the city cameras, but there are miles of individual businesses and cameras along the route they took last night.

Exhausted, I close my eyes for a brief second. We've been here since they brought Mateo in at two a.m. this morning. I glance at my phone. Approximately twelve hours ago. Shaking it off, I refrain from calling Diego back to give him a piece of my mind, and instead, scroll through my contacts until I find one labeled "Fixer" and hit dial.

A rough voice answers. "This had better be good," he warns me. "I was up all night hunting down answers for you here in Chicago."

"Good. I need answers. We're at war and someone drew first blood last night. Mateo was shot. I need you to gather a second team for me. I'll pay double your fee and all expenses, but I need the results fast." I pause to let him digest the offer.

"Sorry to hear about Mateo. Is he going to be all right?"

"A deep graze, but he'll recover. Thanks. But we need to figure out who's gunning for us so we can stop playing defense," I reply. I sweep my hand over my face.

"Double, huh? You sure know how to sweet-talk me. Send me the details, and I'll get a crew on the ground in Miami," he replies. "But you're right—war is at your door. Someone went to a lot of trouble to get that tech on the last deal. The original buyer was into Chicago organized crime for a lot of money. Three days before the bidding opened, someone placed millions into their account. Wife saw it. Husband told her not to say anything.

"He went straight to the cartel and paid his debt. The day after the bid, the husband arrived home in a rage and locked himself in his office. After a couple of hours, he came out, said a lot of sweet things to her and the kids, and left. He never made it home. Police ruled it an accident, but only because they couldn't determine if he purposely drove himself off the bridge or not. After the funeral, the wife found an image on the printer of her and the kids with red Xs across their face. I'd call it suicide by coercion."

My mind latches on to a few things right away. "Which outfit?"

"Italian mafia, run by Scarpioni family, why?"

I'm relieved to hear it's the Italian mafia and not a certain Brazilian cartel, but I keep the past where it belongs.

"Just curious. If he paid the debt, they didn't convince him to take a dive. My guess is somebody else did. If the money was deposited three days before the bidding opened, it means our enemy had insider knowledge."

"Want to know something even more interesting? The rest of the money disappeared completely from their account before he died. Whoever it is was generous enough to let him pay his debt, but they didn't want it to be traced back to them. And when I say disappeared, I mean Slick hasn't been able to find a hint of the transaction, nor a single penny of that money," he drawls, referring to the hacker he has on his payroll.

Same thing happened on our end, but only a handful of people have that knowledge. They're connected.

"Thanks, this information has been a huge help," I inform him. "I'll send the details for the Miami job today. All communications need to go through me. Also, can you have Sterling run this license plate and get back to me asap with the info?" I give him the digits.

"I'm sure Slick would be happy to do it," he chuckles at the nickname every time he says it. I'm sure Sterling loathes it. "Be safe. See you on the ground."

Grayson eyes me expectedly when I return to the room, his arrogant brow arched high and demanding answers. "Did Diego give you any updates?"

I shake my head. "No, I decided to bring in Zane and one of his teams. They'll report directly to me. Diego is not to know," I say, settling in the chair on the other side of Mateo's hospital bed.

He's still sleeping off the anesthesia from the minor surgery needed to close the wound. Thankfully, the bullet grazed his head. It's going to take some time to fully heal, but an inch or two to the right, and he wouldn't be here right now. Fury rises at the thought, but I beat it down. Grayson may kill me if I don't get a handle on it.

"Sterling is also tracking the license plate for the driver."

"Cassie?" a scratchy voice asks from the bed. "Is she okay?" The sheets rustle as he tries to get traction and push himself into a sitting position.

Grayson pushes the button to raise the bed, then jumps up to give him an ice chip. "Here, this should help."

"Is that her name?" I ask.

His brows pull together. "Did she not tell you?"

"You were sitting alone in the parking garage tonight when we arrived," I reply angrily. She left him alone and injured for our enemies to find. "Unconscious and by yourself. I checked the vehicle, but there wasn't a shred of paper or anything in it. I didn't have time to search the structure before the ambulance came to get you. Grayson and I followed it to the hospital. I sent Diego and his men to get prints, but the vehicle was gone."

"She saved us," he pushes out.

"She left you," I retort.

He shakes his head. "She hacked all the nearby alarms. Scared them off." His voice drops to a whisper. "Incredible. Told me to stop being stupid. Anomalies, though." Sleep claims him again.

Puzzled, I glance at Grayson. He's also perplexed. My phone buzzes. Unknown number. "Hello?"

"It's Sterling. Sorry it took me so long. A bit more complicated than I anticipated," he says in disbelief. "Vehicle was purchased yesterday in Miami by Cassie Turner. She traded in a blue Toyota Corolla and paid the balance with cash."

Cash. My gut twists, and I grab a piece of paper and pen from the bedside table.

"Who is she? Does she live in Miami?" I reply.

He reads her credentials. "She's twenty-eight, from Los Angeles, California. Single. Waitress. Annual income of thirty-one thousand dollars. Good credit score. No college. Picture is a female with pink hair and blue eyes."

Sterling pauses, then chuckles. "It's one of the best fake IDs I've ever come across. The backstory is clean and partially accurate. The real Cassie Turner even lived at one of the listed addresses at one time. If I hadn't known she purchased the car with cash, I wouldn't have dug any deeper. When I checked the IRS for her tax returns, the real Cassie Turner came up. The two didn't match. The backstory is simple, but brilliant. If you catch her, I want to meet her. Possibly hire her. Text me if you need anything else." He hangs up.

Blue Corolla rings a bell. I tap on my security system app to review the footage from the cameras at the condo. It returns nothing for that date and time. I try again. It isn't there. I watched the footage yesterday, and today, it's gone. I can't think of why the videos would be missing. I pinch the bridge of my nose. Mateo usually stores back-ups on a private server, but I can't access it until he wakes up.

I growl and look at Grayson. "Why do I feel like we're constantly two steps behind everyone else? Hell, I can't even tell which players are on the board right now. Marcos is missing. Diego's gone off the rails. The condo is bugged. CJ Tech is waiting in the wings. Mateo's shot but saved by a ghost."

He leans back and crosses his arms. "As Marcos would say, let's lay out the facts and work the problem. What did you find out today?"

"The buyer received a huge incentive to bid on the software three days before the bidding started, and he took it because his gambling problem meant he owed the wrong people. He paid them off, but the rest of the money disappeared. Not even Sterling can trace it. Sound familiar?" I say wryly.

He straightens. "Hell yes, it does. So, we have two incidents where the money was deposited, then removed without a trace. In all my years of finance, I've never run across anything like it. There's always some trace. Who killed the buyer?"

"He drove off a bridge, but he might have done it to save his family," I explain. I rub the back of my neck to ease some of the strain. "Cassie, the rideshare girl, is a ghost. Fake ID. Bought the car yesterday with a trade-in and some cash. This is the second time in two days a mysterious woman has popped up and disappeared."

"Third time, if you count the admin from CJ Tech," I remind him.

I perk up and reach for my phone. Maybe I can pull a good pic from the security cameras. "What day and time?"

"Wednesday, around noon."

Scrolling through the security footage from SEI, I stop when I see Mateo and Grayson standing beside a beautiful, tall blonde. I hold out my phone to him.

"That is the woman who said she was from CJ Tech and gave Mateo the encrypted letter," he confirms.

I shake my head in disappointment. "This is undeniably a woman," I murmur, admiring her obvious curves. "The one at the condo barely looked old enough to drive. Tall, gangly. Blue hair. Funny, though. Cocky, given the circumstances." I chuckle at her audacity. "I know I saw her driving a blue car, but I can't confirm if it's a Corolla because the footage has disappeared, like every-fucking-thing lately."

"Rose or Goldie certainly wasn't a teenager," he says huskily, making me raise an eyebrow. "She was intriguing but couldn't lie worth a damn. Interesting thing, she wasn't lying when she said she was with CJ Tech. Only lied about her name, and…" He stops and gives me a startled look. "Diego. Before he arrived, she was calm and collected. He rattled her the minute he stepped into the conversation like she feared him." He frowns heavily. "He wasn't invited to the impromptu meeting but overheard her say CJ Tech and barged his way into the conversation to drill her with questions. I didn't know he knew about the deal."

I try to remember if I'd said anything about it. "I might have said something on the phone to one of you and he overheard." I look away for a second. "I don't know what to think about Diego. He's one of my oldest friends, but I won't pretend I'm not concerned. I need proof he's doing something wrong."

Grayson glances at Mateo and sighs. "I wish Marcos would return." He taps the chair with his fingers. "Without knowing all the other answers, the one fact I keep returning to in my mind—if they have the software, why are they still after us? We're the ones who didn't get paid for the software. We should be hunting them."

Stunned, I curse. Son of a… I've been so focused on the explosion, cyberattacks, and the rest of the mess around us, I didn't stop to think why they are continuing to pursue us.

"What could they possibly want? The only person who might know the answer is Marcos. We need him to get back from wherever he's gone and help us figure this out."

I look from Grayson to Mateo and feel the same fierce determination to keep them safe. My hands aren't clean, and I have no qualms about using every resource in my considerable arsenal to keep my family intact.

CHAPTER 14

<u>HENLEY</u>

My heart races wildly as I aim the gun at my target, but instead of my usual laser sharp focus, the circles swirl and bleed into one another until the paper bullseye morphs into Diego's face. His beady eyes lock on mine with glee, and fear paralyzes me. *Push aside the fear. Breathe. That's it. Aim, exhale, and... fire.* The loud report of the gun cracks the air around me, and Diego disappears in a whiff of smoke.

I set the gun down and wipe my sweaty hands on the towel beside it. I'm terrified of him but need to push through it in case I have to defend myself. Practicing helps me replace my fear and paralysis with ritual. Last night's car chase and shooting raised the stakes, and I can't afford to think this isn't going to get worse. I pick up the gun and repeat the maneuver.

After putting all the pieces together, I concluded they were after Mateo last night, not me. My guess is someone purposely drained his battery, forcing him to call for a ride. Maybe they hoped he'd call Grayson or Thiago, but he called for a rideshare. The app alerted me to the request because I was closest, and I accepted.

My original intent was to follow Mateo home and get his address so I could return later and plant some bugs, not give him a ride. Since you can turn the branding light on and off, I thought the rideshare would provide a measure of disguise if he glanced in the rearview mirror, make him think different vehicles were behind him.

I knew I could leave Mateo for them to find, but I didn't want to chance it. From the corner, I watched the vehicle scream to a halt, and two men jump out of the vehicle.

Instead of the elegantly attired Grayson I met the other day, the man jumping out of the SUV last night to get to Mateo was prepared to go to war. Dressed in black camo pants and shirt, with a gun strapped across his back and one in a side holster, he looked lethal. The transformation was startling, and it made me think of Diego's obvious fear when Grayson shielded me the other day at SEI.

He was followed by a man I've only seen in pictures, but the two-dimensional images didn't capture a tenth of the intensity Thiago Santos exudes. He is every bit as big as I expected, but his fierceness makes him appear a giant among men. Once Grayson confirmed Mateo was alive, Thiago's focus shifted to my vehicle. I shudder to think what he would have done if I'd been nearby. The vehicle revealed nothing, but he did take down my license plate. His body strained to hunt like the predator he is, but the wail of the ambulance siren diverted his attention. He must have called them en route.

When they left, I wasted no time in getting the car out of the garage and to the nearest car wash. After washing the blood out of the seats and vacuuming the glass, I drove to a neighborhood known for its crime and left the car with the keys in the ignition.

When I returned to the rental, I had a small farewell bonfire for Cassie Turner. That ID is burned, and I had to get rid of it.

I load another clip into the gun and start firing at a new target. I'd called the hospital this morning to check on Mateo, but they wouldn't release the info. A quick hack into his records told me his surgery went well and he's in recovery.

My body shakes, thinking about how close we came to getting killed last night, and I need to put the gun down for a second. If I hadn't been able to find and set off those alarms, neither of us would be alive, but I can't stop now.

Marcos encrypted the drive two days before his death, which means I have less than two weeks to find the other file. I'm tempted to let the data disintegrate, but the cost is already too high. Marcos deserves vengeance, and I don't want someone else to benefit from his death.

The banking program I ran on SEI to assess their financials came back clean. There's nothing there to indicate they run a shady business. In fact, they even donate a significant portion of their profits to charity. I also didn't find the money from the sale of our software. If SEI didn't get paid for the deal either, could they be an innocent third-party in all this mess? I haven't found anything to indicate their guilt, but I'm also not going to quickly jump to a decision.

While I was searching through the SEI website for more information last night, I stumbled across their career page. Like a prayer answered, I found a way to get through the door. They're looking to hire a contractor for their IT department. The new hire would fill in temporarily for a recently vacated position while they search for a permanent replacement. Lucky for me, my qualifications are everything they want in a candidate, so I apply for it. Fingers crossed I get an interview.

———

WITH A CLICK OF THE MOUSE, I hit submit and complete the final skills test. "I'm done, Mr. Carlton," I inform the gentleman behind me.

Philip Carlton's head of the IT department at SEI, and thankfully, he loved my qualifications so much, he called first thing this morning. With only two weeks left to get the other copy of the software and decode it, I arranged to come in immediately to interview.

He pulls the results up and beams at me. "Please, call me Philip. You're very well qualified, Miss Taylor, and your contract rate is within our range for this position. We have several more candidates to interview, but we'll be in touch."

"Please, call me Samantha," I implore him with a smile. "I believe I mentioned I can start tomorrow, right?" He scans his notes and confirms. "To be fair, SEI is my first choice, but I need to let you know, I have two more interviews this afternoon. If they offer..." I let my voice trail off and add a slight shrug for effect. Rising to my feet, I hold out my hand to shake. "Thank you so much, Philip. Good luck with your interviews. I know you'll find a wonderful candidate."

He stutters for a second, indecision warring on his face, before he holds up a finger. "Hold on. Let me check on something." He grabs the papers off his desk and hurries out of the office.

I furrow my brow as if confused, but secretly, I hold my breath, hoping my tactics worked.

Five minutes later, he returns with a huge smile on his face.

"We typically approve all IT hires with Mateo Santos, but with him out of the office, I wasn't sure if we could move forward. Thankfully, I caught Grayson in his office, and he reviewed the results and approved your hire. We'd like to officially offer you the contract position in our IT department, Samantha."

With a broad smile, I hold my hand out to him. "Thank you, Mr. Carlton. That's wonderful news, and I accept." *And thank you, Grayson*, I mutter silently.

We iron out the specifics, and I promise to be at SEI bright and early tomorrow morning.

Waiting by the elevator, a pang of guilt hits me. Mr. Carlton, Philip, is an extremely nice man, and when I leave after a few days, he's going to wonder how he could have been so wrong about me. Maybe I can think of something to take the sting out. Winning the lottery? Unbelievable, but not impossible. I sigh.

"Is everything okay?" a gravelly but remarkably familiar voice asks behind me.

I turn slowly to face the man I've only spoken to on the phone and smile widely. "Yes, thank you. Just thinking of the million and one things I must do this afternoon."

I inhale sharply at the sight of him in his custom-tailored suit. It's beautifully cut, speaks of money, and yet it's as if someone dressed a Cane Corso in expensive summer wool. It does nothing to hide the power and lethalness that lies underneath. The danger emanating from him sets off alarm bells and triggers my own highly developed sense of self-preservation, and yet I couldn't move if I wanted.

Thiago's eyes sweep over me from head to toe, then he frowns. "You sound familiar," he states firmly. His eyes narrow on my brown hair and green eyes, and I hold my breath while I wait for his verdict. "Maybe not." Cocking his head to the side, he continues to stare at me, his brow furrowed in concentration.

Intelligence gleams from the depths of the darkest brown eyes I've ever encountered. Combined with the predator instincts, his stare is mesmerizing, like a cobra weaving its magic until you can't help but give in. The appeal of even one night with him...

I swallow and stick my hand out.

"Samantha Taylor, Mr. Santos, I'm starting a position with SEI tomorrow," I say, introducing myself. He won't be satisfied until he gets some information.

"Samantha Taylor," he repeats after me. "Welcome to SEI. Since we're on the fourth floor, I assume you'll be starting in our IT department?"

"Yes, sir," I automatically reply. I wait for him to say something else, but he doesn't, only continues to examine my every movement. The swish of the elevator doors opening releases the magnetic hold he has on me.

His big body brushes mine when he walks past to get in the elevator. Turning around, he gives me a speculative look.

"I'll figure it out," he promises me, a dark smile gracing his hard lips.

The doors close. I raise my hand and grasp the front of my shirt, quickly flapping it back and forth to get air flowing to my body.

STELLA BRIE

Whether it's from the sheer impact of him physically or the knowledge I'm on limited time, I can't tell. I do know it's quite possible I might die of nerves, not bullets, before this is over. He recognized my voice, but the brown hair, green eyes, and professional clothes threw him off. It won't for long, though. I need to get in, get the file, and get out quickly.

THIAGO

The elevator doors close on the lanky brunette, and I frown. She's not even remotely my type, but I couldn't take my eyes off her. Something about her puts my instincts on high alert, and with everything going on, I can't afford to dismiss even the slightest of concerns. I send a note to myself to get her personnel files from Philip Carlton and have Sterling run a more thorough background check.

Grayson texts to let me know Mateo is home, and I nod with satisfaction. He's got a massive headache, but it's a clean wound and he should heal over the next couple of weeks, if we can convince him to take it easy.

My phone buzzes just as the elevator doors open, and I step out to answer it. "Hello," I say, while I stop to get my messages from my admin.

"Hello, this is Agent Antonio Garcia. I'm a Certified Fire Investigator, or CFI, with The Bureau of Alcohol, Tobacco, Firearms, and Explosives, agency otherwise known as the ATF. Is this Thiago Santos?" The man introduces himself.

With a frown, I step into my office and close the door. "Yes, this is Thiago Santos. I've been waiting for someone to call me but didn't realize it would be a federal agency. Do you have any updates?"

"The explosion that occurred last Thursday at eight p.m. was caused by an improvised explosive device, or as we refer to them, an IED. Unlike your basic homemade bomb, this one was sophisticated, complex, and the hallmark of professionals. The explosion originated from the office in the basement of the building. It was deliberate. I'll send you all the information, including my contact information, via email, so you and your lawyer can review it," he says in a clipped voice.

I drop down heavily into my chair and rub a hand over my face. "Did you find any remains in the office?" I ask hoarsely. For the first time in my life, I'm afraid to hear the answer.

"Yes, we found the remains of a body. With the DNA you provided, we were able to match the teeth found at the crime scene to Marcos Santos," he confirms, his tone somber. "With the discovery of his body and confirmation on the location and type of device, this is now an official murder and fire investigation. I'll be lead agent on the case and will be in touch soon with some questions for you and your family. And I'd like to extend my condolences on the loss of your uncle."

"Thank you," I say numbly and hang up.

I immediately text Diego with an order to have a car and driver ready and head out. With my face blank, I inform my admin to cancel all my appointments for the rest of the week. She gapes at me in shock but nods her head.

My body shakes, needing to let loose the barrage of emotions, but I clench my hands into fists and do everything I can to hold it together until I reach the vehicle. Once inside, I instruct the driver to take me home, then close the partition.

Grief explodes out of me like a supernova, and harsh sobs fill the air. Marcos might have held the title of uncle, but he meant so much more. Better than a father to me, he was my best friend and the man who taught me everything worth knowing.

Marcos gave me life after my father took it away. When I was ten, my accountant father betrayed the largest cartel in Rio, and when they discovered the traitor, they offered him a choice. Death or penance. If he chose penance, all would be forgiven. He agreed without hesitation. The penance? Kill his wife and child and dedicate his life to the cartel.

Too much of a coward to kill us directly, he arranged for us to have a car accident on the way home from the beach. Francisca, my mother—and Marcos' sister—and Juliana, Marcos' wife, were killed instantly. Gravely injured, I was taken to the hospital. My father arranged for me to have last rites. But sometime in the night, a miracle happened and I turned away from death. When my uncle went to tell my father, he overheard him reassuring the cartel his family was dead. My uncle backed him up, then personally arranged my "death" with the hospital.

Once the funerals were over and I healed enough to travel, we fled Brazil to Mexico to get my Aunt Mariana and her son, Mateo. From there, we smuggled our way into the US, staying constantly on the move for a year, until we finally landed in Miami and took a new last name—Santos.

"Tio," I roar, grief and fury spilling over until it hardens into the cold steel of vengeance. "I vow your death will not go unanswered nor unpunished. No mercy will be given. The blood of our enemies will run through the streets before I'm done. This I swear." With the sign of the cross, I bow my head and pray for his soul and my own.

We pull into the driveway, and I get out. The white contemporary house crafted of concrete and glass stands strong against the constant winds coming off the ocean. It's a refuge and fortress, like Marcos, who designed it. With a deep breath, I do the hardest thing imaginable and walk in to deliver the news to Mateo and Grayson.

———

WE HOLD the memorial two days later, at our home, overlooking the ocean Marcos loved so much. Although he often lamented it couldn't compete with the ocean near his beloved Brazil, the sight and sounds of the waves crashing reminded him of Juliana and another life and time. He would sit for hours, gazing out over the water, talking to his anjo, his angel.

Grayson, Mateo, and I stand shoulder to shoulder, holding each other up in our grief. Marcos meant something unique to each of us, but our grief is the same, the loss profound. I wipe the tears from the corners of my eyes.

All three of us walk to the table together and grab a shot glass filled with Marcos' favorite tequila. Raising it high in the air, we shout, "Saúde!" After downing the shot, we flip the glass over. With this toast, we celebrate his life and mourn his death.

Besides family, Marcos' two closest friends are here to say goodbye, and they follow our toast with one of their own. Overall, it's a quiet affair. Marcos spent most of his time alone or on rescue trips. We eat, drink, and reminiscence for the next hour, but then everyone slowly trickles out the door.

"The lawyer will be here in the morning," I remind Mateo and Grayson. Mateo's pale and barely holding on. "Go to bed. Rest." He starts to protest, but I hold up a hand. "You need to be at full strength and ready for whatever's coming." He nods and heads to bed.

Grayson hands me a glass of tequila and takes the seat beside me on the patio, the ocean a backdrop to our grief.

"Mateo spent all last night going over footage of the office building," Grayson murmurs next to me. "He's obsessed with finding Marcos' killer." He lifts a shoulder. "I know he should rest, but none of us will be able to sleep until we get answers. We need a target for all this anger and grief. Marcos was the only 'real' father I or any of us ever knew."

"I agree. Let him search," I tell him with a sigh. "We need all the help we can get right now. Zane and his team are at our disposal until this is over." I swallow the rest of the drink and grimace. "I don't know how you and Marcos drink this stuff."

Grayson laughs but looks quickly down at his drink when tears spring to his eyes. "Tequila is only for those with taste and heart." He repeats one of Marcos' many retorts when questioned about his love of tequila.

I stand and clap him on the back. "Goodnight."

CHAPTER 16

GRAYSON

The pounding in my head won't stop, and I stumble into the bathroom to get some ibuprofen and water. Blood-shot eyes filled with grief stare back at me, and I drop my gaze to the counter. The truth is too much this morning. After a shower and food, I'll don my armor and face the world.

An hour later, I'm sitting with Mariana and John in Thiago's home office while we wait for the rest to join us. Mateo shuffles in and leans over to kiss his mother on the cheek. She whispers something to him, and he groans.

"I ate breakfast this morning," he assures her. "I'm taking it easy."

Lie. I raise an eyebrow toward Mateo, and he scowls at me. He hates when I call him out for lying, even when I do it silently. I chuckle.

He must have gotten some rest because he doesn't appear quite as bad this morning.

Thiago strides in with his usual intensity and takes a seat on this side of the desk. I tilt my head to the side and give him a puzzled look. He points to the man walking into the room now—Marcos' oldest friend, Gabriel, who also happens to be his lawyer.

"Hello, everyone. We all know each other, so let's get this business sorted," he states matter-of-factly, and I'm reminded of why Marcos liked him so much.

"Good man. No bullshit," he used to tell me.

Gabriel puts on his glasses and opens the large manila envelope he's holding in his hands. "All the legal jargon about sound body and mind are in here, in case anyone is wondering, but I'm skipping to the essentials." He gives the room a wry look, knowing none will contest his decision.

"'To my sister, Mariana, I leave a trust in her name with enough money to live out her life however she wishes. To my brother-in-law, John, I leave my sister, Mariana. Treat her well. I'll be watching.'"

Mariana and John chuckle.

"'To meus pequenos selvagens'—I hope I said that right—'I leave the following. To Grayson, I leave my prized tequila collection. You're the only one with enough taste and heart in the family to appreciate it. To Mateo, I leave my notebooks with all my ideas. May they spark your own inventions or at least get a few laughs. To Thiago, I leave my Brazilian record collection and posters. May the music fill your soul and remind you of your roots.

"'For my twenty-five percent share of SEI stock, I leave four percent of it to CJ Tech. The remaining twenty-one percent is to be divided equally between Thiago Santos, Mateo Santos, and Grayson Santos.'" Gabriel pauses, knowing we all need a minute to digest this startling news. "'I also leave all my projects and inventions to CJ Tech, with the understanding that all profits and recognition be split fifty-fifty with SEI.'"

Thiago appears to be stunned.

"He left shares to an outsider?" I question Gabriel. When he nods, I continue, "When did he set this up?"

"Two years ago," Gabriel replies cautiously.

"He's been working with CJ Tech for two years, and yet he kept it to himself." Mateo looks confused and hurt.

Gabriel clears his throat. "Closer to five years," he informs us. "I can't give you all the details, but Marcos did clear me to answer some questions."

"Why didn't he tell us?" Thiago asks hoarsely.

"When they first started working together, it was typically one-off projects, similar to how he worked with others. Over time, they clicked. He used to tell me their brains and goals meshed. It evolved into a partnership. They negotiated the percentages on every project, but they counted on each other to develop the tech and bring them to market," he explains to us. "With all three of you heavily involved with building SEI into a powerhouse, it was in good hands, but he needed a partner to develop the ideas crowding his giant brain. There isn't a product he's brought to market in the last five years that didn't have some level of input—sometimes more, sometimes less—from CJ Tech."

He leans back in the chair to gaze sternly at all three of us. "He gave a small portion of SEI shares to CJ Tech with the hope you would continue to support the development of the joint projects they have deemed important. Shared equity makes sure both partners stay in the game." When none of us say anything, he continues, "Per the usual process, I'll notify them individually, but Marcos wanted to be sure you heard it first from me."

He pulls out another large manila envelope. It's sealed with a wax stamp that says "MarcoPolo."

"Who's MarcoPolo?" I interject.

"Marcos. It's his online name," he tells us. "He also wanted me to mail this package to someone named Nyx. One more item is on the will, and it's for me," he says with an embarrassed laugh before pointing to the intricate wooden box beside him. "It's the carved chess set Marcos and I used when we played together. Thiago allowed me to grab it when I arrived. I'm going to miss playing the wily bastard." He rubs a hand along the top. "I'm leaving you each a copy of the will, and if you have any questions, you're welcome to reach out." He lays four envelopes on the desk and leaves.

Mariana and John glance at each other. "We're leaving you

three to talk. Remember, Marcos was a man on his own long before you three grew to adulthood. Over the years, he made many decisions without consulting you, and look where we are now." She waves her hand to reference all we have, including the house. "Give him the same latitude and trust in his judgement that he extended to all of you. Mateo, darling, I'll call you later to see how you're feeling." She gives each of us a kiss on the cheek, picks up her envelope, and walks out the door with John.

As soon as everyone's gone, Thiago explodes out of his seat.

"I don't understand," he utters, his voice raw. Questions spill quickly from his lips, echoing all our thoughts. "How are we the last to know about his partnership with CJ Tech? Did he not trust us? Why would he give this man shares of our company? After his old partner betrayed him, he swore to always keep it in the family. And yet he gave away a piece of our heritage to a stranger. If he trusted his partner so much, why didn't he introduce us all?"

Mariana's words struck a chord deep inside me. I pick up the envelope with my name on it and pull out the will. Skimming through it, I find what I'm searching for and shove the papers into Thiago's chest. "CJ Tech can only sell the shares to the three of us. They don't have enough shares to cause any disruption to the running of the company. Marcos wouldn't have given his partner the shares if he didn't think he'd do the right thing, but even then, he kept our legacy safe. I think the question you need to ask yourself—do you trust Marcos?"

Mateo snorts. "It's not about trust. We would have supported CJ Tech if Marcos requested it. His projects and legacy would have lived on." He folds his arms across his chest.

Marcos and Mateo had a special creative bond, often consulting with each other on projects of their own. He feels blindsided and betrayed by the fact Marcos found a similar relationship with someone else.

"But it's not just about his legacy, is it? CJ Tech contributed to almost all of Marcos' projects over the years. The fact they were willing to stay in the background, hidden, until this last project...

that's what interests me. Why? Marcos brings us a project to broker worth hundreds of millions of dollars, and it's the first project where CJ Tech is publicly listed as a co-founder?" I can't help but speculate on the reasons. "Is CJ Tech behind the theft? Or worse, Marcos' murder? Or are they caught in a bigger web like us? I could list a million possibilities, but we won't know until we speak to CJ Tech. I wish we'd gotten contact info from the woman."

Mateo unfolds his arms and sits up straight. "She told me Marcos sent her to get a file, so there must be something on our in-house servers. I was able to prove the cyberattacks were a diversion to keep our focus away from their attempt to get into the R&D servers. Thankfully, they failed, but maybe CJ Tech decided to go around us and find the file on his own, since his admin was unsuccessful in getting direct access."

"Or CJ Tech is innocent, and Marcos sent them to retrieve the data because he knew we had a mole," I caution Mateo, but I see him shake his head, immediately rejecting the idea. He needs CJ Tech to be guilty.

I glance to Thiago for help, but he's also latched onto the idea. "It makes sense. With Marcos out of the way, he could sell it on the black market and collect one hell of a payday. This all started with the one deal. The fact they sent someone to SEI to get a file tells me it's important." He looks over at Mateo. "Find the file before they do. It's only a matter of time. Even with our new system, they'll get in, and they already have a huge advantage over us—they know the name of the file. Oh, and get me the footage on the food delivery at the condo. It's missing from the original servers."

Mateo frowns and brings up his phone to check the last statement for himself.

"I think our focus is too narrow," I warn Thiago. "If it's not CJ Tech, we just gave our enemy a massive blind spot to hide behind."

Thiago considers my words but quickly dismisses them. "It's not that I don't see your point, but I keep returning to the initial bid. Very few people knew the bid was being re-opened. Marcos would have kept his partner informed as things progressed. It's the only logical explanation that fits." He cuts his eyes to Mateo, who nods in agreement.

"I think you're letting your gut rule. I know it's often right, but try to keep the possibility in your mind," I urge him.

Mateo rules with logic, and Thiago with his gut. I like to gamble and bet the odds. This complicated web of maneuvers feels like an elaborate game of strategy, but to what end?

"I'll follow the money. I'll start with the original buyer, but I'll also investigate Marcos' financials for the last five years. I want to know how much he paid CJ Tech and when. I'll attempt to trace the payments and locate CJ Tech, but something tells me I might have an issue," I tell Thiago.

Thiago nods his agreement. "I'll work with Zane and his team on finding Mateo's shooters and the fake rideshare driver. In addition, I want his team to investigate the bombing at the building." He holds up a hand when Mateo starts to protest. "Send Sterling all the footage. Let him take a crack at it. It's more important you find the file." He waits until Mateo agrees. "One more thing. I'm going to do whatever it takes to flush CJ Tech out of hiding." He delivers his warning on his way out of the office.

Mateo looks at me and shakes his head. We've rarely been on opposite sides, but he knows I'm not convinced CJ Tech's the enemy. He opens his mouth but shuts it quickly. Throwing his hands up in the air, he strides angrily out the door behind Thiago.

When I lay the pieces on the board, I see CJ Tech everywhere, but it feels too obvious. Maybe I'm wrong. If they're the enemy, all their dreams have come true. Marcos is gone, they've inherited part of SEI, and they can claim majority ownership of the software, which will make them richer than their wildest dreams.

The best games are deceptively simple on the surface, almost giving the answer to you on a silver platter. You jump in eagerly, only to find they require strategy and ingenuity to win, but by that time, you're behind. All our bets are on CJ Tech. If we're wrong, we've lost this round and, quite possibly, the war.

CHAPTER 17

<u>HENLEY</u>

My head's spinning with all the names and disguises… and lies… I've used in the last week. It's the part I hate the most, not for the ones who deserve it, like Diego, but for those who don't deserve to be deceived, like Philip Carlton, who's only doing his job. Hopefully, once I get this file and unlock the software, I can find a way to get the video of Marcos' death to the ATF. Then I can return to my incognito existence and leave the cloak-and-dagger stuff to those who are good at it.

I glance down at the new driver's license in my hand, stamped with the state of Tennessee's official holographic image, and I smile because it makes me think of Marcos. In the early days of running, I stole my IDs from drunk girls in bars who looked similar to me. When my stalker found me, I'd switch to the next one and keep running. If Marcos hadn't intervened and taught me how to build a strong, credible background and source quality fakes, who knows where I'd be? Probably dead. Stashing it in my wallet, along with my embossed birth certificate, I continue getting ready.

When I went for my interview, I took note of the business casual attire most of the employees were wearing, even snapped a couple of covert pics. The IT department seemed to be a mishmash of business casual and casual. Erring on the side of caution, I purchased a few simple but trendy dress pants and blouses from a nearby Target. For my first day, I've paired cute black ankle length pants with a floral blouse in greens and pinks.

With my brown wig and green contacts, it's the perfect corporate disguise. I nod at my image in the mirror and shake off the melancholy from this morning. Slipping on the black pumps, I remind myself to stay focused and get the file. That's it. One file, I remind myself, and I'm out the door.

After the interview and impromptu shopping, I'd gone back to the rental and packed up my stuff. I rented it under the previous fake ID, Cassie Turner, which was burned when Thiago pulled the license plate. I didn't check out, though, simply left.

The new studio apartment is only two bus rides from the office, so I've put off buying another vehicle for a few days.

The bus stop is full of people, and I shuffle my way into the crowd to board the next bus when it arrives. Grabbing a window seat, I watch the world go by. I'm a normal person riding an ordinary bus into an everyday job. I love it. When I chuckle at the thought, the woman next to me shifts closer to the aisle. She glances over her shoulder, and I smile, trying to show her I'm not a threat, but I guess she doesn't believe me because she moves several seats closer to the door. I guess there's an etiquette to riding the bus—no eye contact, smiles, or acknowledgement of anyone around you. Got it.

When I get to headquarters, Mr. Carlton is waiting for me in the lobby, but instead of the big smile he was wearing the other day, his expression is somber.

"Mr. Carlton. Sorry, I mean Philip. It's nice to see you again," I state with a smile. When he gives me a weak smile in return, I lean in closer. "Are you okay? You seem upset."

"We found out yesterday one of our key inventors, Marcos, and his bodyguard, Jason, died in an explosion last Thursday," he murmurs quietly. "He was working at an off-site office where he develops some of our more advanced technology, like our newest security system." He shifts closer and drops his voice to a whisper.

"They think it was deliberate. I don't usually gossip, but I'd rather you hear it from me. This is usually a very safe place to work, I promise. It's the first time something like this has ever happened, but I don't want you to worry. You won't be working on anything remotely dangerous or top secret." He pats my hand a few times to reassure me.

Shocked, I stare at him, unable to say anything. *They think Marcos died in an explosion. What explosion? Who's Jason?*

"I-I'm so… sorry," I stutter, still trying to wrap my head around what he just told me. "Did you say last Thursday?"

"Yes, the building blew up around eight p.m. according to the papers. I didn't think anything of it, but I didn't know SEI owned the building either until Thiago, our CEO, sent out an all-employee email with some of the details. He wants to be sure we all cooperate with the ATF investigation if asked," he states nonchalantly, as if he's not excited by all the intrigue, but I see the light shining in his eyes.

I'm going to be sick. The ATF is going to be combing through every bit of footage from the security cameras. Normally, a courier wouldn't draw much attention, but one coming out of the garage, on the same night, at six or six-thirty p.m.… It wasn't later, was it? Shit, I can't remember, but it was close to the time of the explosion. If they see me leaving on the security cameras, I'm going to be one of the prime suspects.

The video is now the only proof of my innocence. Fuck me. I need to make several physical copies and hide them. All the current back-up copies are digital and hackable. The need to run out of the building and secure them right away is strong, but I hold back. This is my only chance to get the other file, so I straighten my shoulders and smile.

Philip leads me to the second floor and drops me off at the HR department so I can give them all my personal information, including my bank account for payroll. Since I don't want the money traced to me, it will deposit into a dummy account, then disappear. It will reappear into the account of an old friend who helped me when I needed it most.

While I wait for the HR manager to return, I can't help but think of how close I'd been to getting caught in Marcos' office last Thursday. If Marcos' DNA was found, it means they put his body back in his office after I left that night. It exploded only an hour or an hour and a half after I left? My mouth goes dry, and I jump up.

I ask the manager's admin for directions to the restroom and fast walk across rows of cubicles and through the bathroom door, barely making it to the first stall before I lose my breakfast. I listen for a second, but it's quiet, nobody but me in here. After rinsing my mouth out, I wet a paper towel and place the cool square on my neck for a second to help get rid of the clammy feeling. On my way back, I spot a dish of peppermints on someone's desk, and I quickly grab one. Hopefully, it will settle my stomach.

The manager's waiting for me in her office.

"Sorry about that," I tell her with a cheerful smile. "Too much coffee this morning." I hurry through the rest of the paperwork, and soon, I'm on my way to my new desk on the fourth floor.

When I get there, Philip is waiting for me. "Set your things down. Unfortunately, I don't have a lot of time to show you around this morning, and I'm going to have to give you the mundane task of helping us update all our executive computers with keystroke tracking software."

I raise my eyebrows. "Wow, okay," I reply, injecting a hint of uncertainty in my voice. "Is this standard?" If so, I'll need to limit my searches to the type of file to avoid suspicion until I can narrow down its exact location, then grab it at the last possible moment.

He nods. "It is now. I'll set you up in Grayson's office and leave you there while I tackle the rest of the VPs on the finance floor."

"Oh, I don't want to bother him, especially being new…" I open my mouth to suggest I take the VPs, but he smiles and pats my hand.

"I'm putting you in there because he's going to be gone this week for Marcos' service and to be with the family," he explains. "The other VPs are in the office this week, and I think they might be a tad nervous with a new person touching their computer."

Puzzled for real this time, I whisper, "I didn't know he was close to Marcos' family?"

Philip looks around and murmurs quietly, "Not many people know, but I've been here a long time and IT sees things others don't, so I figured it out a while ago." He glances around to make sure we're alone. "Marcos was… Marcos Santos. I don't think it matters if you know now, since it's going to all come out with the investigation, but it isn't common knowledge." He motions me into the room.

The office is framed by glass walls on two sides with a stunning view of Biscayne Bay, with South Beach on the other side. The blue green water reflects the bright sun, making the office feel light and airy. I move toward the desk positioned by the windows and take a seat behind it.

Philip shows me what he needs me to do. When he leaves, I quickly modify a couple of Grayson's admin settings, so it will start a hidden application at login that will allow me to use his computer as a proxy. Most people rarely check their admin settings, and any actions I take will be seen as Grayson's, thereby eliminating any potential flags in the system.

I run the new update Philip told me to do and wait while it installs. A picture on the desk catches my eye. It's three young boys standing on a street corner. It's familiar. I grab my phone and flick through the pics until I get to the ones I took in Marcos' office. I hold it up and confirm. The same pic on Marcos' desk is also on Grayson's. Marcos' was taped to the shelf. Grayson's is in a nice frame with the words 'meus pequenos selvagens' etched into the frame. I snap a pic so I can search for the translation later.

Philip returns fifteen minutes later, and I'm standing in front of digital frame on the wall, staring in awe at the image moving before me.

"It's amazing, isn't it?" he remarks excitedly. "It's an NFT by LuckyBet. It's displayed in one of the new digital frames built specifically for NFTs. It has features that can sense light and movement and adjust the positioning of the NFT to best suit its environment, or you can adjust it manually using an app."

This is one area I don't have to pretend to be excited. "It's truly incredible. I want one."

He chuckles. "Hmm, you might want to start with something besides a LuckyBet original. They start around a hundred and twenty Ethereum and go up from there," he quips. "All right. Did you finish? Wonderful, let me confirm, and we can be on our way."

We repeat this on the other two executive floors. There's one for each of the three divisions within SEI. I'm able to modify Thiago's computer, but not Mateo's. Philip tells me he took Mateo's computer to him because he was in an accident the other night and got pretty banged up. I just nod and smile. The less I say, the less likely I am to screw up and forget to lie.

Unfortunately, the updates take all day, and before I know it, Philip's waving me out the door and telling me to go home. At this rate, it will be Christmas before I get the file. I huff with frustration, and my bangs shift. When I raise my hand to sweep them to the side, I see Diego out of the corner of my eye. He walks past me without stopping. I don't dare turn around, and with relief, I hear him walking farther and farther away in the opposite direction.

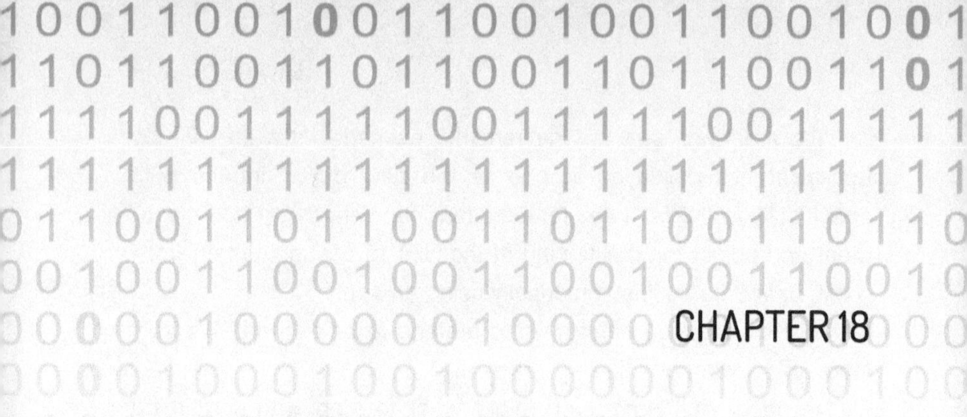

CHAPTER 18

<u>HENLEY</u>

Yesterday was a complete bust. None of the servers I checked contained the file. I've got today and Friday to search before the risk of getting caught—whether it's using their computers or running into one of Santos men in the building—increases exponentially. They'll return to the office on Monday.

The servers I searched yesterday were frequently used by the company. Today, I'm switching to only those used frequently by Marcos… Santos. I snort, still unable to believe this is the family he spoke about all the time. When he spoke of the "boys" and the good times his family had together, I was picturing a gregarious, fun-loving family, with kids running around and relatives all over the place, not three grown men accustomed to dominating the world around them.

In between the tasks Philip gives me, I search for the file, but by the end of the day, I've found nothing. Again. I leave the office frustrated and worried. Time is running out for me and the software. I have eight days until all copies are rendered unrecoverable. Which would be fine if I weren't worried about the invisible man breaking the key and claiming our software for himself or his boss, whoever that may be.

To cheer myself up, I order Mexican food from the little place around the corner from Thiago's condo, but this time, I let a real delivery driver get it and bring it to my new rental. It's still piping hot when it arrives, and I immediately dig into the best burrito on the planet. I did try a burrito from another place in Miami, but it wasn't near as good as this one.

While I eat, I scour the news for any ATF updates on the explosion, but it only says the same thing as yesterday. Agent Antonio is confident the attack is not the work of a terrorist, and they're following the leads.

I wonder if I'm one of those leads. I sigh.

A notification pops up in the lower right corner.

User6732842 has entered the lab.

I put the burrito down and stare at the notification for a heartbeat before racing over to grab my headset from my suitcase. Within thirty seconds, I'm in the lab, watching a man walk around the space with an amused but intrigued, smile on his handsome avatar face.

I'm guessing it's not even close to his real face, but I always find the details people choose to create their avatar to be fascinating. Marcos chose a dark complected avatar with dark hair and eyes, who was almost as rotund as he was tall, with apple cheeks that bunched up when he laughed. A completely nonthreatening figure, which allowed me to be fully relaxed while we were working in the lab.

This man's avatar is all about wealth and power. Tall, elegantly attired in a herringbone suit, with piercing blue eyes and perfectly styled light brown hair, he reminds me of the smooth, aristocratic prince from *Cinderella*.

His eyes sweep down my avatar with appreciation. I'd kept my height but added the kind of curves I so desperately wished I had in real life. My hair is black, reminiscent of the username, Nyx, I usually used. Tonight, I entered as User3938295.

"This is a private lab," I inform him. "My boss will not be happy with you being in here. Please leave."

"Lab?" he says with surprise, a sculpted eyebrow raising high. "Interesting. Although I'm disappointed to see it's empty. You haven't by chance seen a video, have you?"

My breath catches, and I know without a doubt, I'm staring at the invisible man. His ego wouldn't have let someone else get the file. Sending the video to the metaverse tweaked his curiosity. He would have been here sooner, but it took him a while to trace the convoluted route Marcos devised for its delivery.

"You're welcome to look around, but there's nothing here. Not anymore," I taunt him, unable to resist the urge.

He laughs. "Honestly, I don't give a fuck if the video is here or not. I'm not on it, nor did I… eliminate anyone. I was simply curious as to where Marcos sent it." He glances around and nods with satisfaction, like he recently purchased the space for his real estate portfolio. "This space is perfect, and so are you, my dear Nyx." A full laugh escapes him. "I'll be seeing you soon."

Shaking, I pull off the headset and retreat from the virtual space that used to mean everything to me. It's completely tainted now. First with Marcos' death, and now by this egomaniac and killer. I don't care what he says. He's a murderer, same as Diego. And a murderer who knows my avatar's name. I bite the inside of my cheek, trying to think of the implications, but there are thousands of Nyx username variations. I doubt I'll even need it anymore, but I can't seem to make myself delete it. Not yet.

I check on the copies of the video and find one missing. *Damn.* According to the tracking, it was downloaded, then deleted. This guy is good, maybe better than Marcos and me. It gives me an idea, though. Maybe it's time to leave him a few nasty surprises.

For the next couple of hours, I create and install rootkits on most of the videos, then copy and forward them to several locations.

I create a virtual rootkit and place it in the lab.

Pulling snippets of code from various AR projects and other sources, I compile a reasonable facsimile of our AR software. The dupe must be close enough to fool someone of his tech caliber. The most frustrating thing about programming or coding are the bugs that make you scroll line by line to find the smallest of mistakes, like a missing close bracket or a misspelled function. I add some of these into the mix, along with the final rootkit. The bait is set.

Last, I download three clean copies of the video onto individual flash drives. I'll send one anonymously to Agent Antonio at the ATF, one to Thiago at SEI, and the third one via snail mail to a private post office box I set up years ago in San Antonio.

My priority must be the software. Let the ATF and Thiago deal with Marcos' killers. I want justice and don't care who takes them down. Based on what I've learned on this trip to Miami, I don't have enough power or resources to do it myself.

<u>GRAYSON</u>

Only minutes after easing away from the dock, I'm flying across the water toward our downtown offices. The boat hits the first wave, the sprays arcs upward toward the sun, and for a few precious moments, the grief lifts. Marcos and I shared a deep love of tequila and the ocean. Ease your pain, drown the sorrows, celebrate the good life, or provide an escape—those two have seen us through life.

Thiago's in his usual full throttle mode, managing the ATF and Zane's team, and Mateo's irritated with me and still recovering from the shooting. Escape became my only thought. Not to indulge in my favorite reckless pursuits or feed my adrenaline addiction, as is usually the case, but to find some space to process the thoughts crowding my brain.

We all have our tasks, and the best place for me to do mine is at the office, away from the memories and sadness choking the air in our house. Since it's almost four p.m. on a Friday, it should be just about empty, as people leave early for the weekend. Maybe I can avoid everyone and find the peace I so desperately need.

My PA is the only person I see when I get off the elevator, and I raise a finger to my lips. She gives me a sad smile and strolls past without saying a word.

Lots of windows and a view of the water are the only two things I demanded when we moved SEI headquarters into this building. We spend a hell of a lot of time in the office running this billion-dollar beast, and the view of the water calms me in a way nothing else does.

I drop into the chair behind the desk, and the photo of Thiago, Mateo, and me on Ocean Drive hits me in the gut. My throat tightens, and it's hard to swallow the lump stuck in the middle of my throat. This picture is the single most important item I own.

We all have the same photo. Marcos took it on our first visit to South Beach after I moved in with them and gave us each a copy as a reminder of the importance of family, blood or not, although none of us ever needed it.

An orphan who'd never had a family, didn't even have a clue what the word meant, I'd claimed Mateo as my brother minutes after defending him against our second-grade bully during recess. As far as I was concerned, it was set in stone. Unfortunately, social services disagreed, and soon, it was time to transfer me to a new foster family and school about thirty minutes away.

Like most eight-year-old kids, I didn't have any money, but I was a resourceful little bastard and numbers spoke to me. When I discovered an online gambling site, I gambled my way into enough bus money to return to Mateo. I knew exactly where I belonged—with my family—and I refused to let anyone stand in my way. Of course, social services tracked me down and took me back.

Again and again.

The fourth time I landed on Marcos' doorstep, I coolly informed him social services wasn't coming and he needed to let me stay with my family. He opened the door and said, "Welcome home." I'm sure he checked with my foster family, but I'd negotiated my release with them directly. All they'd wanted was the money anyway.

I rub the pad of my thumb across the etching on the frame. Mues pequenos selvagens—my little savages. He used to call us that because we were always yelling and running around, getting into fights, eating him out of house and home. It's the reason we named our company Savage Enterprises, Inc.

I sigh deeply. It's hard to even comprehend he's gone. I can almost trick myself into believing he's away on one of his rescue trips.

Someone calls out goodbye in the hallway, and it jolts me out of my reflection and reminds me to get busy. Diving into Marcos' financial statements will help keep my mind off the grief threatening to tear me apart.

About an hour later, the last five years of transactions are spread across my desk, with all the payments to CJ Tech marked in red, and I'm surprised by the picture in front of me. During this time, they must have worked on close to twenty projects together. About half were sold directly to companies, and the other half brokered through SEI.

The amounts paid and percentages vary, but it's a significant sum of money. The smallest sale was a little over five hundred thousand. After the transaction went through, JF Technologies paid CJ Tech twenty-five thousand dollars, or roughly five percent of the sale, for their share of the project. It's the first payment from JF Technologies to CJ Tech, so I assume it was the first project they ever worked on together. JF Technologies paid CJ Tech an average of five to ten percent for the next four projects as well.

The tables flipped on their sixth project together. It's the first one Marcos brokered through SEI, and I remember it because it was one of the largest deals we'd ever brokered at the time. The project was a machine learning algorithm designed to identify potential insurance fraud faster and more accurately than the standard but very labor-intensive process. Insurance companies lose close to thirty *billion* dollars to fraudulent claims every year, so it's easy to see this why this was a high-value project. It sold for seven million dollars. SEI kept five percent for our fees, Marcos retained ten percent, then paid the remaining eighty-five percent—almost six million dollars—to CJ Tech. I whistle and call Mateo.

"What?" he answers with a snarl.

"I thought you might like to know what I found in Marcos' statements, but we can catch up later," I say coolly, tired of his attitude today.

"Wait, sorry," he replies with less hostility. "Tell me. Please."

"I bet that felt like a trip to the dentist," I retort.

Mateo hates it when I force him to give in. To ease his pain, I bring him up to speed with my findings.

"It's structured like a genuine partnership. The percentages vary for each project. Based on the patterns, I'm guessing they have their own projects and consult with each other on the solutions. Depending on the level of effort given by the other party, the percentage of profit varies."

"I asked him how he came up with the insurance algorithm, and he laughed and told me he had tech-savvy friends," he comments quietly. "I wonder who CJ is and how Marcos met him?"

I shrug, even though Mateo can't see me. "Who knows? You know he spent a lot of time in the deep web. He…" I stop talking when I see my cursor move across my computer. "Umm, are you accessing my computer remotely?"

"Describe to me what's happening," he demands.

I hear his fingers moving across the keys. "Cursor is moving fast. It clicked a folder, now a file." I wait for it to move again. "It paused for a minute, then closed the window. They're gone."

"Got you. Samantha Taylor," he spits out.

I hear him yelling for Thiago in the background. When Thiago gets in the room, he puts everyone on speakerphone and explains what happened.

I hear Thiago swear and mumble something about voices and instincts. "I'm calling Zane," he snaps, then pauses. "Zane, I need you to get one of your guys to SEI to tail a Samantha Taylor."

Why does that name ring a bell?

"Brown hair, green eyes, maybe five foot nine or ten, thin. I'll get Diego to tail her from her cubicle to the outside, where you can pick up her trail. No, I'll have to get back to you." He pauses. "Okay, sounds good."

With a groan, I remember where I've heard that name. "Shit. I approved her employment, but it was for a temporary contract position. Philip raved about her qualifications, but I didn't have time to meet her," I admit with a wince. "You sound like you know exactly who she is… Care to share?"

"I ran into her on the elevator after she accepted the position. When she introduced herself, her voice sounded so familiar to me, but her appearance threw me off and I couldn't connect the two. Then, Agent Antonio called me, and I forgot about her. She's the food delivery driver who planted those bugs in my condo," he says with a hint of disbelief. "It's hard to believe what a few clothes and change of hair will do, but her voice is distinct. Sensual, low-pitched, like someone who could make a fortune as a telephone sex operator."

"Husky?" Mateo asks.

Thiago groans. "Hell, I don't know. Whatever. Moving on. Diego will follow her out, and Zane's team will tail her from there to wher-ever she's going. We need to decide what we're going to do with her, though."

"What about one of Marcos' safe houses?" I throw out the suggestion. "We need time to figure this out, and a few of them are big enough to house a large family."

"Good idea," he replies. It's silent for a second, then he explains what's happening. "Mateo's searching for one now. That one. Yes. Okay, there's a five-bedroom house in a suburb close to downtown. It would make it convenient for us to get to the office if we're needed. What's the address?"

"I'll text it to you both," Mateo says.

A second later, it appears on my phone. "Let me pull together the information I found today and grab dinner for everyone. Say, an hour?" I suggest. "Is Zane and crew going to be there?" Nobody answers. The only sounds I hear are Thiago's muffled voice and Mateo typing away. I hang up.

Well, this is an interesting turn. I wonder if this woman is also Mateo's driver. Sounds like it might be a possibility.

CHAPTER 20

When I walk out of SEI at the end of the day, I'm elated. The sun is shining, birds are chirping, and I feel like breaking out into a song and dance routine like those princesses in the—

Jerked to an abrupt halt, the musical number fades, leaving me confused for a second. I glance down and find a big, meaty fist wrapped tightly around my arm. Following it up, Diego's grim face greets me.

"I'm going to need you to come with me," Diego informs me.

"No," I refuse. "You need to unhand me before I have you arrested for assault." I hold his stare, unwilling to back down. I can't. If I go with him now, I'll end up dead. I jerk against his hold, but he tightens it until I feel like it's going to break. "You're hurting me. Let go."

The absolute glee that crosses his expression unnerves me even further. He's getting off on my pain.

"As chief of security for SEI, I believe you've stolen something from the company, and I'm going to need you to come with me and answer some questions," he announces loudly to the people staring at us.

Two can play that game. "What exactly am I supposed to have stolen? I've only been at SEI for four days. And for the last time… YOU'RE HURTING MY ARM!" When I start shouting, more people stop, and suddenly, there's a fairly large crowd around us. Several women glare at Diego, but he refuses to let me go.

"I have the right to investigate any potential theft of SEI property by its employees. If you'll come with me, we can conduct a quick search of your bag and cubicle. If we don't find anything, you'll be free to go," he states loudly and smiles when several men in the crowd nod approvingly.

"Fine." I glance at a woman to my right who's been glaring at Diego. "Would you mind recording this?" She raises her phone and taps on it. "I, Samantha Taylor, resign from SEI. Effectively immediately." I glance at Diego, who is seething. "I'm no longer an employee. If you would like to accuse me of a crime, call the police. So what's it going to be? Let me go or call the police?"

He gives my arm one last squeeze, making me wince, then holds both hands up.

When I take a step backward, Diego follows. After ten steps, I stop and glare at him. "What are you doing?"

"It's a free country. I'm taking a walk," he says with a smirk.

The woman who videotaped my resignation puts her arm across my shoulders and starts walking away with me. Several other women follow, and soon, I have a huge crowd of women surrounding and protecting me.

Tears spring to my eyes as I look from woman to woman, telling each of them, "thank you." When I glance back, Diego's still following.

A young girl near me pipes up, "I have an idea." She whispers to some of the other women, and soon, they're stripping off pieces of clothing and passing them to me. "We'll exchange clothing, disguise your hair, then scatter all at once."

I grin. "It's a fabulous idea." I whip off my silky T-shirt and pass it over. Pretty soon, I've got an entirely new outfit on, my hair is tucked tight into a hat, and a new bag hangs on my shoulder. I refused to relinquish my pretty peep-toe shoes, though.

Everyone's tense but smiling. At the count of three, we all break and run in different directions. A couple of women run behind me to help shield my back while I closely follow another up one block, then down a short alley to another block. She points to a bus pulling up to the stop, and with a wave of thanks, I jump on it at the last second. When I scan the sidewalk, I don't see Diego anywhere.

Fifteen minutes later, I get off this bus and hop on another to take me back to the stop near my current rental. Although I didn't give HR the address, it won't be long before Diego tracks me down. I need to return and finish setting the trap before he arrives.

Ten minutes later, I'm standing across from my rental watching the entrance to the building. When I don't see Diego, I decide to chance it. Striding across, I enter the little lobby and find it reassuringly empty. I quickly stride down the hall to my rental and hurry inside, then immediately get to work.

Grabbing the drive, I click on the software file, type in what I think is the key, and with a deep breath, I hit enter. When the file opens, I want to shout my relief and victory to the world, but I don't have time to celebrate. Quickly switching the file on the drive with the dupe I created last night, I store the original AR software in a place only known to Marcos and myself. If I don't come out of this alive, the software will be lost forever. I'd rather it be gone than have murderers profit off our hard work.

I load the altered file onto the drive and re-encrypt it with a new key. Something from Marcos' past which would be difficult to find, but not impossible. I set the drive on the coffee table. Then I wipe the hard drive, reinstall the operating system to factory settings, and close the laptop.

Stripping off the borrowed clothes, I throw on jeans, a long-sleeved T-shirt, and my tennis shoes, then pack the rest of my clothes and toiletries. I wheel my suitcase to the living room, grab my gun, and sit down to wait for my visitors.

————

ABOUT THREE O'CLOCK SATURDAY AFTERNOON, they finally arrive. So many times, I almost chickened out, but if I left, I wouldn't be able to get justice for Marcos. I promised myself I'd leave once they knew Diego shot and killed him. I'd mailed the videos to Agent Antonio and Thiago yesterday morning, so they should have them by Monday or Tuesday at the latest. But I need to be sure.

I hear the click on the door and watch it switch from locked to unlocked. My hand tightens on the gun, and I take the safety off. The door eases open, and surprisingly, a tall, good-looking man with dirty blond-brown hair slides through the opening. His eyes dart around the room and grind to a halt when he finds me sitting on the couch.

"What are you doing?" I hear Diego bellow from the hallway.

The guy rolls his eyes.

I raise an eyebrow.

Diego barges into the room a second later. He sees my gun and laughs. "I wouldn't worry. She's a runner."

Ouch, that stings.

He moves casually around the room, and I raise my gun to track his every movement.

"Keep your hands where I can see them," I caution him. I want him to take me to the Santos men, not kill me. The gun is to make sure he listens.

His hand inches back.

"Diego, I know you're reaching for your gun. Remove your hand from under the coat."

He deliberately stares at me and moves his hand farther inside his coat.

I take aim to fire when a hard voice whips out an order.

"Stop, Diego," the blond man orders.

Diego snarls. "Fuck off." Then he plunges his hand into the coat to grab his gun.

A lean hand captures Diego's wrist and twists it up and behind his back, then removes his gun. When he releases him, Diego throws a right hook, but it never hits its target. Next thing I know, Diego's on the floor, and the man is holding him down with a massive boot on his thick neck.

I whistle silently. Diego must have thirty pounds and a couple of inches on this guy, but he took him down without blinking.

"All right, all right. Just got carried away," Diego concedes grudgingly. "Let me up."

With a long-suffering sigh, the man lifts his foot, and Diego scrambles up. Ignoring the man, he turns to me and spreads his arms. "If you're going to shoot me, shoot me."

I ignore his posturing. "Why are you here? I didn't steal anything from the company," I ask him, curious as to what he'll say.

I hadn't stolen anything from the company. The copy of the software was in a folder, not a file, and I found it on an obscure server within SEI's network. I tried to download it, but the server had been configured to only allow uploads. I opened the folder to see if I could grab the file inside, but quickly realized I didn't need it. When I saw the name of the file, I instantly knew the key. With a copy of the software on the drive and the key, I could leave the file where it was stored on SEI's servers. Simple but clever, Marcos.

"We need to ask you some questions," he explains to me.

"Who needs to ask me some questions?"

"Thiago, Mateo, and Grayson have a few questions for you," he states. "A private server was accessed by you this afternoon, and they want to know why."

Interesting. So they know I was on the server. I hadn't expected them to know this soon, but it plays perfectly into what I want. "As part of the IT department, accessing a *company* server isn't illegal. Sorry, but I'm going out of town." I wave my hand at my suitcase. Diego needs to believe I'm reluctant to go with him or he'll get suspicious.

Diego ignores my refusal, his attention captured by the drive sitting on the coffee table in front of me. "Is that SEI tech?" he asks, pointing to the drive. Bending over, he scoops it up and puts it in his pocket.

Goal number one accomplished. "No, it's my personal drive," I return with a sigh. "Why don't you get your bosses on the phone so I can hear from them what they want, instead of demanding I go with you?" Needing some additional reassurance he's going to take me to them, I hold my breath, waiting for him to decide.

"Bitch," Diego spits out.

The guy beside him clenches his hands and glares at Diego.

Maybe he's not on Diego's side, but it doesn't mean he's on mine either. I stand, pick up my phone, and hold it out to Diego.

"Let's call Santos," the calm man suggests.

He waves Diego to his left side and reaches for my phone. I applaud him for his caution. I wouldn't want Diego at my back.

Infuriated, Diego slaps the phone down, charges forward, and uses his full body to slam me against the wall. The gun goes off, and I hear Diego roar. Something hits my head, and pain explodes from my temple before everything goes dark.

<u>HENLEY</u>

When I wake, I'm lying on a couch with an ice pack on my head and a world class shouting match happening nearby. Unable to recognize anything around me, I panic and jackknife into a sitting position. I shove the ice pack away and swing my legs to the floor. With my back pressed firmly against the safety of the couch, I glance around the room and find it full of big angry men shouting at each other. Except for one.

Grayson's kneeling beside the couch, and when I turn my head to stare at him, he slowly raises his hands to show he's not a threat. Dark blue eyes scrutinize my face. He must see something in it, because he sets the ice pack down beside my leg and steps back a few feet.

The panic eases a tiny bit, but the need to run only increases. I search for any windows or exits and discover patio doors to my right. My muscles tense, and I shift my feet until they're flat on the floor.

"Thiago," Grayson murmurs.

I glance at him in disbelief, but the loudest of the shouting immediately stops. I drag my eyes from him to the rest of the room. Diego's standing, red-faced, on one side of the room, with a man in a similar suit next to him. The blond guy from my apartment leans against the wall with a pissed off expression on his face, and in front of him is a big man with a shaved head and scar on his cheek, whose narrowed eyes are pinned on Diego. Thiago, who'd been doing most of the yelling, is now facing me.

He steps forward, and I press against the couch. Grayson holds up a finger, and the two exchange silent words. Thiago stops. His eyes examine every inch of my face, and whatever he sees makes him even more furious.

"Diego, leave. Now. If you don't, I'm going to deliver the worst beating of your life," he tells him in the quietest voice I've ever heard.

"She tried to shoot me. Why do you never take my side? Am I not supposed to defend myself?" he snarls back at Thiago, but the black look he receives in return must finally penetrate his thick skull, and he storms out of the room with the other suited man following close behind.

With him gone, my breathing calms. "I didn't try to shoot him. If I had, I'd have hit him. I'm an excellent shot," I inform Thiago. "He smashed me against a wall, and the gun went off. Something hit me in the head, and I woke here." I wave my hand toward the couch.

"Exactly what I told them," the blond guy mutters from the wall before walking out of the room.

The man with the scar laughs and observes me with a curious glint in his grey eyes. "I'm Zane. You've impressed two of my men. Not an easy feat," he says mysteriously, then leaves me alone with Grayson and Thiago.

Thiago heaves a big sigh and runs a large hand through his straight, almost black-looking hair. "I'm sorry. It will not go unpunished, I promise. Diego wasn't supposed to do anything but follow you. Do you mind if I sit?" He motions to the navy upholstered chair across from me.

"It's your house," I reply with a wince.

A hand reaches down, making me jerk, but it's only Grayson picking up the ice pack. He hands it to me, then sits in the chair beside Thiago.

I hold it to my throbbing temple and sigh with relief when it helps numb the pain. "I didn't steal anything from SEI," I coolly inform Thiago. "Nor have I done anything wrong." Raising my chin, I return his stare with one of my own. I'm positive it has the impact of a gnat, but I refuse to go down cowering.

An arrogant eyebrow raises, and his mouth twists. "You've done nothing wrong? Are you sure? How about identity fraud? Is it Samantha Taylor or Cassie Turner? Or you could give us your real name before your prints come back."

I say nothing, but I can't help worrying about what's going to happen when they run my prints. I haven't exactly stayed on the right side of the law in my attempt to hide from my stalker. But worse… would be *him* finding me again. Maybe I'll be long gone before that happens.

"What about spying? I found the bugs you planted in the condo." He fumes, his anger at me beginning to spill out. "Entering private property under false pretenses. Or leaving Mateo sitting in a garage by himself with a head wound. Running from the scene of a crime." His hands grip the chair, and he's leaning forward like he's one angry thought away from leaping out of the chair.

"I didn't leave Mateo," I protest, oddly hurt Mateo let him think I'd left him.

He raises his eyebrows at Grayson, who's watching me with narrowed eyes, and in a sarcastic voice asks, "Did you see anyone with Mateo in the garage?" When Grayson doesn't answer, he gives me a pointed stare. "I guess not."

I narrow my eyes at him. "Grayson was wearing black pants and matching T-shirt. It surprised me because it's so casual compared to his usual clothing. You both had several guns. Before leaving, you searched my car, but found nothing. The ambulance arrived a minute later." I give him all the details I remember.

Thiago tilts his head in surprise and eases back in the chair. He eyes me speculatively, as if he's trying to figure out if I'm genuine or not.

"Thank you."

I hear a voice say from the doorway and eagerly turn to find Mateo standing there with my laptop in his hands. His glasses are crooked, and his face is covered with at least three days of dark stubble, but he looks so good and alive.

My eyes dart to the wound on his head, and I wince. It's pretty ugly-looking, with the dark stitches holding it closed and the blue and purple bruising surrounding it, but it could have been so much worse.

Striding in, he places my laptop on the coffee table. "It's been wiped clean," he informs Thiago, then stares intently at me. "I mean it. Thank you. If you hadn't stayed that night, I wouldn't be here." His hands open and close several times, but he keeps them by his side.

My eyes lock on his, and for a second, I'm lost to the emotion I find in them. "We saved each other," I say hoarsely, overcome with relief and some residual emotion that's probably left over from that harrowing night. "How's the head?"

"Pounding," he replies. "But slowly getting better, I think. The headaches aren't constant anymore." He moves to my side and eases down. "If you didn't steal anything, why did you erase your hard drive?" His tone is quiet but colored with suspicion.

"After what happened outside of SEI, I knew you'd be coming," I reply, as if it answers everything. It does for me. I accomplished the task Marcos gave to me and secured our software. Making sure his killers can't sell our software is my next task.

There is the slimmest chance the invisible man could decipher the key in the next week. Although, I wouldn't have been able to figure it out if Marcos hadn't left me clues. Improbable is not impossible. If he breaks the key and gets the software, he could sell it.

A breakthrough AR technology for sale would generate signifi-cant chatter on the dark web. If that happens, I'll need to either sell it before he does or release it to the public for free. I refuse to let him profit one dime off our work.

I'm watching the three men communicate silently with each other, and I can't help but wonder what they know and don't know. Thiago's trying to stare me into blurting out my secrets, but I straighten my shoulders and hold my ground.

A stranger suddenly walks into the room, startling me, and I shift closer to Mateo. Thiago stands quickly, halting the man in his tracks.

Bright green eyes, perfectly symmetrical, aristocratic face, and artfully styled blond hair top an elegantly attired man. His ramrod straight posture and measured steps hammer home the picture of an English aristocrat.

"Sterling, this is—" Thiago stops and looks at me for the answer.

"Which name do you like best? Cassie? Samantha?" I throw out there in response.

His eyes gleam with challenge. "What did Marcos call you?"

I bite my lip and debate answering, but decide it doesn't matter. "Nyx."

Loaded silence fills the room, making me uneasy.

"Nyx, this is Sterling. Tech genius," he completes the introduction.

Green eyes light up, and the man gives me a slow smile I'm pretty sure he's given to a million other women. "You did an excellent job constructing the Cassie Turner identity, but Samantha Taylor was brilliant." He taps on my driver's license. "This is a masterpiece. Where did you get such skills?"

I almost die laughing when I hear his faint British accent. I clear my throat. "Marcos taught me," I admit with a wry smile. "Cassie Turner was a level one identity, Samantha Taylor a level three. The higher you go, the more elaborate and deep the backstory you construct." I ignore the stares of the other three when I mention Marcos' name.

"Fascinating. I'd love to hear more details about the criteria for the levels. Also, are you in the market for a job?" He stops when Thiago clears his throat. "Right." He looks at me, and regret flashes across his face. "Sorry, love. Facial recognition confirms she's the rideshare driver, the food delivery girl, the IT hire, and the woman from SEI's lobby."

Air whooshes out of me. They haven't discovered my visit to Marcos' office. Right now, I'm a suspicious person, but the worst I've done is lie and disguise myself. Oh, and plant a few bugs.

"It's fine. Everyone already knows."

Grayson immediately starts choking on his water. Mateo jumps up and pounds on his back until he can catch his breath. They both turn and stare at me, then drop their eyes to my chest.

"Ah, I guess you didn't know I was also the woman at SEI. Really, is it so far-fetched? I didn't realize a padded, push-up bra would make me appear that different," I quip with a roll of my eyes. When all four men's attention shifts to me, I cross my arms over my chest and burrow into the couch behind me.

"Have you found anything from the explosion yet?" Thiago directs his question toward Sterling.

Of course, tech genius would be assigned to the task. I glance at Mateo and see the same irritation on his face.

He opens the laptop he's holding. "It's a lot of footage. I did discover one thing, though." All three men crowd around the computer, and I freeze. "Here."

"It's Marcos' car leaving the garage Monday morning," Mateo retorts. "I already pointed that out to you."

"It's his car, but he's not driving it," Sterling says, steel lacing the proper accent. He taps a few buttons. "See. Right hand. The driver's skin is white, not dark complected like Marcos. He's wearing a gold ring with some kind of animal on it. I haven't searched for the ring yet, but does Marcos have anything similar?"

I jump up and peer over Sterling's shoulder. Mateo crowds in behind me. I squint. It's a beaver. "It's either a Brass Rat or a Grad Rat." I glance at Mateo, who's peering at me with a puzzled expression on his face. I return to staring at Sterling's screen. "Can you zoom in?"

Sterling magnifies it again, but the image starts pixelating.

"I can't tell," I say sadly. If the invisible man went to MIT, it would explain a lot. "It's definitely an MIT ring, although Marcos didn't attend there."

Both Grayson and Thiago are gazing at me speculatively.

Sterling pulls up an image of a brass rat and compares the two. "I concur. I'll do my best to enhance the image, but I doubt it will be effective. It does generate some doubt about Marcos' time of departure, though." Sterling closes the lid. "That's it so far, but I'll keep searching." He strolls out of the room like he's going to a garden party.

I slide to the left to return to the couch, but Mateo grabs my arm. I hiss at the pain and ease my arm from his hand.

Mateo looks stricken, but before I can explain, Thiago's sliding the sleeve of my shirt up. When it gets stuck at my elbow, he switches tactics. With a couple of quick maneuvers, he has my arm out of my sleeve while the rest of me is still completely covered. His large hand gently holds my arm to the light. The skin is mottled and red, with a combination of broken blood vessels and several darker red circular imprints from where Diego gripped my arm and squeezed.

"Who did this?" he says nonchalantly, his thumb lightly rubbing across the inside of my arm.

Angry at the question, I raise my head and glower at Thiago. "Who do you think?"

"Desgraçado." He practically growls when he says it.

Where have I heard that term? "What does that mean?" I ask softly.

Instead of answering, he carefully slides my arm into my sleeve. Dark eyes drill into mine, and I shiver at the rage reflected in them. He spins on his heel and stalks out of the room, Grayson right behind him.

I move to the couch, and Mateo follows. "It means 'bastard.' How did you know it was an MIT ring?"

I meet his direct gaze and realize I don't want to lie to him. So I tell him the truth. "I dated a guy named David who went to MIT, and he had one." I don't admit I had one too.

<u>MATEO</u>

She's full of secrets, but whether she'll trust us enough to tell us what's going on, I can't predict. She's a walking contradiction. It's obvious Marcos trusted her to some degree, or he wouldn't have sent her to get the file from SEI nor would he have left her something in his will. Yet she has done nothing but lie and deceive us since we met her.

Does she work for CJ Tech? Or did Marcos instruct her to say that to us? If she located the file, why didn't she take it from the server? Does she know what's on the file, or is she simply doing what she's told? Philip Carlton manages our IT department for a reason. He's well qualified and extremely tech knowledgeable. If "Samantha" impressed him enough to break protocol and request her immediate hire, she's skilled. How much? I don't know, but maybe if I get her to show me what she did in the garage, I can start to put a framework around it.

After she fell asleep on the couch last night, I carried her to the bedroom we'd assigned to her. She must have been exhausted, because she didn't even twitch. I debated removing some of her clothes to make her more comfortable, but she looked so peaceful, I just covered her and left.

Thiago returned in a worse mood than he left. Diego ghosted him. I wish he'd found him and delivered the beating he deserves, but I can't say I'm unhappy with this turn of events. When we were children, Diego was a monster, tormenting everyone weaker than him. He delighted in it. When I tried to explain to Thiago why I didn't like him, he went to the "alleged" victims, but none would tattle on Diego. Some even joked about it until it seemed like I was exaggerating his behavior.

Grayson never saw or heard him do anything, but he knew I wouldn't accuse someone without reason. He had a little chat with Diego, and whatever he said to him worked. He stopped hurting the kids in our neighborhood.

Yawning, I walk into the kitchen and find Thiago and Grayson up, dressed and working at the kitchen table. I shake my head. Their most productive hours are early morning, while mine are late at night. Thankfully, they gave up making me see the light of dawn a long time ago.

"Coffee? Food?" I practically growl the words.

Grayson points to the counter, where a breakfast buffet is laid out. Fruit, bagels, pastries, cereal, and two boxes of coffee with the words 'Mimosas in Miami' emblazoned on the box. A popular breakfast spot not far from here.

Shuffling over to the smorgasbord, I grab a paper cup and fill it to the top with the delicious, dark brew. Then I pile everything but the cereal on a plate and make my way to the table. All I do for the next fifteen minutes is eat and drink coffee. I don't contemplate world problems or even peek at my laptop. Finally full, I get up, throw away my plate, and get a second cup of coffee.

When I sit down this time, Thiago and Grayson stop working.

"Did she say anything after we left?" Thiago jumps in with his question first.

"She dated someone at MIT who had a ring," I reveal. "But that's it. She fell asleep pretty quickly."

Grayson raises an eyebrow, wanting to know if I carried her to bed, and I nod. His eyes gleam with interest. Surprisingly, Grayson, the most cynical person I know, who also hates liars, seems the most willing to give her the benefit of the doubt.

"Not only is she Rose, Cassie, and Samantha, she's Nyx. And she learned to create her impeccable fake identities from Marcos," I reiterate last night's findings. "Marcos left Nyx a package in his will. The fact she's even mentioned is important. Besides Gabriel, only family and CJ Tech were in the will. It makes me think she's either one of Marcos' rescues or she works for CJ Tech in some capacity, maybe both. Either would fit with the current facts."

Thiago considers my assessment and nods. "I came to a similar conclusion while we were driving around searching for Diego last night," he admits. "It still doesn't tell me where her loyalties lie. With Marcos? CJ Tech? Herself? Until we start getting some real answers from her, I want her to stay here, where we can keep an eye on her."

Grayson swivels toward Thiago. "Are we holding her against her will?"

Thiago hesitates for a brief second, but then shakes his head. "No, but if she doesn't cooperate, I'll be forced to turn her over to police. We have enough evidence of her using fraudulent identities to gain access to the condo and to secure employment with SEI, and with our influence, they would likely press charges."

Grayson grunts, clearly unhappy with Thiago's comment.

"I'm also uneasy turning her over to the police," I state slowly, trying to figure out the best steps forward. "Maybe if she gets to know us, she'll give us more information. Right now, we're strangers. Why would she trust us when Marcos apparently told her not to trust anybody and sent her to SEI, a company we own, to get a file?"

Thiago runs a hand down his face and sighs. "We'll give it a shot. Get to know her and see if it helps."

"All of us, Thiago, not just me," I say pointedly, looking directly at him so he understands I'm specifically talking to him and not

Grayson. I know Grayson's on board. He's intrigued, and it's such a novelty for his jaded soul, he won't be able to stay away until he's solved the puzzle.

"I hear you," he grudgingly replies, then eyes Grayson. "Were you able to trace CJ Tech through the payments Marcos made to them?"

"No, the payments bounced across multiple accounts and eventually disappeared. I also had Sterling try, but he got the same result," he says smugly. "In addition, I asked our accountants and attorneys to run the name through their databases to see if the company is registered anywhere or if taxes were filed for them. None. So, at best, we're dealing with a shadowy corporation who can't be found and apparently hasn't paid taxes at any point in time. Yet Marcos trusted them enough to leave them shares of SEI in his will. Something isn't adding up, but I can't figure it out."

"Good morning," a husky voice calls out, and we all shift toward the doorway.

Cassie… err, Nyx? All the names are driving me crazy. She's standing there in her bare feet, wearing the same clothes as yesterday, but her hair is a bold pink and her eyes are blue today. She's pale, but I can't tell if she's in pain. I straighten my glasses.

We all lock on her face, unable to look away. She backs up a step.

"Are you wearing a wig and contacts?" I blurt out to divert everyone's attention.

A blush stains her cheeks. "This is the real me," she replies, sweeping a hand from head to toe. "Well, obviously, the hair is colored, but it's the color I choose most often. Okay?" She bites her lip while she waits for me to answer.

Something in me relaxes when she answers me truthfully. I smile and wave her over to the counter. "Breakfast and coffee are over there. It might be cold, though. Grayson and Thiago brought it in hours ago."

"Sorry, I'm not a morning person," she replies softly. "I often work late and can't get motivated enough to wake up early." She warms her coffee and a plate of food, then pauses. She looks hesitantly at us, then to the barstools by the counter.

"Come sit with us," I tell her.

She needs to get comfortable with us. The sooner, the better. We need answers, and I know Thiago won't wait long to get the information he wants, not with an unknown enemy and Marcos' murderer out there.

Up close, I notice her eyes are more grey than blue. I wonder if they change color.

"So, do you really want us to call you Nyx?" I ask with a frown.

She laughs. "I can see you don't care for it. Call me Cassie," she says with a shrug, as if the name we call her isn't important.

How can your name not be important?

She rubs her temple, and I hear Thiago growl. I give him a "cut that shit out" look, and he clenches his jaw but keeps his mouth shut. Reaching for my messenger bag, I pull out the ibuprofen and set it by her plate.

She smiles gratefully and swallows a couple tablets. Tucking into her breakfast, I watch while she scarfs down an impressive amount of food. I smirk at Grayson, who's watching her every move with fascination. I'm not sure he's ever seen a woman eat this much food. All the women he knows eat miniscule amounts to retain their figures. My eyes return to Cassie and linger appreciatively on her tall, lean body. I wonder how she stays so thin.

Finally, she slows and glances at us three. "Thank you for grabbing my suitcase. I noticed it in my room this morning."

"Cruz made Diego grab it when they left your rental," Mateo informs me.

"Cruz? Is that the blond man's name?"

"It is. He reports to Zane," Thiago confirms before leaning forward.

She immediately freezes.

"Cassie, we're not forcing you to stay here, but we need answers. If we don't get them, our enemies are going to bury us like they did Marcos," Thiago explains bluntly. "If you leave, I'll be forced to turn you over to the police to see if they can get the answers we need. I don't want to do it, but I will. I hope once you spend some time with us, you'll be able to trust us enough to share your secrets, but the clock is ticking." He leaves the rest unsaid.

She swallows. "I understand."

Thiago continues to stare at her for a few more seconds until he's satisfied with whatever he sees in her eyes. "We're going into the office to catch up after being out last week. I'll see you two tonight." With his laptop in hand, he strides out of the kitchen.

She grabs her plate and dumps the rest of the food in the trash. "I'm going to get a shower and change clothes."

———

AN HOUR LATER, she strolls back into the kitchen with a more relaxed expression on her face. Relieved, I push the chair beside me out for her to sit.

She sits and peers at my screen. "What are you doing?"

Her body wash fills the air, and I groan silently. It's the same one she wore the night of the shooting. I don't know what it is about the smell, but it definitely turns me on. I clear my throat.

"I'm reading the log files for the server you accessed yesterday. Why didn't you download anything?"

She looks at me with surprise. "You can't download files from that server. It's set to only allow uploads," she replies matter-of-factly, like it's common knowledge.

I try to download a file I saved to the server two months ago, and a system message pops up, stating the server doesn't support this function. I dive into the backend, enter my admin credentials, and bring up the audit log. This server is restricted to only a handful of people in SEI. The last change was almost three weeks ago. Cecilia Martinez, server admin, disabled the download function on this server.

"Apparently, one of our server admins recently changed this functionality." I hesitate for a second but decide to share my findings with her. How are we going to get her to trust us if we don't share in return? "The server is restricted to only a few people. I didn't ask her to change the settings."

Her blue eyes widen. "Cecilia Martinez," she murmurs, her brow furrowed. "Isn't that the alias of the last woman Marcos saved on one of his rescues?"

I tilt my head. "What? No, she was an IT person I hired, then had to let go when we were hit by the cyberattacks." I pause. It's too coincidental. "What were you searching for on this server?"

"The file Marcos sent me to get," she answers cautiously.

When she doesn't say anything else, I realize she isn't going to. Marcos told her not to trust anyone with the file information, and it's one line she won't cross.

"I get it," I assure her. "I do." I explain about the cyberattacks and tell her about the pattern I discovered. "They were concentrated solely on the servers in the R&D department and the personal computers of Cecilia, Marcos, and me. Whoever set up the attack knew we could access the file you were sent to retrieve. Cecilia was the anomaly I couldn't account for in my equations. If Marcos wanted to protect the file, he would have asked her to change the settings as a precaution."

I grab my phone and call Philip. "I need the address for Cecilia Martinez. Can you forward it to my email?" When he agrees, I hang up.

She taps her finger on the table. "Can I have my laptop?"

I give her an incredulous look. "No, it's out of the question." My voice is cold when I answer.

With a smirk, she shrugs, but her eyes dance with knowledge.

An email appears marked "Address," and I open it immediately. Son of a bitch. My eyes immediately find hers. She knew. Cecilia's last known address… was this house. The exact house we're sitting in right now. I cross my arms across my chest and motion for her to fill me in.

"I create the identities for the people Marcos rescues because as Sterling said, I'm very, very good at it, and he has enough to do to get them settled. I created one for Cecilia Martinez in Miami about two months ago. I assume the address confirms she was Marcos' rescue?"

"Yes."

"The cyberattacks were focused on you three. If you weren't aware of Cecilia's relationship to Marcos, then who knew?" she questions, then scrambles to assure me. "Besides me. I didn't hack into your company."

I chuckle at the thought of her hacking SEI. "You didn't even cross my mind," I say absently, trying to think of who would know of their relationship. Philip Carlton, of course. Maybe someone else from the IT department?

The chair scrapes loudly on the floor when she gets up and stalks out of the kitchen. Puzzled, I try to think if I said anything terrible, but nothing comes to mind.

HENLEY

"You didn't even cross my mind," I repeat in a deep, condescending voice.

Hacking SEI would be tough, but I *could* do it. In his intellectual arrogance, he doesn't even consider me a capable threat. It's so infuriating, it makes me want to launch an attack to prove him wrong. I won't, but I *want* to. With a sigh, I flop down on the bed and drag the pillow under my head.

I lie there, contemplating what to tell them. Thiago's threat is real. He'll turn me over to the police if he doesn't get answers.

If I tell them I'm CJ Tech, I put everything at risk, including my life. Six days. If the invisible man doesn't crack the key by Saturday, the data will be unrecoverable and I'll have the only copy of it. If he finds out I'm CJ Tech, he'll stop at nothing to get to me.

I'm hoping the video of Marcos' murder will divert their attention to Diego and off me. It should be in Thiago's hands, and the ATF's, by Monday or Tuesday at the latest. It proves Marcos died by gunshot on Monday, well before the explosion, which was only used to cover up how he died. Diego behind bars eliminates the threat closest to me.

The other potential issue is what I overheard this morning. To the Santos men, CJ Tech is a potential software thief who murdered his partner, exploited his trust to inherit shares of SEI, and doesn't pay his taxes. Not once have they considered CJ Tech could be me, or even a woman, which is aggravating. I can prove I didn't murder Marcos, but the only way I can prove I'm not behind the theft is to follow through on the plans I made with Marcos to make sure the software is distributed to all who need it. Cost should not be a barrier to entry when it comes to using technology to save people's lives.

I ignore the part about the taxes. If nothing is real, how do you pay taxes? Instead, I donate a significant amount to my favorite charity. They do more with it than the government ever would.

I still can't wrap my head around why Marcos would give me shares of his family's company. It never even occurred to me to betray his trust and delve into his background, so I didn't even know he was part owner of SEI. Maybe I can just return the shares.

"Are you okay?" a voice above me asks.

Startled, I open my eyes, but when I see it's Mateo, I relax.

"I'm fine," I assure him. When he continues to stand there, I rise to my elbows. "Do you need something?"

"Yes," he replies huskily. "I want you to show me what you did to set those alarms off so I can be more prepared next time." He holds out his hands.

I nod. It's a start. A small secret or two to help tide them over until they get the video. I grasp Mateo's hands, and he steps back and pulls me up until I'm standing in front of him. In my bare feet, he's about five inches taller than me, and I have to tilt my head to see into his eyes.

He releases one of my hands to capture a pink strand between his finger and thumb. Rubbing back and forth, a surprised expression crosses his face. "It's so soft."

It's been so long since someone physically touched me with such sweetness, I stand absolutely still. "Thank you," I murmur.

He tucks the hair behind my ear and turns on his heel. My other hand's still held in his, and he clasps it tighter to pull me along.

He leads me over to the couch and motions for me to sit. Reaching into his pocket, he pulls out my phone but holds it out of reach when I go to grab it.

"Promise me you won't use it for anything except to show me what you did in the garage that day, and you'll return it to me when we're done," he demands.

When I nod, he hands it to me.

My anxiety eases. Having something tech in my hands is like having a safety net or a lifeline or my third limb. I unconsciously rub my fingers over it, and he laughs knowingly.

He sits down thigh to thigh beside me on the couch with his phone in hand. The warmth of his body along with musky smell of man and soap wraps tightly around me, and something deep inside stirs to life. Desire, attraction, but more than that, a long suppressed craving for the intimacy only lovers know. I tried to find it in a couple of one-night stands, but the brief interludes couldn't fill the emptiness of being truly alone. My eyes close, and for a moment, I just breathe in the two of us together, the smell almost a taste on my tongue.

He chuckles. "Are you going to turn on your phone or just hold it?"

The deep timber sound caresses my ear, making me shiver.

"Are you cold?" Without waiting for my reply, he's already twisting to the side to pull the blanket from the arm of the couch. Laying it over my lap, he tucks it around me. "Better?"

Worse, better, I don't even know anymore, but I nod and turn on my phone.

He leans over my shoulder to peer at the apps, then compares it to his. "Quite a few of the same apps," he comments, then holds his screen up for me to see.

We do have a lot of the same apps, but I focus on the ones

used to identify security vulnerabilities. He probably uses his to test new security systems at work. Mine are customized to be more helpful when hacking and escaping bad situations.

I tap on one and show him how I modified the application to connect with security systems and search for weak spots in the design or in the setup.

"You use the information to fix the security system, but I use it to exploit it. Once I have the information, I pull up a second app and search the database for the two parameters—system plus weakness—and it gives me instructions on how to hack it. When we were in the garage, the first app helped me identify our options, and the second app told me how to set off the alarms."

"Where did you get the second app?" he asks, opening the app store.

I reach over and tap the close button. "From the dark web. A couple of hackers developed it. I helped them with something, and they sent me the app as payment. Better than money. I'd share it with you, but they control the distribution to keep it out of competitors' hands."

Over the next hour, we talk "shop" and our favorite applications and modifications. I don't get too deep or share all my phone's secrets, because I may need a surprise or two later to escape. Plus, I know he's only fishing for information. It's still fun to bounce ideas around, especially with a massive brain like his.

"Maybe you should go straight and retire from hacking. Delete all those illegal apps on your phone and come work at SEI," he says, only half-joking.

The absurdity makes me die laughing. I worked hard for all those illegal apps, and nothing on this earth would make me give them up to go work a boring job at SEI, even if the scenery is rather nice.

Firm lips capture the laughter spilling from me, and for a second, I'm stunned to feel him kissing me, but when he starts to ease back, I can't bear the thought. I wrap my hand around the nape of his neck and dive into the kiss, my lips and tongue consumed with the need to know how this man tastes and kisses.

The spark between us quickly flames to life, and I moan, wanting more of him. This sexy, brainy man, who ordered me to find safety in the garage, who can geek out with me on something as simple as an app, and who... doesn't trust me in the slightest. My lips cling to his when I pull back. Breathing heavily, I can't help swiping my tongue across for one last taste.

He traces my lips with his finger. "You have a great laugh," he says huskily.

"Thanks?" I respond self-consciously. When I study him, I see the same conflict I'm feeling in his eyes.

"How did you meet Marcos?" His dark eyes are intent behind his glasses, needing to know the answer to this simple but complex question.

I shut off my phone and return it to him. He smiles and puts it into his pocket.

I sigh and stare at my hands. Without my phone, they're restless, fidgeting constantly, until his hand reaches out to cover them. I lace my fingers through his and grip it tightly.

Flicking my eyes to his, I stare at him and let the words flow. "I met Marcos in a chat room on the dark web. On the run and desperate, I posted a request for tips on how to create a better identity, one that would hold up to scrutiny, so I could get a job or a bank account in another name. I had tech skills, but I didn't have a clue how to do something illegal." I was so innocent back then.

"It was pure luck Marcos replied and not someone unscrupulous. He helped me create a couple of identities. From then on, any time I had a question about what I was doing, I posted and he answered." I smile at the memory. "Eventually, I leaned on him to learn more. How to set up multiple bank accounts, find small hacking jobs for money, and the best practices to secure my computer from other hackers. Basically, how to live and survive in the world I suddenly found myself in."

He squeezes my hand and sighs. "He rescued you."

As if it's the answer to everything, and while simple, it fits.

"Exactly. We chatted regularly for a few months. He fed me pointers and information, and I slowly learned how to hide myself. One night, I went offline and didn't return for a couple of weeks. When he found out why, he stuck his neck out and truly rescued me," I say with a shiver.

Those two weeks were dark. I didn't think I'd escape.

His hand sweeps through my hair, his expression troubled by what he sees in my face. "You're safe here. I promise."

I place two fingers on his lips. "Don't. Don't promise me safety. It's an illusion. Nobody is safe. You enjoy the days you get and let tomorrow come or not."

"Marcos used to say the same thing." He grimaces. "I prefer to see things optimistically. Dreaming for a better tomorrow gives you hope today."

I shrug. I used to feel the same way a long time ago, but it's impossible now. "I can't," I say helplessly, looking away from the optimism shining out of his eyes. "Dreaming is a luxury I haven't had in a long time."

He gently grasps my chin and turns my head toward him. "Who took this away from you?"

"Before I tell you, please don't trivialize the situation or try to fix it or me," I implore him, having had bad experiences with both in the past. "In college, I picked up a stalker, and being an over-achiever, I attracted a brilliant one. Genius level, Marcos thought. No matter what I did, I couldn't hide from him. If I asked anybody for help, he ruined them. Evidence of theft, financial problems, cheating, you name it. If they left me, they'd get part of their lives back. Not all of it, because they still had to be punished, but most of it. It didn't matter who it was. My own mother lost her house, her career, and all her friends."

I take a deep breath. "When Marcos offered to help, I declined. He refused to accept my answer. When he asked why, I told him, and you know what he did? He laughed. Told me you couldn't ruin a ghost. He didn't exist in the real world." I laugh.

"For the next two weeks, Marcos barely responded to messages. I thought he'd had a change of heart and left me to fend for myself like all the others. When he returned, he made me change everything about myself to become a new person from the inside out. All my habits, my appearance, my digital signature and coding style, my name, accounts, location, you name it. He never told me how he was able to hide me, but it worked. While I live a reclusive life, I haven't seen my stalker in almost five years."

Pride shines on Mateo's face. "Marcos was really, really good at rescuing people. When we were young, he rescued all of us, his family. It wasn't enough, though. When he made his first million, he committed twenty-five percent to a fund which he used to seed more rescue missions. With every dollar he made, he put aside the required funds so he could continue helping others find safety." He sighs heavily, grief etched in the sad smile he gives me. "I don't even know how many he helped. Or anything about it. I'm ashamed I never asked."

"Three hundred and forty-three," I inform him. When he appears confused, I expound upon it. "Including me, he saved three hundred and forty-three people from some incredibly scary situations—stalkers, cartel targets, political activists, abusive husbands, you name it."

He blinks, and I see him processing the information, wanting to ask more questions, but I'm done answering tonight.

I shake my head. The therapist Marcos forced me to see every week for four years taught me to recognize my boundaries and enforce them. I still reach out to her when I need help coping or to reset.

Understanding dawns, and he gives me a tender look. When he leans forward, I hold my breath, longing to feel the spark between us ignite again, but instead of the passionate kiss I was expecting, he presses his lips firmly to mine in the lightest and sweetest of kisses.

"Thank you for sharing something with me."

I cup his scruffy jaw. "Feel free to share it with Thiago and

Grayson," I murmur. "Your uncle was truly a remarkable man. He was my mentor and only friend. I'm sorry for his loss, but I'm more sorry the world will never know how much he did for others."

The door opens, and Grayson strolls in with a large brown bag in his hand. "Well, you two are cozy."

HENLEY

When I discover the food is from my favorite Mexican food joint, I jump up from the couch to help spread everything out on the counter. I missed lunch while I was plotting and planning, and I'm starving.

I pull out several fat rolls wrapped in aluminum foil and practically drool in anticipation. Then a large bowl of salsa. Each time my hand goes in the bag, it brings out lovely, delicious food—beans, rice, pico de gallo, guacamole, and queso. A second bag is filled with chips, warm tortillas, tacos, and several to-go containers stuffed with red pork tamales and chicken verde enchiladas.

Wait, we're missing something. I double check, but it's official. There are no sopapillas hiding in the bottom. Another bag appears in front of my face, and excited, I glance up and find Thiago staring at me with an amused smile on his face. I blink. The man should smile more often.

Pivoting, he sets a few more bags on the counter by the fridge and pulls out water, Cokes, several cases of bottled beer, and some limes. After stocking the shelves, he grabs a bottle for himself, then looks at Mateo.

"Zane, Sterling, and Cruz are coming over. We'll need more seats. I'm going to shower."

When I hear who's joining us for dinner, my stomach sinks. I guess if I'm going to have a last meal, I'm glad it's this one. Grabbing paper plates, napkins, and plastic silverware from the bag, I lay them beside the food and back up to check—A hard body stops my momentum. Twirling, I find Grayson standing practically on top of me. He smells of soap and the subtle scent of his expensive cologne. After his shower, he'd exchanged his usual suit for a pair of dark jeans and a button-down. High style as usual, but eminently more approachable.

A bead of water rolls down from the damp hair on the top of his head, along his temple and across his sculpted cheek. I reach up to smooth it away, but when I realize what I'm doing, I freeze, leaving my hand hanging in mid-air.

Grayson leans over and places his cheek next to my hand, his eyes never leaving mine. They're not quite as cold as when we first met, but they're not warm either. A hint of something is shining out of their blue fathomless depths.

My thumb captures the drop, and I absentmindedly wipe it on my jeans while he straightens.

"You might be my favorite person on the planet," I quip, trying to ease the tension between us. "This is the best Mexican food in Miami, and the chicken burrito is hands down the best I've ever tasted anywhere."

His eyes crinkle. "Maybe it tastes good because you've never had authentic Mexican food," he teases. He reaches past me and grabs a chip and some salsa. Shoving it in his mouth, he gives an exaggerated moan.

"Please, I live in Texas," I retort, then stop when I realize what I've said. I just told him where I live—something I never do.

"Easy. Take a deep breath," he orders me, his eyes pinned on me like a laser. "Texas is a big, big state."

I nod and breathe in and out. Again. He must think I'm crazy. I watch him slip to the fridge and grab two beers. Removing the tops, he hands one to me and takes one for himself. He taps the necks together.

"I hope you have one of those for me," a gruff voice says from the doorway.

When I glance over, I see the blond man from the other night. The one who laid Diego out on the floor. I smile at the memory. He must be Cruz.

"I'll get it," Grayson interjects. Crossing to the fridge, he grabs a beer and shoves it toward the guy with a look.

A deep chuckle emerges from the man, and I raise my eyebrow.

Grayson sighs and stares at the ceiling like he's asking for patience.

Mateo and Thiago come into the kitchen together. Thiago's hair is also wet from the shower, but he's wearing a well-worn pair of jeans and a T-shirt. Formal or casual, the man still exudes the same lethal aura, and the air changes when he enters the room like a lion prowling through a crowd.

Zane and Sterling arrive a minute later, and they all stand to the side so I can fill my plate first.

I place a serving of everything on my plate, add a side order of the chips, loaded with salsa and queso of course, then pick up my beer and head to the table. The room is utterly silent, and I look around for the reason, but they're all staring at me. Even Thiago gets an amused glint in his eye when he glances at my plate before he moves to the table and pulls out a chair for me. I tilt my head in gratitude, then lay everything down.

Cruz gets his plate and grabs the seat next to me. Someone clears his throat, and with an apologetic glance, he moves down two seats.

I shrug. I'm sure none of the Santos men want me to make friends with anyone who might help me escape and evade the police. I'm not a prisoner now, but the more they discover, the higher the possibility my status could change.

Zane and Sterling sit across from me, and I see their plates are just as full as mine. Mateo sits beside Cruz. Grayson sits down on my left, and Thiago grabs the seat on my right.

When I see everyone else pick up their fork, I dive in and take a bite of the burrito first. I close my eyes at the sheer flavor exploding in my mouth. I wonder if I could convince Juanita to open a second restaurant in Dallas? I could easily promise to order from her every week. I hum happily when I bite into the tamale. It's perfect too. The masa is steamy, and the pork shredded. Maybe I could order twice a week.

Zane coughs, or grunts, I can't tell, but I glance up from my plate to find him staring at me. I turn to Thiago to see if I missed anything, but his eyes are locked on Zane.

"What have you found?" Thiago asks him.

I slow my eating so I can focus on the conversation.

Sterling shares a glance with Zane, then swallows. "We were able to capture footage of the car chase. Cameras picked it up about a mile from the office. We followed it to the garage and were able to capture several different angles of the occupants."

I take the last bite and set my fork down.

"And?" Thiago prompts him, but Sterling's silent.

I lean back and pat my stomach. My eyes cut over to Sterling and see him staring at… my plate. I laugh.

With an exasperated sigh, Thiago shakes his head.

"Slick, finish your report," Zane orders with a chuckle.

"Who's Slick?" I ask, frowning.

Zane slaps Sterling on the back. "Fanciest blue blood you'll ever meet. I call him Slick."

With a scowl, Sterling flips his laptop so the screen is facing us. There are a multitude of pictures. Mateo reaches out and clicks on an image.

Diego's face is clear, as if the picture had been taken during the day. A passing light caught him full on the face, hanging out the side of the car with a gun in his hand.

I shiver. If Thiago hadn't brought in Zane and his team, Diego could have easily stalled the investigation on his end, and nobody would have ever known he was behind it. Once he saw Zane, he knew his time was up, which is why Thiago couldn't find him last night.

Mateo curses. Grayson shoves his plate away. But Thiago, he rages. In a tirade of Portuguese, he jerks the laptop closer and scrolls through each of the images until he stops on one where the gun is pointed directly into the passenger seat at Mateo. He snaps a picture of it with his phone.

"That must have been taken when they shot out the passenger windows," I murmur, remembering the frightening sound of the window exploding behind my ear, followed by the one on the other side.

Before Thiago can say anything, Zane interjects, "We're looking for him, but he's gone underground. He's street smart and knows Miami inside and out. We won't find him overnight."

"Try not to kill him when you capture him," Thiago states softly. Interestingly, his head is turned toward Cruz, not Zane. "I want to have a long chat with him about loyalty and family."

Cruz nods, then puts down his fork. "I found Marcos' car, abandoned, near the everglades. Wiped clean." He pauses. "Blood in the car. Backseat."

I grip my hands together in my lap. Grayson reaches down and lays his hand over mine. His thumb moves softly across the back of my hand in a soothing motion.

"Is it Marcos' blood?" Thiago asks hoarsely.

"It is," Zane confirms. "Lab results came back immediately. I can't figure out the scenario, though. Was he kidnapped on Monday, beaten, possibly killed, then returned to the building? Is the explosion a coverup? What's the motive?"

"If it was the person who stole the software, whether it's CJ Tech or not, why would they go after Marcos?" Grayson asks, bewildered by the latest discovery.

Six days. Today's almost over, though, so it's nearer to five days. My leg starts bouncing, but I say nothing. Thiago's large hand clamps down on my knee, and I stop.

"We have one other item, but we can discuss it with you before we leave," Zane says casually.

I freeze. All I want to do is look at Zane after his statement, but I force myself to get up and grab the honey, along with two sopapillas. It's definitely a two sopapillas night.

When I sit down, Cruz slaps the table and motions to Sterling. Bright green eyes stare at my plate in disbelief before he slaps a twenty in Cruz's hand.

"Did you bet on my getting dessert?" I ask incredulously.

Mateo pipes up. "Actually, the first bet was on whether you could finish the food on your plate, and the second bet was on whether you would eat dessert."

I give them a quizzical look. "It's not like I went back for seconds. Although, I did think about it since I missed lunch, but I wanted to be sure I saved room for dessert. Dessert is a priority."

Zane busts out laughing. Then the big man stands and heads over to the sopapillas and grabs two for himself. "Always save room for dessert. It's a good motto."

After dinner, I help clean the kitchen, then sit down on the couch. There's a TV in the corner, but it doesn't interest me. Without a computer, I'm kind of lost. My eyes dart around the room, hoping to find something to read or do, and I spot a shelf full of puzzles. Perfect.

I sweep everything off the coffee table and dump the pieces out of the box. Grabbing the corner pieces first, I set those in place, then set about finding the rest of the edge pieces.

The puzzle not only gives me something to do, but takes my mind away from the discussion Thiago is having with Zane about me. There's nothing I can do about it anyway. I'll just have to wait and see which of my secrets has come to light.

<u>THIAGO</u>

"**H**er prints came up in the criminal database for a Henley Davis, deceased, along with an inactive warrant. Issued in 2015 for first-degree arson. What do you want me to do?" Zane states quietly, his face marked with distaste, which tells me he likes her.

Surprised, I try to reconcile the woman in the house, with her bold pink hair and air of innocence, starting a blaze big enough to be charged with a felony.

"Investigate it. I'd like to know if Henley Davis is her real name, and since she's obviously alive, why they would think she's dead? It's not a far stretch from arson to explosives, but honestly, I don't see it," I tell him. "Also, if she's Henley, I'd like to get a full background check done."

He hesitates. "You're paying the bills, but I need to remind you it's sometimes best to leave the past where it belongs... dead and buried. Something happened to her, but just because she survived it once doesn't mean she can do so again." His voice is hard, likely thinking of his own situation, but it also reminds me of mine.

"Understood. Just do an exploratory visit," I tell him, amending my first orders. "Number one priority is Diego. Let me know when he pops his head up. I want that bastard."

He nods, and without a word, he vanishes into the night.

When I return to the house, Cassie's bent over the coffee table, putting a puzzle together. I stop, and she peers up at me. I try to picture her as a hardened criminal, but I can't. Maybe it's the pink hair or the wide blue eyes or, as Grayson said, the inability to lie. We know she has secrets. Hell, she even admitted it to us. But it's a long road from secrets to being a killer. I head to the backyard, where Grayson and Mateo are waiting for me.

Relaying Zane's information on the fingerprints and warrant, it surprises me when Mateo interjects in her defense.

"Over five years ago, I bet it's her stalker." When Grayson and I look at him with a puzzled expression, he shares their discussion from earlier. "If it weren't for Marcos, she firmly believes she'd be dead by now."

I swivel toward the backdoor, wanting to go in there and swear she'll be safe, but I don't take a single step. I couldn't even keep her from Diego's cruel hands.

Grayson doesn't seem surprised, but he's good at assessing people. "I could see it in her eyes when she woke up on the couch, as if waking up in an unfamiliar place is her worst nightmare visiting her from the past. He must have caught her sleeping at some point." His eyes are dark with anger.

"Anything else?" I give Mateo a side-glance.

"She also helped me find the connection between Cecilia, Marcos, and me." He goes on to explain the settings on the server and our former employee's connection to Marcos.

"Find out who knew about their relationship. It's not something Diego's likely to see, which means we could have two SEI traitors," I order him. "Don't spare anybody. Even if you think they're innocent." I can't help but glance at the house.

"On it," he replies. "Any word from Agent Antonio and the investigation?"

"We met today, and he went through a list of questions about our relationship with Marcos, our locations leading up to the explosion and after, and the standard litany of whether SEI had any enemies," I inform them with a half-smile. "I gave him the usual spiel of how SEI couldn't be the powerhouse it is today without having stepped on a few toes or companies along the way. We have plenty of enemies, but none who knew of our relationship with Marcos. Or his with SEI. Of course, I didn't know at the time that Diego was a traitor, but I'll call and update Agent Antonio."

My voice is raw when I speak about Diego. A good friend for twenty years, then he betrays my friendship and trust in the worst possible way. I examine the wound on Mateo's head. If he'd been any closer, I'd have buried two family members in a week. Before this is done, I'll bury Diego and scatter his ashes to the wind. He will have no rest, no peace.

"Besides shooting Mateo, which I have to confess has crossed my mind a time or two—" Grayson jerks to the side to avoid Mateo's fist, then continues, "How deep does Diego's betrayal go? How far back? Instead of CJ Tech, could he have sold the bidding information to the buyer and his mysterious backer?"

Reeling at the thought, I contemplate the nuances of the deal. "He could have easily heard me speaking to one of you about the timing, but the bid amounts would have had to come from someone in R&D. Mateo's department is the only one who reviews and assesses the bids. It doesn't go to finance, or even to me, until R&D selects the winning bid." I watch the same conclusion happen on Mateo's face. "We have two traitors in our house."

CHAPTER 26

<u>GRAYSON</u>

When I hear her enter the kitchen, I step through the door to tell her to bring her coffee and breakfast to the back patio, then return to my seat. The patio is shaded from the hot sun and has a large dining table in the middle, perfect for eating and working. I prefer to be outside, so I made this my office space for the day. First Monday I haven't gone into the office in a long time. Feels almost like playing hooky. I grin.

She steps out with her plate and hands full, and I quickly pull out a chair for her to sit. Like Mateo, she says nothing until she's eaten most of her plate and drunk her first cup of coffee. It's funny how similar those two seem to me.

I study every inch of her, noting the slight curves and lean lines of her body, the brightness of her pink hair, and I'm stumped. Except for her height, she lacks the physical attributes I find most appealing in women. Why do I find her fascinating? Is it all the roles she's played? The layers I get a glimpse of before she hides them again? I sigh, knowing I need to stick to the women I know, not one woman who can be hurt by my actions. Nobody wants a repeat of the past.

My dates are sophisticated, confident, and quite adept at utilizing every tool in their armory to draw my attention. Perfectly polished with the innate ability to wear clothes to showcase their bodies.

Her jeans and T-shirt are loose and covered with folds and wrinkles, like she pulled them directly out of the suitcase. Did she not unpack? I tilt my head to the side and consider the possibility. Surely not.

"Did you find plenty of hangers in your closet? If not, I can grab some from mine."

She sets her fork down precisely on her plate and raises an eyebrow. "Breakfast was delicious, thank you," she says with laughter in her voice.

I nod and dip my head to acknowledge her statement.

"As for the number of hangers in my closet, I wouldn't know. I didn't count them," she replies, then stands and takes her plate to the kitchen.

Count them or use them? Minx. She's deliberately baiting me. A few minutes later, she returns with a fresh cup of coffee.

She purses her lips and blows on the dark liquid to cool it off, then takes a sip. "What are you working on this morning?"

Dragging my eyes from her soft-looking lips, I debate answering her, but maybe it's the only way to see how much she knows about the deal that went wrong. "I'm trying to figure out how the money disappeared from our account after we brokered a software deal." Not an ounce of confusion or puzzlement shows on her face. She knows about the deal. "You wouldn't have any ideas on how to trace the transaction, would you?"

"If I had access to my computer, I could show you how it was done," she states confidently. She rolls her eyes when she sees the skepticism on my face. "Fine. I'll explain it, and if you want me to give you a demonstration, then you can give me my computer."

I lean back and motion for her to continue, although I still don't believe she knows the answer.

She taps her finger on her chin. "This would be so much easier to show you. They're playing the long con," she begins. "If they have enough details ahead of time, they can easily move money in and out of the bank without detection, especially if it's a large commercial bank like the one SEI uses." She takes another sip.

I give her a sharp look. She knows the bank we use. Interesting little tidbit she just dropped.

"Money is nothing but a number. If it's a large number, many numbers combine to create the one number. Banks monitor transactions, patterns, and ledger balances, and if the 'thief' doesn't trigger any alerts related to those variables, they can move money around all they want."

I sit up straighter. She's brimming with energy and excitement, like she finds the subject of money as fascinating as I do.

"All they need is three pieces of information a few days before the transaction takes place—the bank information for each party and the estimated purchase amount. Banks calculate the ledger balance at the end of every day, and they use this as the next day's beginning ledger balance until it's recalculated at the next day's close. The ledger balance includes all confirmed transactions, which gives the 'thief' an idea of how much money is moved in and out of a bank during a twenty-four-hour period. If you expand it to thirty days, it gives a broader picture of the banks' balance and transaction activities for a longer period."

She takes a sip of coffee and raises an eyebrow.

"Basically, they need to know the low balance and high balance for the bank over the last thirty days," I summarize.

"And the amount of money that can safely be moved within a twenty-four-hour period," she adds. "In addition, the ledger balance is not representative of the available balance, which gives them a small safety net for any software miscalculations."

She puts the coffee cup on the table. "Most of the money for the purchase likely came from other corporate accounts at the same bank, with a small percentage flowing in from other banks. The software they deploy conducts transactions all day and all night to stay in those parameters. The money is constantly on the move, and the same amount reported as a deposit one day could be split into a pending debit and a wire transfer when it moves. Credit, debit, credit. The transactions are small, incremental amounts and consist of odd numbers, like $1.54 or $74.69 to reflect near similar conditions of transactions made within the past thirty days. Once the software is deployed, it not only moves the money around, but it tracks the original transaction source and type, destination, and amount, so the money can continue its original journey once they release it."

She pauses to see if I've understood her explanation.

"Essentially, they mimicked the bank's transaction patterns to move millions of dollars so they could make us *think* the money was in our account. I'd have noticed if it was in pending status," I argue.

"When a transaction moves from pending to actual, the money is reflected in available balance, correct?" When I nod, she continues, "And you have money constantly flowing out of your account too, right? So the available balance fluctuates and changes throughout the day, and money designated as available becomes unavailable due to new transactions.

"If you were to examine the days surrounding the sale amount, I'm sure you'll find lots of tiny transactions that could easily be overlooked. Some of the money you received from the sale likely came from your own account as well as other accounts in and outside of your bank. They had to keep the money moving to evade detection by the bank's machine learning algorithms, which monitor for possible money laundering by establishing patterns by a given customer."

Stunned, I sort through the implications of her scenario. "They used the bank's existing patterns to identify how to move the money. Then they manipulated millions of transactions to make us think the money was in our account, and at the end, simply dispersed each transaction back to its original owner or intended recipient? You're saying—it's a giant shell game?" I roar and jump to my feet to pace around the patio. I shake my head. "The algorithms required to enable those types of real-time transactions and pattern management must be insane."

"Most of the transactions are recorded entries but not actual transactions. Plus, they have up to twenty-four hours to net out with the final transaction amount," she says absentmindedly.

"What are you saying?"

"For example, let's say I give you five dollars, you give Mateo two dollars and Thiago three dollars, then they each give me two dollars, and Thiago buys a car for one dollar." She glances at me when I snort, then continues, "At the end of the day, the net transaction is one dollar to an outside bank. The remaining four dollars stays in this bank and is calculated on the ledger balance."

"How the hell do you know all this? Or do I even want to know?" I ask her, astounded by the depth of her financial transaction knowledge. "I'm on the board at several large banking institutions, and I've never heard of anything even remotely close to this level of sophistication."

She bites her lip but says nothing.

"I'd rather you not tell me than lie," I assure her softly. "Why don't I get your computer, and you can show me?"

Her head's down and she's looking at her fingernails, but she nods.

When I come back, she's staring out at the garden, a sad expression on her face. "Hey, if there's anyone who should be sad, it's me. I'm out a hell of a lot of money, and the 'thief' has the last piece of software Marcos worked on." I set the computer down and smile with relief when her eyes light up. "Show me."

An hour later, I lean against the chair and analyze the information. Our overall account increased by the amount of the purchase, but from millions of transactions instead of a single deposit. Before the bank calculated their next ledger balance, the money was gone.

Her grey-blue eyes peer at me with apprehension, but I'm not angry. She didn't pay me with pretend money. I'm just amazed by the way she thinks. It's like her brain is a combination of Mateo's and mine. Fascinating.

"I'm not angry with you. I'm trying to think of what we can do to prevent this from happening again," I explain, trying to make sense of the thoughts swirling around in my brain. We're already using the most sophisticated accounting software on the market. What else can we do? "If you have some ideas, I'd love to hear them."

She opens her mouth, but the buzz of my phone cuts her off.

"Sorry," I say and grab my phone. "Thiago, what's going on?"

"Diego's been spotted. Cruz has him in sight. Zane's in North Carolina, so Mateo and I, along with a few hand-picked men from our security team, are headed to back up Cruz." He puts me on speaker. "Sorry, changing clothes. Everything okay there?"

"We're good. Rose helped me trace the money, and long story short, we never had the money. They used an elaborate shell game to play us from the start," I bark, still pissed off. "I'll give you the details when I see you. Do you need me to come with you? You could send someone from security here to stay with her."

Rose shoots me an angry look.

I raise my hand, silently asking her to fill me in, but she just waves her hand and stomps off.

"I could use you. I'll send Roberto to... Rose? Why are you calling her Rose? Doesn't Mateo call her Cassie? Can we not agree on one name to call her?" He sounds irritated, but I ignore it.

"Send me updates with your location, and I'll meet you once he gets here," I tell him. And I'll call her whatever the hell I please.

I head to her room, but the door is closed. "Rose, I'm heading out. Do you want me to order you some lunch?" Silence. She must be pissed if she's not responding to lunch. I chuckle. "I'll call back later and see how you're doing." I didn't think she was the type to get mad about me leaving, but maybe it's because she's stuck here.

The front door opens, and I find Roberto standing in the doorway.

"Hey, Roberto, Rose is in her bedroom. Just leave her in there. I'll call and check on you both in a little while," I greet him and point toward the back of the house.

He narrows his eyes, and I tilt my head.

"Everything okay?" I question sharply, putting my hand near the gun in my back holster.

"All good, sorry, just listening to the chatter," he explains, pulling the device out of his ear to show me. He hands me a new one from a case in his pocket.

I take it and head out. Unable to help myself, I stare at her window while I'm backing out of the driveway, but the blinds are completely shut.

CHAPTER 27

<u>HENLEY</u>

I agreed to stay in the house with them, not with someone from SEI security, especially not a man Diego hired and managed. As soon as Grayson's car backs out of the driveway, I head down the street. Thankfully, I have money stashed everywhere from jean pockets to resealed tampons. Three blocks from the house, I catch the bus into South Beach.

I need a phone. Heading into a busy 7-Eleven, I grab a ball cap, sunglasses, a pack of ponytail holders, and a burner phone. When I leave, I use one of the elastic bands to put my hair into a tight bun, then pull the cap on over it. I'll be less noticeable without the pink hair flying everywhere. Spotting a little sandwich café nearby, I grab some lunch and figure out my next move.

"Excuse me." When the mother next to me raises her head, I ask, "Is there a public library in South Beach?"

She assesses my clothing and wrinkles her nose. "South Shore Branch Library. You can catch the bus across the street, and it will take you close. Get off at Alton Street."

"Thank you so much," I reply with a forced smile. A few minutes later, I'm out the door and getting on the bus. Right before I get off, I ask someone for directions from the stop to the library itself. It's a two-minute walk.

Easily spotting the yellow building, I enter the double doors and make my way over to the computers. This is perfect. Logging into several locations, I find a couple of the videos have been downloaded, then deleted. I laugh. Hopefully, the rootkit works, and I can get remote access to their computer. I check, but they haven't opened the file yet.

Messenger reports several entries into the lab, but they exited quickly.

I search for updates on the ATF investigation and find a new press video of Agent Antonio walking into the building, carrying a familiar envelope. My heart starts beating faster. Clicking on the footage, I put on the headsets provided by the library and press play.

"After examining all the footage from the security cameras, we've narrowed down our suspect pool and will be concentrating on a handful of individuals. The driver of a black SUV, a disgruntled security guard, and a courier who were all seen in areas of the building close to the explosion. That's all for now. Thank you." Agent Antonio gives his statement, then walks into the building.

Well, the good news is he had the envelope I sent with the flash drive, so hopefully, he'll watch it soon. If not, he'll start to investigate the courier—aka me—and I doubt my disguise will hold up to scrutiny.

I wonder who the SUV driver might have been? I search for pictures of the footage, but nothing shows up.

Relieved to know the drive got into his hands, I spend some time checking emails and paying bills for my place in Dallas. I log into the security cameras and check the perimeter of the building and the inside hallway. When I get to the camera closest to my door, I spot a pink sticky on my door. Zooming in, I see it's courier notice with a request to call them and arrange the delivery of a package. I grab the number and call.

"Hello, Courier Express, how may I help you?"

"Hello, I've received a note to pick up a package, but I'm out of town. What are my options?"

"Do you have anyone who can get the package for you?" she asks me.

"No, I'm sorry, I don't," I reply.

"Give me your name," she says with a weary sounding sigh.

I reel off my address because I'm not quite sure what name will be on the package.

Silence. "I asked for your name, not your address. Never mind, I have it," she retorts. "Nyx?"

It's from Marcos. "Yes, it's me, I'm Nyx," I assure her.

"Okay, it's a business-sized envelope. We can store it in a locked box at our office. We require a hundred-dollar deposit and a hundred dollars for the first month's rent. When you pick up your package, we'll refund the deposit. If we need to store it for longer than a month, the rent increases an additional twenty-five per month."

Without thinking, I whistle. Convenience hurts.

She chuckles. "I know, girl, but if we don't charge an outrageous amount, people will leave their stuff here forever. What's it going to be?"

I agree to the amount and pay the fee.

"Thanks so much for your help," I tell her, then hang up.

A hand touches my shoulder and I let out a short scream. Whipping around, I find an older lady standing there with a sour expression on her face.

"We don't allow phone calls in the library," she informs me, her lips pursed. "We're also closing in five minutes." She walks away to speak to a young man nearby.

I glance at the old-school white and black clock on the wall and see it's five o'clock. Gathering my things, I head out.

When I get to the bus stop, I try to trace the correct colored route to get where I'm going, but it's like tracing a single noodle through a bowl of spaghetti. A young man steps up to help me find the right bus numbers.

My bus finally comes, but with rush hour, it's another hour before I get to the neighborhood. When I near the house, flashing red and blue lights shine bright against the night. I stop. The driveway and street are filled with police cars, a plain sedan, and an ambulance.

"Shit, shit, shit," I repeat over and over. Did someone else die? My heart starts racing at the thought of one of their deaths. I just met them.

A couple of EMTs come out of the house, pushing a gurney, and I catch sight of a black zippered bag. Someone is dead. My feet start moving, and before I know it, I'm running toward the body. Strong arms come from behind and wrap around me. I start wailing on them, trying to force them to let me go.

"Easy, Cassie, I've got you," a voice croons softly in my ear, and I gasp.

Twirling around, I throw my arms around Mateo's warm, living body. "Who died?" I ask with a hiccup, tears flowing down my cheeks.

"Roberto," he answers, his voice hoarse with emotion. He pulls me in tighter and rocks back and forth. "We thought the killers kidnapped you or something."

"Is she ok?" a gruff voice asks.

I ease out of Mateo's arms, wipe my tears away, and face Thiago. "What happened?"

His eyes dart to the cops standing a few feet away, and he pulls me in close and wraps his massive arms around me.

Startled, I jerk backward, but he tightens his arms until I can't escape.

"Stop fidgeting," he orders me in a harsh but low voice. "Some idiot called the cops when he heard gunshots. They know about Roberto, but I'd rather they not know what's going on with Diego. Do you understand? Nod yes or no."

When I nod yes, he continues to murmur in my ear. "Here's what you're going to tell them. You left the house, went to South Beach, did some window shopping, then returned. We'll talk later about where you've been and about telling people where you're going." He squeezes me. "So glad you're home, honey." With a quick pivot, he settles me under his arm and walks me into the house.

Honey? Unwilling to risk his wrath, I play along.

A middle-aged man in a brown wrinkled suit and a young woman wearing pressed black pants and a button-down shirt wait for us in the house. They introduce themselves as Detective John Hagen and Detective Marley Jones from the Miami Police Department.

"You can call us John and Marley. We understand you've been out all day, but we'd like to ask you some questions."

"Sure, go ahead."

Detective Marley takes the lead. "What time did you leave the house?"

I see Grayson slide into the room and lean against the wall. His blue eyes are dark, and his face is set with anger. I deliberately turn my head to the detectives.

"I left about two minutes past twelve," I state clearly, glaring at Grayson. He raises an eyebrow in response.

"What did you do when you left?" she continues, while Detective John observes me like a hawk.

"Went to the bus stop about three blocks away and hopped on a bus to South Beach. Stopped at a 7-Eleven for a hair tie, sunglasses, and a hat." I conveniently leave off the burner phone but give her all the rest. "The sun is brutal around noon, and I forgot to bring those items with me. I'm sure you understand."

"I do," she says with a wink. "What else did you do?"

"Ate lunch at a little sandwich shop. Last, I went to the South Shore Library until it closed at five p.m. Then hopped the next bus back." I finish up the tale of my day.

"Do you happen to have any receipts?" she inserts smoothly.

"I do," I reply, pulling the one for lunch out of my jeans before making a show of searching for the other receipt. "I must have misplaced the other one, but here's the one for lunch."

After copying the information from the receipt, she hands it back to me. "You're good to go. We appreciate you giving us your statement." Her voice is filled with warmth now that I've provided her with an entire afternoon full of alibis.

"Thank you. I hope you catch whoever did this," I say fervently, praying she catches Diego or someone else does soon.

I sit in the living room for a couple of hours, but when the police show no signs of leaving early, I head toward my bedroom. When I open the door, I inhale deeply and walk slowly into the destroyed room. I open my mouth to yell, but a big hand clamps down it.

"Shhh," he whispers. "I don't want the police to hear. Nod if you understand."

After I comply, he releases my mouth but keeps me in his arms.

I whimper at the destruction around me.

The stitching has been ripped out of my suitcase. Everything's been dumped out on the bed. My clothes are wrecked with holes or tears, and a terrible smell is emanating from the center of the pile, where someone has peed on them. Wrinkling my nose, I motion for him to move away from the smell.

I'm shaking at the thought of someone rifling through my things, violating my privacy. Similar scenes from the past flash in my head, bringing familiar feelings of helplessness and vulnerability. My skin crawls like a thousand ants are scurrying across my body or a thousand eyes are on me. Nowhere to hide. I'm having a hard time breathing. I drag in a ragged breath, then out, in, out, in, out. Unable to get air, I slide to my knees, and the edges around my vision darken.

Large hands wrap around my head to hold it up.

"Breathe with me," a hard voice demands. "In, take a deep breath in. Come on, querida, breathe in." He takes a deep breath in and waits for me to join him.

Desperate, I latch on to the dark eyes in front of me and inhale. Then exhale with him. Again, together, slowly. Over and over. When

I can breathe easily again, the tears flow down my cheeks and the shaking starts.

"He's not here. Do you hear me? I promise. Your stalker isn't here. He's never been here. This is all Diego's doing." Thiago's voice is forceful as it tries to break through my fear.

"Not here. Promise?" I ask, desperately needing him to say it again.

"I swear to you, with everything I have, he isn't here. It was Diego," he promises.

I cry harder, unable to stop the tears from coming.

I hear murmurs above me, but I can't hear the words.

Thiago shifts to his feet, then leans down to pick me up in his arms.

"Keep them busy," he orders someone behind us. Stalking down the hall, he enters a large bedroom, then kicks the door shut.

Settling into a large chair, he holds me tightly in his arms, while I cry tears of fear and rage until I'm finally empty again.

Lifting my head, I visually trace the strong bones of his face, from his broad forehead to the granite jaw locked with emotion, and whisper, "Thank you." Leaning forward, I kiss his strong cheek.

He smooths the hair from my face and scrutinizes me in return. Seeing the lingering fear I'm trying to hide, he grips my chin between his finger and thumb. "I won't let Diego get to you. I—"

To his shock, I cover his mouth with my hand. "Don't promise me safety. Promise me you'll get Diego. He's dangerous. You don't even know how dangerous," I plead with him, feeling the weight of what I know weighing me down. The walls are closing in around me, but I don't know what else to do. Maybe he'll get the video tomorrow.

"I promise. I'll get him, and I'll bury him," he says solemnly, watching me closely.

"Good. He deserves to die," I tell him, not caring if he thinks I'm heartless. "And the next time any of you leave me alone in a house, I want my phone and gun. It's non-negotiable. Or I'll just go with the police right now." I lift my chin and wait for him to agree.

"We'll go to the range tomorrow, and if you can show me you know how to shoot, I'll agree to your terms," he replies with his condition.

"Deal," I state clearly and hold out my hand.

His large one engulfs mine. "Deal."

CHAPTER 28

<u>THIAGO</u>

She's sound asleep when Mateo opens the door an hour later. I carry her over to the bed, stopping only for him to remove her shoes before I lay her down and cover her with a blanket. I turn the bathroom light on so she can see if she wakes up, then follow him out the door.

"We're leaving, Mr. Santos." Detective Marley flashes a wide smile and a look of appreciation toward Grayson as she shakes his hand. She comes over to Mateo and me, her expression changing to something more solemn, and shakes both our hands. "We'll be in touch with anything we find. I'd reconsider our offer for protection if I were you. You're surrounded by close calls." —she glances at Mateo's head— "and is it two or three deaths now?"

"We have our own team, but thank you, Detective Jones," I firmly reply. "Detective Hagen." After shaking their hands, Mateo sees them out.

"Did they find anything?" I ask Grayson, reaching for the glass of bourbon he's holding out to me. Taking a large sip, I let its warmth soothe me.

"Three men, Roberto fought two. He took down one. They found him a block from here on someone's lawn. The men were skilled and searching for something, but it doesn't look like they took anything." His voice is gruff when he lays out the facts. When we first got here, he'd gone ballistic, thinking she'd been kidnapped and he hadn't stayed here with her.

Mateo throws his hands in the air. "Since when did Diego become smarter than us? He must have known Cruz was onto him to be able to double back here. But how? Where's Sterling? Wasn't he supposed to track Diego?"

A voice laced with steel answers from the doorway, and Mateo jumps. "Sterling got jumped. He was racing to tell you the comms were hijacked when they took him down."

I slide the safety on and return my gun to my side holster. "Is Sterling going to be okay?" I wave a hand at my seat and grab him a glass of bourbon. Handing it to him, I grab mine and sit on the couch across from him.

He takes a long swallow, then sets it down with a smile. "You boys sure do buy the good stuff. He'll be fine. Everyone thinks he's a cream puff because of the giant stick up his ass, but he did a stint in the SAS. Three dead and he wounded the other, but the fourth guy got off a lucky shot when he went down. Hit Sterling in the side. Through and through. Laid up a while, but he'll be fine."

Grayson whistles. "The SAS. Hell, now I'm impressed with the bloody bastard," he says in a near perfect mimicry of Sterling's British accent.

Zane chuckles.

I bring Zane up to speed with what happened here. "The cops didn't find any signs of forced entry," I state quietly, letting the information sit like a bomb in the room. "Our entire security team is compromised. She knew it. I'm sure that's why she left the house. I'm going to take her to the range in the morning and make sure she knows how to shoot, but we're never going to leave her without a gun and a phone again. If she hadn't left... I would've had another death on my hands, or worse."

"I'll send for Raider and get him to recruit a new team for you," Zane replies. "Do you want to hear what I found in North Carolina, or wait?"

I heave a big sigh but motion for him to continue.

"Henley Davis died five years ago. Her prints match a coroner's report for a young woman found dead in a cemetery from overdose. I looked up the old warrant, which is inactive due to her death, and found the detective who issued it. He's still active duty, so I went to see him." He rubs a hand across his shaved head.

"Detective Tyrone Jackson gave me the facts. Henley was renting a room from an older couple. The house burned down with the couple in it, and when they discovered the fire started in her room, they issued the warrant. When I started to question the evidence, he suggested we go to lunch and talk about it." Zane takes a drink.

I lean forward, my gut churning with anger, knowing I'm not going to like what I hear.

"Over lunch, he told me everything. Henley and her mom came to him with evidence of stalking. When he investigated, he was disturbed by what he found. The stalking started in college but didn't end there. She transferred out her junior year, but he continued to follow her to every subsequent university. Defeated, she returned home to her mother, and he foreclosed on their house, demolished her mother's career, and basically destroyed their lives.

"The detective tried to help, but the stalker trapped him in a web of police corruption so deep, he was facing prison. With two daughters at home and no other income, he was forced to back off. The mother disappeared two weeks later. Henley said she ran off, but he isn't sure if she truly believed it or if she didn't want to face the truth." He swallows the rest of his bourbon, but when I get up to refill his glass, he shakes his head.

Grayson, Mateo, and I share a look. No wonder Marcos got involved.

"After the fire, he got a call from the stalker, ordering him to issue the warrant, so he did. Over the years, he buried it as deep as he could, but couldn't delete it until Henley died. He stared at me for a while, then said, 'If you want to help, let the dead stay dead.' On a hunch, I pulled out Marcos' picture and showed it to him. Asked if he knew him." He stands.

"The detective said he met a man like him five years ago. He was a good man who would go to the ends of the earth to help his friends." Zane ends with one final statement. "He picked up the tab and told me, 'She sent money for my daughters to go to college and paid off my house, and the only good I ever did was to help that man bury her.'"

"Merda. Marcos staged her death," Mateo murmurs quietly. "And we just dug her up." He drops his head in hands.

"Not necessarily." Zane smirks. "We couldn't erase her fingerprint match from the FBI database, so I had Sterling file a fake police report stating we discovered the fingerprints in an abandoned car in a junkyard, where a recent homicide took place, along with dozens of others. We were just tracking them all down, blah, blah, blah." Zane stands.

"Thanks, Zane. We appreciate it."

Satisfied, he heads to the door. "I'll be in touch after I get a few hours' sleep," he states as his parting shot.

I pinch the bridge of my nose. "I'm taking her to the range tomorrow. While we're out, I want you to move everything to our house. It's more secure."

Neither Grayson nor Mateo protest.

———

"HOW DID you know what to say to help me calm down?" she asks quietly while staring out the window.

She's barely said a word all morning, and I worried last night had been too much. "My father was a hard man, selfish, prone to drinking and finding new ways to torment his wife and child. He really liked surprising us, said it kept us on our toes. I hated it. For years, small things, such as someone suddenly appearing around the corner, could trigger a flashback. Marcos learned to help me. I did the same for you," I reluctantly reply, hating to reveal anything about the past, but I don't want her to feel she's alone.

She flashes me a grateful look, and I shrug. The traffic lightens considerably, so I let the car off its leash, needing the extra exhilaration this morning. I check to make sure she's not afraid and see a wide smile on her face.

"I need to get one of these," she says, rubbing the leather on the seat beside her leg. "Is that why you all left Brazil? To get away from your father?"

"My father killed my mother, my aunt, and me when I was ten," I inform her. When she swivels toward me, I tell her how Marcos saved me by letting my father think he'd succeeded in his plan to kill all of us. How we went to Mexico to get Marcos' other sister, Mariana, and her son, Mateo, and made our way to Miami. "He created a new family for us. New backstories, name, everything."

Her mouth twists. "He was truly a remarkable man," she murmurs sadly.

"Zane found an old warrant out on you for first-degree arson, so I sent him to check it out," I tell her. "He met a Detective Tyrone Jackson, who gave him the true history of what happened." I catch her smile out of the corner of my eye. "He also discovered Henley Davis died five years ago. Marcos did the same thing for you that he did for me. He faked your death." I tell her what the detective told Zane.

She's shocked at the information. "Marcos would never tell me what he did, only that I had to become a new person to hide myself," she discloses, her eyes locked on the past. "Henley Davis is dead. I'm dead. Dead. I don't know why it bothers me. It's not as if I ever thought I could be Henley Davis again, but it's the way I still think of myself. If I'm not Henley, who am I?"

"I was ten when Marcos faked my death, but I understand what it means to have your identity and everything you know stripped from you," I assure her, recalling the pure homesickness I experienced for my culture and people, and the restrictions we lived under for most of our lives, unable to reveal our past. Thankfully, I'm unrecognizable as an adult and can live a life completely in the open. Marcos couldn't, and neither can Henley.

"You can still be Henley if you want. Mateo, Grayson, and I need one name to call you instead of the half dozen identities you seem to possess." She laughs. "So… can we call you Henley?"

The full-blown smile she returns causes me to shift uncomfortably in my seat. "Yes, please."

Her mood is lighter, as if the lies and disguises had been dragging her down. I wish Marcos had told her, but maybe it's for the best he didn't, because it did save her. I gear down to take the exit. Five miles down the road, we're turning into the gun range.

There's a lane reserved for us, and I point her to it. She gets everything ready, puts on her safety goggles and plugs, and picks up her gun. Her stance and grip suggest professional lessons, not self-taught, and her motions are smooth and controlled. She shoots a clip, and I bring the paper forward. All the shots are accounted for on the target.

She takes out her ear plug and raises an eyebrow.

"I appreciate you showing me, and a deal's a deal," I tell her. "We have the lane for another twenty minutes, if you want to keep shooting?"

Determination raises her chin. After last night, she needs to feel control is in her grasp, and this will help.

I shoot her an arrogant look, knowing she doesn't want my pity, and step out of the way.

She empties another clip.

When I bring the target forward, the shots are less scattered than her previous round.

"You might want to relax your shoulders more, drop them down a bit," I advise her as I demonstrate what I mean.

She gets into her stance and looks at me questioningly.

Moving in behind her, I rest my hands on her shoulder. "Relax, that's it. Drop them a little bit more. Perfect." The delectable smell of her drifts up, making me draw in a deep breath. I'm tempted to move forward and feel her body against mine, but I force myself to move to the side.

She glances around to make sure I'm not close, then fires her last clip.

The target shows a couple of shots skewed to the left, but it's to be expected when adjusting your stance. The rest are grouped tightly together.

I smile approvingly and watch the pink spread across her cheeks when she blushes.

After tidying the lane, she picks up her brass and washes her hands, and we head out.

Our house is close to the range, and twenty minutes later, we're rolling through the gated entrance. Hugo waves at us from inside the security hut. It's an exclusive neighborhood, and as we wind through the streets, she swivels her head in astonishment. Most of the houses or mansions around us are hidden, but she gets an occasional peek of one through the trees.

"Where are we?" she asks nervously.

I pull into our driveway and up to the house. "Our home. This is where Marcos, Mateo, Grayson, and I live, or lived." A pang of sadness hits me when I realize I can't say that anymore. "Marcos chose this lot because it overlooks the ocean, and he designed the house. What do you think?" I wait for the usual gushing comments most women give when they see the massive structure.

"It's stunning, but a bit stark," she replies, her eyes flicking from one end of the façade to the other. "A lot better than most of Marcos' designs."

And that's it. Polite but dismissive. My mouth quirks. Her not liking the house eases something inside me.

Suddenly, she busts out laughing.

"What's so funny?"

"The night Mateo got shot, I didn't intend to be his rideshare. My original plan was to follow him home, so I could break in and plant bugs in his house," she admits, waving a hand toward our house before breaking out into more laughter. "I was so naïve. I can't imagine what I would have tried to do to get in here." She gives a self-deprecating laugh and follows me into my home.

CHAPTER 29

HENLEY

The outside of the massive modern house is all white stone with black metal framed windows and doors, which makes it seem like a giant fortress. I shrug. Maybe it's prettier at night when the light shines out of all the windows. I'm relieved to find the inside of the house is another story. Spacious, clean lines, but with large furniture in luxurious fabrics, mainly in shades of neutrals like black, tan, greys, and whites, but with the occasional pop of green. It's soothing and extremely comfortable-looking. The inside is a home, not a showcase.

"Agent Antonio called about an hour ago. Said he wants to speak to you," Mateo informs Thiago when we walk into the living room.

I tense.

Thiago picks up his phone and groans. "I turned it off at the range and forgot to turn it back on. I'll call him. Mateo, can you show our guest to her room?" Without waiting for a reply, he's gone.

"Why don't I give you the grand tour?" Mateo offers with a

smile. He holds out his hand, and I reach for it with mine. "Living room, dining room, and kitchen are all together."

We walk in a huge circle from the large living room, across to the dining room, through a butler's pantry, and into the modern kitchen lined with black cabinets. We pass by the piece de resistance, a massive marble topped island with six barstools, and we're suddenly in the living room again. Mateo walks over to the floor to ceiling accordion doors and slides them open so we can step outside.

We stroll through the large, manicured backyard filled with large palm trees and bright tropical flowers, which fill the air with a lush fragrance. In the rear is a round overlook. It's basically a large circular patio with outdoor furniture, a fridge, pedestal, and firepit, but its unimpeded view of the ocean is the real showstopper. Entranced, my hand slips from Mateo's, and I walk to the edge of the concrete and stare out at the waves crashing onto the shore.

A hand grips my ankle, and I jump.

"Take your shoes off and we'll go for a walk," Mateo suggests with a grin. I lift one foot, then the other, to allow him to slip off my tennis shoes and socks. He stands and shucks his own off, then pulls me down the steps and onto the sand.

It's warm, almost hot, in the afternoon sun. My foot stretches with every step I take on the constantly shifting sand, but it feels so good. I can't take my gaze off the view in front of me. The ocean is calling my name as loudly as it did on the way down to Miami when I spontaneously stopped for lunch.

What a difference between then and now. Terrified to be in public, I couldn't stop worrying my stalker would find me and track me down. And yet in the last two weeks, I've been everywhere. So focused on getting the files and trying to figure out whether SEI was involved with Marcos' death or if Diego was the only traitor in their house, I hadn't given one thought to my stalker. My world is big again, making me feel lighter and freer.

When we reach the water, I walk straight into it. The hem of my jeans gets soaked, but I don't care. The cool water rolls over my feet, recedes, and returns. I scrunch the wet sand beneath my toes as if I can trap the water beneath them. Mateo laughs and pulls me with him to walk along the shore. His hair whips around his head in a riot of carefree waves, making him look younger than his thirty-two years.

While we walk, I watch the waves race each other onto the shore, where they deposit fish, crabs, and an assortment of shell pieces before returning to the ocean to get more treasures. The crabs are tiny, sort of see-through, and they scurry across the sand to reach the water or bury themselves in a hole. A bigger wave hits the shore, covering me to mid-shin, and I see a shell tumbling in its depths. I swoop down to grab it before the water claims it.

It's the first almost whole shell I've seen. I hold it up to the sun and examine the brown and white ridges on the back, before turning it around to see the smooth pink and white interior.

"What did you find?" Amused, Mateo grips my hand in his so he can see what's I'm holding. "Those are pretty common. I'm sure we can find you a better shell, and one that's not broken."

I wrap my fingers tightly around my new treasure and glare at Mateo. "I don't mind common. Rarer or prettier doesn't mean they're better. I like this one. Besides, it fits me. A broken shell for a broken soul."

He frowns and cups my jaw. "You're not broken," he says fiercely.

"I am, though. Marcos made me see a shrink every week for four years to talk through all the bad stuff, so I could learn how to deal with it and see it wasn't my fault. It sucked. Sometimes I hated her, most of the time I hated myself, but my therapist helped me get to a place where I could live with myself and the decisions I've made." I reveal another piece of myself to him. "But I'll never be whole like I was before it all started. A piece of my soul chipped off along the way, and it's just… gone."

He pulls me into his arms, his hand holding my head against his chest, and sighs. Yearning for a full hug, I slide my arms around his lean body and spread my hands against his back. Rubbing up and down, I close my eyes and commit every bit of this moment to memory. The slight breeze against my skin, the warmth of the sun and his body, the fit between the two of us, the tangy smell of the ocean mixing with Mateo's scent, and the roar of the waves. Memory is stronger when you use all your senses, so I take the time to cement each one in my mind.

It's important to recognize perfect moments when they happen. Whether they last or not, memories are the only things you think about when you are left with nothing. I should know.

He gently slides away from me, then turns me to face the ocean with him against my back. Wrapping his arms around me, he leans down and murmurs, "You're right. We're all broken in some way or another. Revel in the imperfect—"

"Because it gives us purpose." I say the last part with him. It was one of Marcos' favorite sayings. Then again, he had a lot of them. "Secretly, I think he was a philosopher at heart, not a programmer."

Surprise flashes across Mateo's face. "I never thought about it, but you're right. For someone who should be so practical, he often led with his heart." His brow furrows, as if he just pulled back a curtain he didn't know was closed.

I lean my head against his chest and stare at the ocean. "I can't imagine having this in my backyard. I'd never leave," I say dreamily.

I glance up to find him observing me. His head descends slowly, giving me plenty of time to move away, but I couldn't, even if I wanted to.

Firm lips capture mine, and I'm lost. Unlike the tentativeness we both felt the other day, this kiss is filled with intent and passion. He shifts me in his arms and pulls me in tight, and I wrap my arms around his neck, trying to get closer, until I'm practically inside his skin. He dives into me, tasting and possessing, and my mouth surrenders to his need. As the kiss ebbs and flows, his hand moves from my waist to the small of my back to fuse the two of us together.

The ocean roars in the background, rising and breaking. It's a sensual beat fanning the fire in us, until it feels like we're going to burn up with the sun. His body hardens, and I automatically arch into him, wanting to feel his desire against mine. Rubbing upward, I moan, and he harshly exhales.

Pulling his lips from mine, he stares down at me, a question in his dark brown eyes. "I need to touch you," he pleads hoarsely.

I nod, and the banked heat in his eyes transforms into a roaring blaze. His next kiss is wild and demanding, deliberately smashing through the boundaries of my control. Within seconds, I'm drowning in our combined passion, but at the same time, my hands and lips are greedy for more.

His hand slips between us and pulls open the button on my jeans. Sliding down the zipper, his knuckle caresses the bare skin underneath making me gasp.

Widening my stance, I raise one leg to the outside of his hip. All I can think about is having his fingers inside me. I break the kiss for a second, needing to catch my breath. My eyes drop to watch his warm hand slip beneath my underwear and down until he's palming me. I grip his shoulders and arch into his touch further. Blunt fingers slide through my folds and into the heart of me. I moan, loudly.

"You're so wet, so ready. It's killing me," he murmurs, his eyes flicking from my moving hips to my face. "Você está linda." His thumb caresses my nub, and the sharp pleasure makes me cry out.

With a groan, his mouth plunders mine, covering it completely, owning every sound escaping from my lips.

With a groan, he thrusts toward me.

My hand finds the button on his pants, but he places his hand on mine. "No, don't unbutton. I don't have anything with me."

"I could..." My voice trails off when he shakes his head.

"Next time," he promises me. His cheeks are flushed against the warm brown of his skin, and I can see the tightness around his eyes, indicating the tight rein on his passion.

Expecting his fingers to move faster, I'm surprised to feel them slow. Trembling with need, I watch him close his eyes and breathe heavily, like he's completely savoring the feel of his fingers sliding inside and out. His thumb slowly rubs the bundle of nerves at the top until I'm hanging on the edge.

Releasing his shoulders, I spear my hands through his hair and bring his head down for a scorching kiss of my own. When he hits a particularly sensitive spot, I moan and break away from his lips.

He opens his eyes. "God, you feel so good," he admits with a smile. He twists his wrist until the top of his hand is rubbing against my nub, while his fingers thrust in and out rapidly. The friction of his palm and increased speed is exactly what I need to drive me straight over the edge. Sensation explodes from my core outward, and with a cry, I come until I'm practically seeing stars.

Breathing heavily, I drop my leg and stand quivering for a minute or two. I'm not sure any of the boys I ever dated or one-night stands ever made me come as hard as he just did. Maybe this is the difference between boys and men. Taking a step away from him, I wobble for a second, and he grabs my elbow to help steady me. I laugh.

"It's been a while. Give me a second," I say breathlessly. The cry of a seagull overhead startles me, and I remember we're standing on a beach, in full daylight. Frantically turning my head side to side, I'm relieved when I don't see anyone.

He chuckles. "It's a private beach," he assures me. "Although, I like knowing I made you forget where you were."

I jokingly roll my eyes. "You certainly did. Mmm, thank you. That was one hell of a kiss," I reply, stretching up to place a sweet kiss on his lips.

Buttoning my jeans, I smooth down my shirt but don't attempt to tame my hair. Isn't the tousled look supposed to be beach-y? He's staring at me with a puzzled expression on his face.

"What?" I glance down to make sure I buttoned my jeans correctly.

"Nothing," he says with a wry smile. "Let's go get dinner."

"I'm starving," I warn him.

"When are you not?"

I punch him lightly in the arm and plow forward, with him trailing behind me. When I turn to find him, he's in deep thought.

Shrugging, I turn my face to the sun and savor the last of this perfect moment. When I'm all alone again, this moment will feed my soul for a long time.

CHAPTER 30

<u>GRAYSON</u>

I answer the doorbell and find Hugo from the front gate, piling boxes and mailers on our steps. Picking one of them up, I see Mateo's name on all of them, so I start bringing them inside. There's roughly fifteen boxes and mailers.

Mateo rounds the corner and stops when he sees the packages. He returns to the stairs and calls out, "Your packages are here."

Light footsteps rush down the steps, and Henley appears wearing a pair of plaid pajama pants Mariana got Mateo for Christmas one year, that I know he's never worn, and a grey T-shirt with html code on the front, a favorite of his. She dives into the packages and starts stacking them together.

"Is there somewhere I can open these?" she asks, her arms loaded with boxes.

"If you go past the stairs and to the right, there's an office," I tell her before bending down to pick up a pile and follow her.

Mateo does the same, and I wait for him. "Interesting attire

Henley is wearing this morning." I scowl slightly. I miss calling her Rose.

Mateo's cheeks flush, but he shakes his head. Something happened, but he's not gone totally overboard yet. Good to know.

"What is all of this?" I ask.

He gives me a side-glance that says nothing and everything.

"Are you kidding me?" I state loudly, striding into the office and setting my load on a nearby table. "Did you order clothes?"

She pulls out a pair of tennis shoes from the box in her hands, then tosses it aside. "Yes, clothes, shoes, underwear, socks," she replies before grabbing the next package.

I stare at her in disbelief. "Did you not see the clothes in your closet?"

"I did," she answers quietly. "I appreciate the effort you went through to get me the clothes. I did keep a few of them, and I'll send you the money to pay for those items. As for the rest, the tags are on the clothes, so I'm sure you can return them."

"I bought them for you," I inform her, irritated by her response. "You don't enjoy nice clothes?" Sliding my fingers into my hair, I resist the urge to pull at the ends in frustration.

"Of course I enjoy nice clothes, but the clothes you bought aren't practical," she returns with a shrug, then opens the next box. She pulls out three pairs of leggings, then breaks down the box and tosses it aside.

Dumbfounded, I watch her open every bag and box and pull out the most casual, boring clothes I've ever seen. Wait, I eye a blue shirt that looks oddly familiar. Snatching it up, I unfold it and realize it is the exact same shirt she had on last Saturday when she was lying on the couch with the ice pack on her head.

"You would rather wear this shapeless, boxy, long-sleeve T-shirt, than the beautiful blue blouse I bought to match your eyes? Why?" I ask with complete confusion.

Her face fills with anger. "Where am I supposed to wear the beautiful blue blouse that matches my eyes? Huh?" she asks belligerently.

"I don't know. To dinner or a movie? A play? A date?" I snarl when I say the last one but shake it off. "Does it matter?"

She gives a hollow laugh. "You truly don't understand, do you?" A sheen of tears appears in her eyes, and I step forward to comfort her, but she holds her hand out to stop me. "My world is a two-thousand-square-foot loft where I eat, sleep, and work. I don't go anywhere, and nobody comes over. If you have friends or colleagues or a life, they can be used against you. I don't want anyone else to suffer because of me."

She wags a finger at me. "No, you don't get to pity me. It took a lot of sessions to get to the point where I'm happy, and you're not going to ruin it." She glances at Mateo. "Although, if I'd known I was dead, I might have said yes to a date more often. Fine, I'll take the blue blouse and go out on a date. Thank you for the sugges-tion." With that final statement, she crams all the clothes into her arms and stalks off. "I'll pick up the shoes and mess later."

"I don't understand what's so bad about wanting to give her nice clothes. If she only wears them for herself, I'd be happy," I retort. "They didn't cost much." A chime sounds, and I raise my phone to glance at the notification on the screen. "$432.17 has been deposited in your account." I guess this is to pay for the few clothes she kept, including the blue blouse. Shoving my screen into Mateo's face, I storm out of the office when he starts laughing.

Thiago's standing by the front door when I cross the hall. "Grayson," he calls out, and I stop. "I'm going to meet Agent Anto-nio. He says he has something to show me but doesn't want to talk about it over the phone. After that, I'm going into the office. Is everything okay? Where's Henley?"

"It's fine. Go. If you need us, call. I'm going to stay here today," I say abruptly, suddenly changing my mind about going into the office. Pivoting on my heel, I race up the stairs to my room to get changed.

Twenty minutes later, I'm standing by Henley's chair in the dining room. "I'd like to take you out today," I inform her.

Her expressive blue eyes travel over the polo shirt and shorts

I'm wearing down to the brown deck shoes on my feet. When her gaze flicks back to my face, she looks intrigued.

"When you get done, go upstairs and put on comfortable summer clothes. You know, shorts, T-shirt, and tennis shoes. Meet me at the front door in fifteen minutes."

Without waiting for her reply, I head to the garage to gather a few supplies and load up the golf cart.

Fifteen minutes on the dot, I'm waiting by the door. A couple more minutes go by, and I can't help wondering if I bet on the wrong odds. It happens, not often, but it does.

She rounds the corner wearing a T-shirt and pair of silky shorts which I bought for her, and I can't help the satisfaction I feel in seeing her in something so flattering to her figure. She paired it with her own tennis shoes, but I'm good with the compromise.

I whistle, and she blushes. Who knew she was covering up those legs? Long and lean but with muscles popping out, I could stare at them all day. Good thing I'm planning to do exactly that.

"Do you run?"

Her hands tug on the hem of the shorts. "Yes, I usually run several times a week, although I haven't done it since I've been here. How did you know?"

I pull her hands away from the hem. "Stop, you'll wrinkle them. You've got great legs, trust me. Women would kill for legs like yours."

I open the door and motion for her to grab a seat on the golf cart. Following, I jump on, release the brake, and we're off.

Two blocks over from our house is a small private marina reserved for the residents of this neighborhood. Boats of varying styles and sizes bob softly in the water, waiting for their chance to hit the water.

Pulling up to the front, I motion for the attendants, and in seconds, everything on the cart is unloaded and stashed on the boat. I toss the keys to one, and he parks the golf cart. Striding around to her side, I start walking down the dock.

"Have you ever been on a boat?"

Her brow furrows while she thinks about it. "No," she murmurs.

She follows at a slower pace. Her eyes are wide as she studies each boat, occasionally stopping to read the names on a few of them. She laughs and points to the one beside mine. *Laundered Money*.

"That's not funny." I mockingly growl when I reply.

"Ironic, though," she says breathlessly.

She steps up to mine and reads the name *LuckyBet*. She smirks. "I wanted to steal the NFT from your office. It's amazing. It appears to be water, but I wasn't sure. It constantly shifts and changes into something entirely different each time you look at it. I'd love to see the others you've created."

Uncomfortable, I step onto the boat and hold out my hand. When she places hers in mine, I grasp it firmly and help her aboard.

She tilts her head, and I shrug.

"Mateo and Thiago know I'm LuckyBet. Marcos did too. He's the one who encouraged me to create the first one," I explain. "I love numbers, but sometimes, I need to escape them. The NFTs give me a different outlet." I clear my throat.

Pulling her to the top deck, I show her where to get a drink and sit. "Let me make sure everything's stored away, and we'll get moving," I say, leaving her to explore or make herself comfortable.

The attendants stored everything properly, so I untie us and head up. She's sitting, her face to the sun, with a water in the cupholder nearby. She shields her eyes to smile at me, and I give her a brief one in return.

Maybe this wasn't such a good idea. I wanted to show her something more, something different than a two thousand square foot loft. The breeze hits me, calling me out into the ocean, and I smile. We'll cruise around for an hour, then return.

Once we're out on open water, she moves from the front to the middle, practically hanging off the side to see everything around us. Delighted with her response, I cruise along the shore, pointing out spectacular houses and scenery you can only view from the water.

Eventually, she makes her way to the front and downs her water. I grimace when I see the pink on her arms and legs.

I slow the boat to a crawl and motion her over to take the wheel. She blanches, but I patiently wait for her to decide she can do it. When she moves forward, I back up and slide her into position directly in front of me. I lace my fingers through her hands and place them on the wheel. Moving up against her, she stiffens, but I ignore her reaction. Sliding my hands until they're only lightly touching hers, I guide her hands right and left until she gets a feel for how much it takes to move the boat accordingly.

"Don't touch anything else and don't steer us into any rocks," I tease her.

Once I'm out of sight and in the cabin, I reach down and adjust myself. Taking a few minutes to let my body subside, I drink a glass of water, then grab the sunscreen and a towel. When I return, I can't resist taking a picture of her standing at the wheel, with her bright pink hair flowing in the breeze and a massive smile on her face.

"Give me your arm," I order her.

Suspicious, she looks from me to the sunscreen, then shakes her head. "I'll put my own sunscreen on, thank you very much," she says pertly. With a sad glance at the steering wheel, she takes the tube and towel from me.

I leer at her legs and flash her my best smile, hoping she'll change her mind.

She throws me a disbelieving look. "Please, I'm not even your type," she sputters, laughing at my antics.

"Women are my type," I reply with a wink.

"Hmm, beautiful, sophisticated women who meet your criteria are your type. Women who know how to use their charm and sensual beauty to get exactly what they want out of life. Women similar to yourself, who play hard and work hard, but don't want the entanglement of anything long term," she asserts.

Shocked to hear such a clear assessment of myself from her, I say nothing.

"I don't have a lot of experience, but I'm not innocent," she says with a chuckle. "There's nothing wrong with knowing what you want and going after it. You don't seem happy with the status quo, though."

I shift my eyes from the water to her face and raise my eyebrows. "Having a bevy of beauties around is every man's dream." If I only believed it myself.

She tilts her head and considers my statement. "I'd agree if the pictures didn't tell another story. Your smile doesn't match your eyes. You should work on that if you want to sell the playboy act. I think the reason you have a 'bevy of beauties' instead of one is so they'll be too distracted competing with each other to focus on you. One woman would see right through your smokescreen."

I laugh harshly. "I'm not a good guy or a nice guy. Don't wish that on me."

"Oh, I believe there are plenty of women, just not as many as the pictures would have one believe. And nice?" She laughs.

"None of you are nice," she retorts. "Mateo wants you to believe he's nice, but he doesn't have the patience for it. He's arrogant and dismissive to those who can't match his superior intellect. You're obsessed with making money and betting on the next big thing, and Thiago's focused on conquering the world. 'Nice' is the last word I'd attribute to any of you."

I rear back. "That's harsh," I state, offended by her statements. "We've been good to you."

"Yes, you have, but you want answers. If you didn't, I wouldn't be here right now," she says with a shrug. She bends down and rubs sunscreen into her leg, and my eyes involuntarily follow every pass of her hands. She rises, and I jerk my eyes to hers. "Is there a bathroom on this boat?"

I give her directions to the head downstairs and contemplate her words. If I'm fair, it's a good assessment, but it's a shock to the system.

When she comes back, she's holding a tray of food in her

hands. Setting it down on the table, she gives me an embarrassed shrug. "I was hungry," she blurts out. Turning away, she grabs another water and sits down to eat.

"I'm sorry. I don't want you to feel self-conscious when you eat. It's refreshing to be around you," I admit reluctantly. When she snorts, I shake my head. "I'm serious. You lie atrociously, dress like a vagabond, exhibit the appetite of an elephant, and have more secrets than Fort Knox, but I like you." Not exactly eloquent, but for some reason, I don't feel the need to be perfect around her.

She puts her fork down and stares at me. Suddenly, she busts out laughing and clapping. "Truth, all of it," she says, agreeing with my assessment. "Bravo, it's the first real words I've heard come out of that handsome mouth of yours."

"So, you think my mouth is handsome?" I ask huskily.

Her eyes widen, and she loses it. She's literally cracking up. "Seriously?" She sighs. "I bet that voice gets you quite a lot."

I grin. "Probably more than it should."

Suddenly serious, she fingers the shorts. "I want to apologize for this morning. You did something very nice for me, and instead of calmly explaining why I couldn't accept the clothes, I berated you for not having the foresight to know they wouldn't fit into my life. Given I haven't shared much with you, I realize it wasn't fair of me. I'm sorry."

"I wish you would take them. I don't care if you wear them to the grocery store or to the mailbox. You deserve to wear beautiful things. For your own pleasure," I implore her.

"I'll sort through them, and if there's anything I really like, I'll pay you for those too," she reluctantly agrees.

"No, they're a gift," I insist, hating the idea of her paying me for them.

She shrugs. "Then I'm not taking any of them," she states firmly.

"You're the most stubborn woman I've ever met. Take the damn clothes. If you don't, I'll throw them in the firepit," I warn her.

Bewildered, she studies my face. "Fine, I'll take the damn clothes," she says ungraciously before tacking on, "Thank you."

"You're welcome. Let's eat," I remark casually, knowing I barely won that argument. If I hadn't seen her fingering the fabric several times today, I wouldn't have known she liked them so much. I wasn't bluffing, though. I'd have thrown them in the fire.

CHAPTER 31

HENLEY

After cruising around all day, we return to the house to fix dinner for everyone. Grayson grills some steaks and baked potatoes, and I throw together a salad. Since nobody else is home yet, he and I sit down at the kitchen island to eat dinner together.

"Can I ask you a personal question?" I swivel to face Grayson, who's sitting next to me. He's chewing a bite of steak, so he lifts a shoulder in answer. "How did you become part of the Santos family?"

His eyes cut to mine as he contemplates whether to answer me or not. Given what Thiago told me, I know he and Mateo are cousins, but only the two of them came to America with Mariana and Marcos. So where did Grayson come from? Apparently, it's the biggest secret on the planet, because the answer doesn't exist anywhere.

"I saved Mateo from an overgrown bully with the mind of a slug in the second grade and earned the undying gratitude of the family. They were forced to adopt me when my parents kicked me out for violent behavior," he replies, a devilish smirk on his face.

His nonchalant answer tells me this is a sensitive subject for him. "You could have said you didn't want to talk about it," I remind him. "I have secrets too, remember?" I sniff and stand up to put my plate in the sink on the other side of the island.

He gives an exaggerated groan and waves his hands in the air. "Fine, I surrender. I did save Mateo from a bully in second grade. He was the new kid and way too smart for the public school he was forced to attend. The bully took offense to his intellectual snobbery and popped him one."

His voice is tight with some hidden emotion this time, but he's obviously not comfortable sharing. I understand this more than he probably realizes, so I don't push him for more.

I snicker. "So, he's always been like that, huh?" I say, switching subjects. I'm amused by the picture in my head of a dark-haired little boy with tousled hair, figuratively looking down on a poor eight-year-old because he wasn't brilliant. "Best friends from that moment, huh?"

"On my part. Mateo took some convincing," he says with a chuckle. "Once he realized I wasn't quite the dunce he thought, I was allowed to be in his presence."

"Hey, that's just mean," Mateo says with a low whistle as he enters the kitchen. "True, though. Then you had to go and ruin it by forcing us to adopt you. Instead of a best friend, I got a brother."

Grayson pours Mateo a glass of the delicious Malbec we're drinking and hands it to him. The two toast each other. I'm guessing there's a lot of history behind that statement.

"And you..." Mateo wags his finger at me, his mock outrage making his eyes sparkle behind his glasses. "I think you're really smart, and I'm devastated you would go behind my back and malign me in this dastardly way." He clutches his heart and staggers dramatically.

I snort. "Really smart? One day, you'll apologize to me for that statement," I tease him, knowing I'll eventually have to tell them I'm CJ Tech. "Until then, I guess I'll have to find friendship and solace someplace else. The two of you are obviously not who I thought you were. If you'll excuse me, I'm going to take a shower." I sniff and raise my chin in mock offense.

When I step out from behind the island, Mateo sprays red wine everywhere.

My eyes dart between the two of them, trying to figure out what just happened, but they're having one of those silent conversations. Men.

When I walk away, I hear them both groan.

———

AFTER BEING out on the boat all day, my skin feels tight and a little burned, but a shower and some moisturizer help tremendously. Descending the stairs, I hear Thiago's voice and head to the kitchen. He's sitting at the island, eating one of the steaks Grayson grilled earlier. All three of them are wearing serious expressions on their faces when I walk up, but the discussion ends abruptly.

"I can go to my room and do something if you prefer?" I offer, feeling uncomfortable with the tension in the room.

Thiago studies me for a second. "Agent Antonio never showed up for our meeting. I called his office and was immediately put through to his supervisor. They grilled me on the details of our last conversation. They didn't say anything specific, but I'm guessing he's missing. Sterling's checking on the situation."

I reach out behind me for the barstool and slide onto the seat. "I wasn't aware you two were going to meet today. Did he say why?" My mind is racing in a million different directions, but I can't help but think his disappearance is because of me. Did they kill him?

Thiago apparently finds this an interesting question, because he shifts his entire body until it's facing me. "He had something urgent to show me that would blow the case wide open. Why? Is there something you're afraid he's going to show me?" His stare is predatory, like he's contemplating whether he needs to take down a possible threat.

Needing to think through this, I don't answer him. I want to tell him. I'd do anything to dump it on someone else's shoulders right now and run far, far away. But if they got to an ATF agent, there isn't anything they won't do. You can't even see the other man on the video. It's got to be Diego.

"Nothing to say?" he questions me softly. Leaning back, he crosses his arms and stares at me unblinking for a few minutes. "I hear you helped Grayson figure out how they made the money disappear." When I give a slight nod, he continues, "Okay, here's another question for you. Care to elaborate on how you know so much about banking?"

Finally, a question I can answer. Grayson plants his hands on the island and leans forward to listen. "Since you know my real name, I don't have to hide my past anymore. When I was fifteen, I entered a competition to win a national scholarship to a prestigious school, and I won. My entry was an algorithm designed to detect patterns and anomalies in banking. It was the first one designed with machine learning in mind, and it helped seed the current anti-laundering methods they use today."

Mateo's eyes narrow, and he picks up his phone. Likely wants to double check my story.

"Try not to search too many times for Henley Davis," I caution him, hating the fact he's using a regular browser to investigate. Did Marcos not teach him anything? "I'm supposed to be dead, remember?"

He nods but doesn't say anything else.

"Why didn't it work against our thieves, then?" Grayson asks with a skeptical look on his face.

I laugh. "You did hear me say I created it when I was fifteen, right? Twelve years is a long time. Technology evolves rapidly. In college, I was already working on new variations to improve upon it. Since then, anyone could have taken my work and expounded on it. Mainly, though, my original algorithm focused on identifying individual patterns to find potential money laundering accounts, not in using the bank's own system and patterns to move the money. It's brilliant." I can't help but admire whoever took it to another level, even if it scares me to know they can manipulate money in such quantities and with incredible speed and accuracy.

"Yeah, brilliant," Grayson mimics sarcastically. His expression suddenly shifts, and he looks surprised. Then he gives me a satisfied smile, like he knows something I don't.

Mateo, on the other hand, appears angry and hurt when he looks up from his phone. He shoves it toward Thiago. "You could have told me."

"What's it say?" Grayson asks Thiago.

Thiago holds the phone up, his face inscrutable. "It's an article from a North Carolina newspaper. 'Local genius wins national scholarship to MIT for winning entry.' Impressive." He hands the phone back to Mateo, but Thiago seems more lost in thought than angry.

I meet Mateo's glare with one of my own. "So, you think you have the right to be angry?" Mateo jerks his head in answer. "Because you've shared your every secret with me, right?" He deflates a bit. "My life is more important than your need to know something so trivial."

He raises an eyebrow at the word "trivial."

"The stalking started when I was at MIT, and it got so bad, I had to abandon the dream I'd had since I was a child. I was devastated. It was worse when I realized leaving didn't work. Over the next year, he followed me to four more schools. Defeated, I went home, thinking I'd be safe. Instead, his behavior escalated. My mother lost everything, a good detective almost went to prison, and a sweet old couple lost their life because they gave me a room to rent. I wished I'd never gone to MIT," I say bitterly.

I study all three of the Santos men sitting around the island in this great big house with its private beach and ocean right outside the door.

"Marcos never judged me. He knew I'd done some incredibly illegal things, not just for survival, but to gain the kind of security only money can give you. And I didn't judge him," I remark, pointedly staring at Thiago. He knows Marcos did what he had to do.

"With all this at your disposal, I'd bet odds the Santos hands aren't quite as clean as you portray, and it doesn't matter to me."

They couldn't have built SEI if they weren't tough. I just hope they're prepared to do whatever it takes to win. Decision made, I take a deep breath. "I came to Miami for two reasons—to get the files Marcos instructed me to get and to dig up information to give to the FBI or the press to take down his killers. At first, you were my prime suspects." Mateo throws his hands up, and Grayson scoffs. Thiago doesn't move a muscle.

"Once I found out you were related, I knew you weren't involved because Marcos loved and trusted his family more than anything or anybody," I inform them. My eyes lock onto Thiago's, and I watch the comprehension dawn on his face.

"Are you saying he was dead *before* you came to Miami?!" he roars and surges to his feet. The barstool goes flying behind him. His hands reach out and grip my shoulders.

"Yes, he died on Monday, before the explosion," I reveal, my heart thumping wildly in my chest while I stare at the hard man in front of me. His hands flex on my shoulders, and I flinch. Noticing, he immediately removes them from my shoulders and starts pacing.

"How did he die?" Thiago throws the question over his shoulder.

When I don't answer right away, he stops and sweeps everything off the island. Plates, dishes, and food crash to the floor.

"Answer me," he roars.

My eyes dart to Mateo and Grayson, who are also furiously waiting for me to tell them. Tears roll down my cheeks. "He was... shot."

All three of them are devastated. Mateo leans over like he's going to throw up, and Grayson walks off to stare out the backyard toward the ocean. Thiago looks the worst, alternating between guilt and anguish. He grips the edge of the marble countertop, preparing himself for what I say next.

"How do you know?" he whispers.

The video is an albatross of guilt around my neck. "If Agent

Antonio is missing, he's likely dead, and I might be the reason why. I sent him a video. Well, I sent him and you a video, but you never got yours. Oh God, if you had gotten it, you'd probably be dead now, too."

A fist pounds on the island. "Tell me," Thiago commands.

"Marcos recorded it and streamed it to a secure place where we keep… files. I went to see what he uploaded and watched it happen," I answer hoarsely, barely able to say it out loud.

"Why didn't you call the police?" Mateo yells next to me.

"And tell them what? MarcoPolo is dead, and I don't know what city or country he lives in, but I thought someone should know?" I shout back.

It finally gets through to all three of them. I had to watch this happen and couldn't call for help or tell a soul.

"How did you figure out MarcoPolo's identity?" Mateo's logical brain needs the steps to reconcile getting from point A to B.

"At first, Marcos thought I was behind the money and the software deal going bad. Given what I can do with money and the fact I could connect JF Technologies to the software and to him, put me first on his list of suspects. He hacked my system." I smile ruefully when I tell them. "And after he cleared me, he knew I was the only one he could trust."

All three of them protest loudly, and I wait until they're done.

"Now that I have more facts, I realize it isn't that he didn't trust you, but the individuals around you. He knew information was getting leaked but didn't know by who or how many. During the last few days of his life, they were following him and monitoring his communications. He sent me a letter via courier with instructions on what to do if something were to happen to him. His priority was securing the software."

Thiago swears loudly in Portuguese.

The only word I recognize is food, which means fuck. Marcos used to say it a lot when code didn't perform like he expected.

"I just don't understand why he didn't come to me or any of us," he says wearily, his voice bleeding with a million different emotions, as if he can't decide what to feel. The same bewildered expression is on Grayson and Mateo's faces too.

"Maybe he tried and it was intercepted," I offer with a shrug. "I know he didn't have a lot of time. SEI brokered the last deal, and Marcos told me not to trust anyone, so you were all suspects in my book. My first priority was getting the files he left for me, the second was his murder." I stop when I see Grayson sneer, and it hurts. I hunch my shoulders. "Maybe I made the wrong decision, but it was the last request he made of me."

He stops sneering, but I can tell he still disagrees. I watch the other two nod in agreement with him.

Pushing their reactions aside, I bring their focus back to the current situation. I point at Thiago. "If you didn't get the video, someone intercepted its delivery, which not only means they're watching you, but they're physically close to you and in your office. I made lots of copies, but they're hunting them down and destroying them," I reveal. "To get the other copy, I need to leave."

"I don't need the video," Thiago interjects. "Tell me who's behind this and I'll take care of it." Grayson starts to protest, but Thiago kills it with one slice of his hand.

"I actually do need the video. If I don't get a copy, they're going to try to pin the building explosion on me. I was there that day, and even though I left around six-thirty p.m., I heard Agent Antonio say a few days ago that the courier was one of the primary suspects. I'd hoped I could send the video to him and he would drop the investigation, but..." I trail off.

"Meu Deus." Thiago swipes a hand down his face. "Fine, we'll go get it, and—" He stops when I shake my head.

"All three of you need to stay here and keep up appearances. If they got to Agent Antonio within a day, they'll get to one of you. You're safe as long as they don't think you have the video. Ask Zane if he can send someone with me... to Dallas," I tell him.

By the look of stubborn rage he's wearing, Thiago's adamantly opposed, but I know he won't risk Mateo or Grayson's life. It's the only way.

"While I'm gone, I'll think of a way to safely give you or show you the video without your watchdogs picking up on it."

Thiago has a wordless conversation with Grayson and Mateo, then grabs his phone. "Zane, I need protection for Henley for a few" —he glances at me questioningly, and I mouth days— "days. Driving?" I nod, and he confirms. "Leaving tomorrow."

CHAPTER 32

HENLEY

Zane and Cruz arrive at Thiago's house in the morning. Similar to when I left Dallas, I pack mostly comfortable clothes and I'm done in a few minutes. I head downstairs, drop the duffel bag by the steps, and walk into the kitchen. All three men are standing there with scowls on their faces.

"I need breakfast and cash. As much as you can give me," I inform them. "I can Venmo you money from one of my accounts." Spotting a bagel and cream cheese, I quickly toast it and smear some creamy goodness on top.

Grayson curses until the air is blue, but Thiago ignores him and gives me the order to follow him. Entering his office, he goes directly to a safe behind his desk. Still eating my bagel, I turn around to give him privacy, and he chuckles.

"It doesn't matter if you see the combination. I'm sure you could steal considerably more directly from my bank account without me knowing about it," he muses. Placing several stacks on the desk, he quickly counts them. "There's twenty thousand. Think it will be enough?"

Thank goodness it's in one-hundred-dollar bills or I'd have a hard time finding enough pockets to stash it in. "With the three thousand I have on me, it will have to be." I slide the money into different pockets, the travel money pouch I have on under my shirt, and into the purse I've slung across my body.

"I don't like it," Thiago states emphatically. "My gut is telling me something is wrong, and I can't tell you how often it's right. Please reconsider. Zane and his team can get the video and bring it to us."

"And if they're ambushed, it's gone forever. Whoever is behind this is well funded and sophisticated. Right now, one of our few advantages is me. They don't know who I am, only that I'm interesting because I have a slight connection to CJ Tech and to you three. They might send one or two after us, but not a full force. I'm sure Cruz can take care of that piddly number." I turn and look at the man leaning on the doorway. "Isn't that right?"

"I may get a big head if you keep flattering me," he drawls.

Thiago snarls at us both. "It's not funny." He comes around the desk and grips my arms. "Don't take any chances. There have been enough deaths around here. Promise me, Henley."

I stare at him. "I promise," I assure him with a smile.

"Grayson's right—you are a bad liar," he says gruffly. "Let's go."

Mateo, Zane, and Grayson are waiting in the foyer.

Mateo pulls me into a fierce hug. His eyes are full of remorse, but when he opens his mouth, I place two fingers on his lips.

"No promises, remember?" I remind him. He grabs my hand and places a kiss in the center of my palm.

I close my fingers tightly to hold it close. Quickly, I turn to Grayson.

He reaches out and straightens my jacket. "You're always a fucking mess, Henley. When you return, you're going to start wearing all the beautiful clothes in your closet. No more fucking wrinkles or rags that should have been thrown out long ago. Got it?"

I must be getting through that thick armor of his. "Hmm, you do swear a lot when you're worried. Nice to know you have a tell," I remark softly. I dart a glance at Cruz. "Ready?"

Zane puts a hand on my shoulder. "Do you have your gun?"

I pat his arm. "I've got it, and it's loaded. Don't worry, I'll take good care of Cruz."

He snorts. Cruz chuckles. We get in the boring grey car waiting at the curb. Nondescript and designed to blend in with millions of others.

———

I JINXED US. The black SUV behinds us roars up and rams us. Our car swerves wildly before Cruz gets it under control. Shortly after leaving the Santos house, they started following us. A few minutes later, a second SUV and a motorcycle joined them.

"I can shoot, but not from a moving car," I inform Cruz. "If we don't switch, they're going to kill us." A bullet pings off the roof, then another shatters the driver's side mirror.

He smashes the pedal to the floor. "As fast as we're going, we need a straight stretch of road to switch, and I think there's one in about a mile. I'll lift, and you slide into my seat." Without taking his hands from the wheel or feet from the pedal, he lifts his body. I climb over the console and slide into his seat under him.

My foot blindly follows his leg down until it reaches the pedal. He shifts his boot until I can take over the gas pedal. Lifting off, he maneuvers his right leg toward the passenger seat. With a tight grip on the steering wheel, I peek under his arm at the road.

"Got it, go."

He doesn't waste any time in diving into the passenger seat. I grab the seatbelt and yank it on.

"Brace yourself," I yell, just as the SUV rams into us again.

Cruz hangs on to the seat until it's over, then opens the window and slides half his body out. They weren't expecting us to switch sides, and he easily takes out the SUV nearest the passenger side with a couple of shots.

One down, two to go.

The SUV rams us again, but instead of backing off, he keeps us bumper to bumper. I change lanes, slow down, speed up, swerve, but nothing works. The guy on the motorcycle pulls along the driver's side, and I flinch, but instead of shooting at us, he tosses something on the hood of the car.

Cruz grabs my head and shoves it down just as bright light flashes, followed by a loud bang. I slam my foot on the brake, causing the SUV to slam into us at maximum speed. Our car spins, then flips a couple of times before coming to rest upside down on the side of the road. Dazed, I lie there, examining the ground through the windshield. A wildflower growing through the cracks of the asphalt catches my eye. Hardy little thing. I blink. Thank you, God, for my seatbelt and the airbags. I glance at the sky and smile.

"Cruz?" I shove the airbags out of my way and frantically scour the car for the blond-haired man, but it's empty.

Releasing my seat belt, I push through the window on my back. Strong hands suddenly grip my shoulders and yank me out. Getting my feet under me, I manage to stand and turn.

"Cruz," I gasp out, looking at his bloody face. It's streaming from several cuts, two that appear to be pretty deep. I trace the rest of his body, but I don't see anything alarming until I get to his leg. Based on the angle, it's broken. Even with him in bad shape, I can't help the broad grin that escapes just knowing he's alive.

He grunts and slumps forward. I throw my arms around him and try to brace us as we slide to the ground.

"What is it? Your leg?" I lightly grip his arms to hold him up.

"Shot, gun," he murmurs.

I didn't hear a shot. I slowly bend down, like I'm trying to listen to something he's saying. "Mine is somewhere in the car," I whisper.

"Back," he mutters, and his eyes drift close.

"Absolutely," I say loudly. "We're going to get you some help." I slide my right hand under Cruz's body and pull out his gun. It's heavier than mine, so I grip it tighter. I glance down and turn it to the side. Red dot. It's ready to fire.

The crunch of boots on the gravel tells me someone's getting closer. I look up and see it's the guy from the motorcycle. He's pointing his gun at me.

"Leave him and come with me," he orders.

I gently shift Cruz to the ground with my left hand. Standing, I'm careful to keep my right arm straight and the gun behind my leg. I take a couple steps toward the guy. When he sees me complying, he points the gun with a silencer toward Cruz. I simultaneously bring up Cruz's gun and fire. It's loud and kicks back hard. If I hadn't had a tight grip, I would've dropped it. The man falls to the ground. My ears are ringing from the shot, but I stumble over to make sure he's dead. Sightless eyes stare at me from inside his helmet.

Unable to help myself, I start crying. I've never killed someone, and even though it was to save someone else's life, the guilt is overwhelming. I need to find the SUV. Sniffing, I scrub at my eyes several times until I can see where the other vehicle went. There's nothing on this side of the road, but when I hear shouting, I look across to the northbound lanes and see pieces of the black SUV all over the road, along with a jackknifed semi. I wince.

A minivan pulls up, and a man and a woman get out and run toward me. The man asks if I'm okay in a heavy accent that sounds like Spanish.

"Hello. Can you take my friend and me to the hospital?" I ask, pointing over to Cruz on the ground.

He reluctantly says yes, but I can see he's confused on why I want him to take me to the hospital. I'm sure the gun in my hand isn't helping things. I shake my head and point to the motorcycle dude. "Bad men are chasing us, and I need to get him to the hospital."

He walks over to the man and sees the gun still in his hand.

"Yes, sí."

I rush over to Cruz. "I've found someone who's going to take us to the hospital. Can you stand?"

He grimaces, but between the man, woman, and me, we get him up and into their vehicle and lay him down. I sit with him and hold his hand. Tears silently flow down my cheeks.

When we pull up to the emergency room twenty minutes later, he's unconscious. I run inside and get help. "We were in a car accident, and I think he flew through the window. His leg is broken. And he's got a gunshot wound somewhere in his back, I think." They rush outside to get him on a gurney, then disappear into the cool dark interior of the hospital.

I turn to the man standing beside me and point to his phone, which he reluctantly gives me. Thiago answers on the first ring. "Santos," he barks. I hear Grayson in the background.

"Phones are compromised. Dump them. Tell Zane to get to Cruz immediately. Hospital closest to you. Tell Mateo to leave new cell numbers on our favorite server." I hear him shout my name as I hang up. Removing the SIM card, I hand it back to the man, and he glares at the card in my hand.

Pulling a couple thousand out of my purse for a new SIM card and his help, I hand it to him. "Thank you."

His eyes widen, and he opens his mouth but closes it when his wife pinches his arm.

As I exit the hospital, I notice someone's car running in the valet. Sliding in, I put it in drive and head toward my favorite Miami car dealer.

CHAPTER 33

<u>HENLEY</u>

Ten thousand dollars doesn't buy much these days, but with the right deal, it can get you a car with an expedited fake ID and a stolen license plate from the shadiest dealer in Miami. The Nissan Sentra only has one hundred and fifteen thousand miles on it, and it runs beautifully, so I'm lucky he sold me a good car.

I was even able to bribe his equally shady niece to run to Wal-Mart and grab a few items for me. Band-Aids, a splint for one of my fingers, butterfly strip for the deep cut on my forehead, a burner phone, and some new clothes that weren't torn or bloody.

With a grimace, I glimpse the bright purple sequin T-shirt out of the corner of my eye, which of course she paired with matching joggers with "Cheeky" on the butt, and shake my head. I swear she did this on purpose. Never trust a sixteen-year-old with an attitude who's smart enough to charge you a fortune, then make you wear the most atrocious outfit she can find. She probably took pictures. Truly devious. Grayson could learn a thing or two from her.

The wind flows through my hair, and I lean my throbbing head against the seat. I'm not sure if there's an inch of my body that doesn't hurt right now, but when you look at it, I came out a hell of a lot better than Cruz or the bad guys.

I wonder how long their phones have been compromised. For a while, is my guess. It's how they knew Roberto was the only one at the house that day. How they knew Agent Antonio had something damning. There are two departments that could touch their phones without raising suspicion—security and IT. I frown. There are also apps on the market that allow you to tap into someone else's cell phone remotely and get all kinds of information, including any sounds or conversations the phone's microphone picks up from its surroundings. It could be anyone.

On the other side of Tallahassee, I stop for everything. Ibuprofen, gas, snacks, and a map. Hoping to avoid the interstate construction I hit on the way to Miami, I find an alternative way around it to save time.

It's hard to believe it's only been three weeks since I drove down to Miami. So much has changed in so little time. Nervous or scared, it didn't matter. I did things I wouldn't have dreamed of doing before Marcos' death, and I feel more capable and confident in myself than I have in years. I don't know what's going to happen next, but unlike before, I don't *fear* it.

Twelve hours later, I pull into the garage down the street and hide the car under one of the extra tarps I keep stashed in my back-up car's trunk. Walking home, I keep an eye out for the usual riffraff, but it's quiet tonight. Light shines out of the second floor of my building, and I'm relieved to see my home but strangely anxious too. Entering a code, I unlock the outer door, then my front door, and shuffle into the loft. It's musty smelling, so I crack a window.

After downing a few more ibuprofen and a glass of water, I kick off my shoes and drop onto the couch. An ambush and twenty straight hours of driving, I'm out in an instant. Sometime Saturday afternoon, I wake for about an hour to eat and take some more pain meds.

It's Saturday. Scrambling up, I rush over to the desk and search both the dark and deep web for any mention of new AR software. Nothing. The deadline has passed. Does this mean the invisible man didn't break the key? I set up a couple of search monitors to alert me to any chatter on AR software and stagger back over to the couch. For three weeks, I've been waiting for the other shoe to drop, and I'm massively relieved, but I'm also kind of feeling lost without them to share it with.

Frowning at this thought, I ease down onto the couch and burrow into the blankets again. It's astounding how much everything has changed in the last few weeks. The whole time I was in Miami, it felt temporary, allowing me to throw caution to the wind and focus on what I needed to do.

How do I return to this life... by myself? I won't even have Marcos to work with every day. I will truly be alone again. My eyelids drift down, and I allow myself to bury my head in the sand and fall asleep.

Heaving, I jerk upright, my hands scrambling over my chest in a last-minute attempt to stop the bleeding. Slowly, things like the blanket and couch start to register in my head, and I flop down in relief. It's just a nightmare, I reassure myself. The scene on the side of the road in Miami flipped inside out until I was the one on the ground dying from a gunshot wound while the motorcycle man stood over me.

Bleary-eyed, I blink at the clock on my phone and see four-twenty a.m. Sunday morning. Energized by the long sleep, I use the restroom and grab some coffee. My stomach growls, but when I check the cabinets, I find only empty shelves or out-of-date food. Grabbing a back-up phone, I add the delivery app and order breakfast from one of my favorite places, Rita's. They don't open until five-thirty a.m., which means I won't get food for another two hours by the time they cook and deliver it. I sigh and fill my cup.

Returning to the computer, I pull up the Miami news, and a large, grainy picture of a brown-haired courier exiting the garage is splashed on the home page of the website. Yesterday's date. Shit. They've released the photo. Scanning the article, it states ATF has put out an APB for information or the whereabouts of this courier. Me. I squint, trying to see if I can make out any features, but the picture isn't that good.

The loose clothes I'm wearing camouflage a good portion of my body. A jacket, helmet, and wig practically obscure anything noticeable. My face is really pink in the picture, reminding me of how hot I was in my disguise.

There's nothing I can do about it now except stick to the plan. Logging into my storage accounts, I find two videos left, but I know they're corrupted, so I don't bother making a copy of them. I check my email and see a notice from the San Antonio post office with a preview of the mail that arrived in my box. It's the envelope I sent with a physical copy of the video on a drive.

I check on my copy of the software, and it's safe and secure. Sighing with relief, I try to think if there's anything else. Remembering my quick message to Thiago, I pull up SEI's network and enter my credentials. Unauthorized user. I enter them again. Nothing. I enter Mateo's credentials, and it starts re-routing me to another IP address. I close the window, cut the Wi-Fi access, and erase all recent activity.

Biting the tip of my nail, I try to figure out if there's any way to get into SEI's network without hacking, but I think all avenues are blocked. I have no way of getting their new phone numbers.

The bell rings, and I tap on the camera app on my phone. It's the delivery guy. "Please leave the food at the door. I've added a tip, thank you." I watch his every move until he leaves.

Rushing out the door, I grab the bag of food and scurry inside. I pull out a large to-go box filled with breakfast. It's literally called Everything Breakfast. It includes a pancake, a slice of French toast, two eggs scrambled, hash browns, sausage, bacon, and a small portion of cinnamon oatmeal. Reaching into the bag, I pull out syrup, butter, jelly, and two homemade biscuits.

I eat and make a to-do list. Tomorrow morning, I need to go by the courier's office and get the package Marcos sent. Then fill my back-up car in the garage with gas and get it packed with everything. I'd rather take that one instead of the Nissan I bought in Miami because the tag and license will hold up better to scrutiny. With an APB out, the last thing I need is a cop to pull me over for suspicious tags. And I need to get food, drinks, and snacks for the return drive to Miami on Tuesday.

<u>HENLEY</u>

Returning home, I drop the large envelope on the couch and eye the red wax seal with MarcoPolo stamped into it. While it might seem innocuous, the last time I opened a package from Marcos, it upended my entire world.

Leaving it for a minute, I grab a drink and down some ibuprofen to combat the pain and stiffness. Dark blue and purple bruises are starting to show in various places all over my body.

With an exaggerated groan, I stalk over and pick up the envelope. Opening it slowly, as if it's a rattlesnake waiting to bite me, I pull out several items. A formal-looking envelope made of heavy weight cream paper with my real name on it. Several pairs of AR glasses we've been working to improve. The headsets used today are bulky, so we're trying to find something lighter, with a better fit, that could be slipped on as easily as any other pair of glasses in an ambulance or an operating room. A couple of flash drives.

Opening the stiff envelope, I pull out a letter on equally formal stationery. The letter is dated five months ago.

My dearest friend Nyx, or I guess I should call you Henley,

If you're receiving this package, it means I, Marcos Santos, also known as MarcoPolo, have passed on to another place. If I'm lucky, I'll get to spend eternity with my angel and love, Juliana, but with all the things I've done, good and bad, I'm not sure where God will choose to put me. Maybe I'll have saved enough souls that the worst of my transgressions can be forgiven.

Every six months, I update this letter and package to include my most important projects because I can't bear to pass, knowing they'll never be used to help others. I know you'll help them get to market and into the right hands. The reason I know is because I see in your eyes the same burning need to use technology to make the world a better place. You're not driven to solve the intellectual problems of the world, but the problems of its people.

I've also left you shares in a company called Savage Enterprises, Inc. or SEI. Not a lot, but enough to give you working capital to bring these and other projects to life. I know I haven't told you much about my life, but I would never jeopardize the family who means everything to me. They're not going to be very happy with my decision, but I've safeguarded the shares. You can't sell them outside of the family, nor does it give you majority share. When you're ready, reach out to my friend and attorney, Gabriel. His information is listed below. He's prepared to put the shares into any name you wish to use.

Yes, my real name is Marcos Santos, and while you'll likely hear a lot of things about me, both good and bad, you'll realize you know me better than most others. Not my name or my family, but me. The dreamer who only wants to make the world better for the good people living in it. The bad ones—let God sort them out.

Although you know about the glasses, I haven't had a chance to tell you I've got them working. The code is on the flash drive. I've also been working on a vest to help with the early detection of breast cancer. This project is a labor of love in honor of my wife Juliana, who was diagnosed with breast cancer when she was eighteen. If you get this working, please donate all proceeds to breast cancer research in her name.

Please continue to send twenty-five percent of all projects to my charity. The support is critical to keep the rescue missions running. My friend Zane will get everyone to safety and set up with new lives, but he needs money to do it. Better that than the government, eh?

Hopefully, I'll be sitting down in another six months to rewrite this letter, but if not, I'll miss you, my friend. It's been an honor working with you. You came along at a time in my life when I needed more than rescue missions and family. I needed to dream again.

If you meet my little savages, tell them I said to behave because I'll be watching them.

And by the way (I always drop this at the end of the letter to make sure you're feeling warm and gooey and won't hate me for not telling you sooner), Henley Davis is dead. It was the only way to save you, and I don't regret it. You turned right around and saved a piece of me.

Make sure to pour me a shot when you go to Nacho Tequila!

Always your friend,

Marcos Santos

Mmm. Nacho Tequila. The letter gives me an idea. I put everything back into its original envelope and store it in the backpack I'm taking on the trip. Picking up the laptop next to it, I slide it into the bag. A shiny brass key catches the corner of my eye, and I snatch it up, placing it securely in the inside zippered pouch. I'll need it to open the post office box in San Antonio. Everything else is already in the car.

My eyes linger on the place I've called home for the last five years, wondering why my beautiful loft feels so empty and small now. Three weeks ago, only Marcos' death could get me to leave the place, but now, it's as if I can't wait to escape to Miami. Maybe it's time to sell and move on to a new place. By the ocean. Somewhere warm. I pull up a map of the United States on my phone. Anywhere but North Carolina. No need to repeat the past.

The lights in the loft flicker, and I put my phone down. That's new. I scream when the alarm goes off, then clamp a hand over my mouth. Bringing up the cameras, I see Diego and three other men opening a door at the far end of the building. How the hell did they track me here? Shoving the thought aside, I tap on an app to close all the fire doors in the building to create additional barriers between us.

I grab the backpack and slip my feet into my tennis shoes. Waterproof jacket, I remind myself. The lights flicker again and go out. The alarm also shuts off. They cut the power. Using the phone's flashlight, I rush over to the entry closet, pull out the jacket and slip it on. Then I pull up the hood. Spotting a pair of tennis shoes in the bottom, I wedge them into the front of the backpack.

My eyes dart to the cameras on my phone to watch as Diego and his men spread out. It's only the first door of five now, but it means they'll be here in about seven minutes. I slip my arms through the straps of the backpack and secure the one around my waist. Flying over to the desk, I shove everything off it, then climb on top.

I throw the painting on the wall to the floor and open the black metal hatch. A click of the switch inside, and an emergency path lights up. Six minutes. I step on to a little platform and close the hatch, then slam my hand on a large red button to my right. Special water sprinklers turn on with a whoosh and start spraying. There's no time to use the actual steps. Leaning back, I place my hands and feet on the cold metal handrails and carefully slide down them like a sailor navigating the narrow stairs of a ship. When I get to the bottom, I peek at the time. Four minutes. I yank my jeans up over my knees and start running.

Water drips on me from the top and sides of the tunnel and covers me up to mid-calf, making it hard to run as fast as I want. It must have rained recently. Breathing heavily, I reach the end of the tunnel and bring up my phone. Less than one minute. I hit the red app. There's a huge rumble, and a loud noise above me. Warm air hits the tunnel, shoving me back a step with its force.

Shucking off my wet tennis shoes and socks, I grab the pair from my backpack and squish my feet into them. Gripping the metal bar, I climb the ladder and push open the hatch. Keeping my eyes peeled for anyone in the garage, I slip through the opening and gently let it close. Running to the far corner, I pull the sheet off my back-up car, roll it up, and get in. Tossing it into the floorboard, I put my seatbelt on. Thank goodness the car's already packed.

Turning the key, the Maserati Quattroporte rumbles to life, and I carefully ease out of the parking space and make my way to the entrance. Turning right, I slowly roll up the block toward the flames shooting into the night sky. When I get about a half a street away, I watch the fire consume everything. The red button I hit caused specific sprinklers to drop from the ceiling and spray an accelerant guaranteed to keep the fire burning until the building is gone.

To prevent firefighters from entering the building, I added a special plaque to the wall to let them know. Anyone else would overlook it. It worked. They're standing across the building preparing to spray a special foam. A dark figure crosses the road shaking a fist at them, and when he turns to point at the building, I see Diego's furious face in the fire's light. *Damn it.* He must have turned back for something.

Sighing, I pull away from the curb and turn right at the corner to take me away from the fire. Hitting the interstate, I go the speed limit until I get out of Dallas, then I push it. Will I lose everything by the time this is over?

CHAPTER 35

HENLEY

While I wait for the post office to open, I check the Miami news. Expecting to see my courier pic, I'm relieved to see it's been replaced with a picture of a sultry ballroom decorated like a 1920s speakeasy. I scroll down the page to make sure my pic is gone and spot three familiar-looking men wearing black tuxes and masks beside three beautiful dates in flapper dresses and beaded masks. The picture is from last year's Annual Miami Masquerade Ball sponsored by Savage Enterprises.

I skim the article and learn it's an annual charity ball to benefit the Santos Foundation, which assists families who have been rescued from dire situations. *Sounds like Marcos' charity*, I muse. For years, I've given him twenty-five percent of my profits to put into his charity. Like he said, it's better than giving it to the government, especially when the company doesn't legally exist or report its revenue. I always deposited the money directly into his account, so I never knew the name of his charity was the Santos Foundation.

This year's extravaganza is being held at 1 Hotel South Beach in an indoor-outdoor setting to promote the theme of this year's ball—

technology and nature. The exclusive, high-end affair is invitation only.

I tap on the side of the phone while I try to figure out a way to get inside. Maybe I could try to do some of the tech setup or AV equipment or something.

I'm searching for the name of the vendors and run up on a juicy tidbit. As this year's selected premier choice of venue, 1 Hotel is auctioning off six tickets to its guests for the chance to win an invitation to the event. Clicking the link in the article, I book a room at the hotel for the rest of the week. When I check out, I blanch at the total but hit submit.

A woman hurries by with a package under her arm, and I see the post office is open. Taking my backpack with me, I enter the building and head to my box. Inserting the key, I pull the envelope out of the narrow slot and close it. Then I step up to the self-serve package center, drop it into a priority mail two-day envelope, and mail it to the post office I opened in Miami under Marco S. Polo.

Getting on the road immediately, I head toward Miami. I'm going to need a dress for this fancy ball. Using my phone's voice assistant, I call French Kiss and ask to speak to my favorite—and only—stylist, unless I were to count Grayson. I snicker at the thought, although I'm sure he'd jump at the chance to pick my clothes.

"Peyton speaking," a voice drawls into the phone.

"Hi, Peyton, this is Henley," I say tentatively, not sure if he'll even remember me.

"Henley, darling. How are you? Did you get the job?"

"Good, thank you. I'm working with them on a couple of projects," I reply, which is sort of true. "I realize this is extremely short notice, but I was hoping you could help me find a dress and a mask. There's this ball tomorrow night—" I hold the phone away when he starts screaming.

"Seriously? Darling, I'd love to help. French Kiss doesn't carry formal wear, but I know several amazing and talented designers, including myself. We'll find you a dress. What's the theme of the event?" he asks in an excited voice.

"Technology and nature. Indoor and outdoor. The dress must have deep pockets. I'll need to carry several devices that evening, and it would be best if there was a way to hide them." I bite my lip, hoping he doesn't protest my only condition.

"Ooh, I love a challenge. When can you get here?"

"I won't make it to town until tomorrow night, but I'm staying at the 1 Hotel for the rest of the week. Could we meet there? Maybe around seven p.m.? Ask for Henley Night," I suggest. I created a new identity on Sunday that combined my real name, Henley, with a variation of Nyx. Henley Night. I loved it.

He whistles. "Mmm, you sure know how to live. Of course we'll be there. Bye!" He hangs up before I can ask who all is coming.

———

THE NEXT DAY, I check into the hotel. "Excuse me, I read a notice in the news about an auction you're holding to win a ticket to the Miami Masquerade Ball. How do you enter a bid?" I ask while signing into the hotel's app on my phone. I opted to use it instead of the key.

The front desk lady gives my leggings and long sleeve T-shirt a side glance, and I grimace.

"Please excuse my attire. I've just driven across country behind a moving truck, and leggings were the only thing that was comfortable." I give her a wry smile.

"Oh, where are you moving from?" she asks politely. Reaching down on her right, she pulls out a locked box and a pulpy-looking card.

"Palm Springs," I reply, watching her eyebrows go up. "A friend moved out here and absolutely loves it. So here I am, and I can't tell you how thrilled I am to be near the ocean again."

"I love it here," she assures me. "Here's the card for the auction. It's made from seeds, can you believe it? The hotel is going to plant all the entries in the garden when the event is over." She points to a spot on the card. "You simply enter a bid on this line."

I bite my lip. "Is there a range for the auction? It would be incredible to go to the event and make some friends in my new town." I smile wistfully at the card, but not at her. I don't want to lay it on too thick. "Can I return this to you later?"

"I'm sorry. You need to fill it out now. The hotel is drawing the winners in an hour to give the guests time to purchase their outfits and masks," she states firmly. She leans in closer. "I can't give you a range, but I did see a wealthy gentleman write one hundred thousand dollars for his bid. The hotel manager was extremely pleased." She stands straight and gives me a conspiratorial smile.

Here goes nothing. I write two hundred and fifty thousand on the line and hand it to her. Her eyes widen, and she hurries over to the manager to show him the bid.

He strides over and pulls up my hotel reservation. Tilting his head, he gives me a puzzled look. "Miss Night, did you not wish to stay in one of our ocean view suites?"

"I booked last minute, and the hotel website only had two rooms available, so I grabbed the first one," I explain to him.

"We always keep suites open for our most valued guests," he says with a smile. Turning to the girl, he tells her to upgrade me to an ocean view suite. "Thank you for your bid. It was most generous."

It sure as hell was generous, and if I win, it's counting toward the twenty-five percent I pay annually to Marcos' charity. Hmm, I wonder if I should deposit the money somewhere else now? I'll have to ask Zane.

"Thank you! An ocean view suite sounds amazing after my long drive," I exclaim. "I do hope I win."

The girl winks at me, and I slide a couple thousand across the counter to her. Now, everybody's happy.

A little over an hour later, the manager knocks on the door and hands me an envelope.

"I won?! Wow, that's so exciting, thank you!" I say breathlessly. "And it goes to such a good charity. Win-win, right?"

He beams at me. "Absolutely. Congratulations. We would like our six winners to meet in the lobby at eight p.m. tomorrow evening for a photo. Please don't forget your mask."

"Sounds good, and I won't forget," I say, smiling as he walks away.

———

PEYTON AND A FRIEND arrive at seven p.m. with a rack full of dresses, bags of shoes, and tons of mask accessories like feathers, rhinestones, and sequins. I open the door, and they roll right in but stop when they see the view from the windows.

"Wow, I've been living in Miami for fifteen years, and I've never stayed in a hotel room like this one. Did you rob a bank?" He eyes me.

"They were having an auction to win a ticket to the event tomorrow evening, and I threw in a bid for charity. When I won, they upgraded me to this suite. Can you believe it?" Having had both Thiago and Grayson mention how bad a liar I was, I try to stick as close to the truth as possible.

Peyton puts his hand on his hip and cocks it to the side. "I thought you already had a ticket?" His eyes are sharp as he questions me.

When I looked in the envelope earlier, it had contained two tickets. "I have two now. One for me, and one for a guest," I say with a flourish, whipping the guest invitation out. "Would you like to go with me?"

This will be perfect. Anyone searching for a single woman will look right past me.

"Are you serious?" Peyton asks, his mouth agape. "This would put me on the map. I could go schmooze all those fabulous people and tell them I'm a designer. Hell yes." He pulls me into his arms and swings me around. "Now, we really have to find you the perfect dress."

His friend gasps, then grabs my hand. "I'm Sebastian, I'd like to be your friend too," he says while batting his eyelashes in an outrageous manner. He twirls me around and nods at Peyton. "You're right—she's the perfect clothes hanger. Not too much here." He points to my chest. "Or here." He points to my rear end. "Tall. Lean. Clothes will hang on her like a dream. Darling, you just keep getting better and better."

We all bust out laughing.

"Before we get started, I don't want a repeat of last time. Been there, done that. Tell me, what color will your eyes and hair be tomorrow night?" Peyton stares me down and waits for me to answer.

"Pink hair, blue eyes," I reply. I'm going to this ball as myself. With a mask, of course.

CHAPTER 36

<u>THIAGO</u>

I slam my hand down on the desk. "Where the hell could she be?" I glare at Zane and Sterling, waiting for them to answer me.

Bright green eyes give me a haughty stare in return. Sterling opens his mouth but shuts it when Zane puts a hand on his shoulder.

"We're looking, but unlike most of the population in this world, she's turned hiding into an art form," Zane replies heavily. "We have to trust she'll make it to where she's going and back in one piece."

I see the guilt hanging on him and I force myself to ease up. "Sorry, the one thing I wanted to avoid has happened. She's alone. No back-up. It's driving me crazy imagining all the possible scenarios. How's Cruz doing?"

"About as pissed off as you," Zane retorts with a groan. "If he could get out of bed and walk, he'd be on the hunt for her. She saved his life. For now, I've called in a few more members to help. Raider's vetting candidates for your security team so we can get it running at full capacity again in the next few weeks. We need the extra manpower to alleviate the stretch we're feeling right now."

I rub a tired hand down my face. "I wish we didn't have to attend this ball tonight," I say, giving Grayson a hopeful look, only to snarl when he shakes his head.

"The ball provides us with capital for the next year or two," Zane reminds me. It's weird to hear it come from him instead of Marcos, but he's running both the rescue and charity now. I share a wry smile with him.

"You're coming, right?" I confirm.

He grumbles but shakes his head. He's usually raring to go. Every year, he and Marcos do their due diligence, meeting donors, shaking hands, and telling carefully curated rescue stories. But they're both sharks and highly competitive, and every year, they'd compete to see who could shake the largest money tree. The bets were often astronomical and insane. This year, it will be a somber affair for all of us, but he's right—the show must go on.

Zane and Sterling stand and head toward the door.

"The car is arriving at seven-thirty tonight," Grayson calls out.

Zane flips a hand up to indicate he heard. Then the two are gone.

Mateo's squinting at something on his laptop. Bringing it to my desk, he asks me if I can tell who's in the car. I frown and zoom in a little, but it's too dark. The car is a Maserati Quattroporte.

"Nice car, but I can't tell who's driving," I admit with a shrug.

He brings up another image. "See anything interesting in this picture?"

I pull the laptop closer and look at the crowd of people standing in front of a fire in Dallas. Scanning their faces, I stop when I see a familiar face. Cold anger burrows into my very bones.

"Diego's in Dallas." The potential implications of that simple statement reverberate through me. "Do you have any information on the fire?"

Mateo pulls up the article, adjusts his glasses, and starts reading. "Firefighters in Dallas are standing in front of an industrial loft conversion in downtown Dallas this evening. The fire started in the middle of the night, and due to heavy amounts of a class B accelerant in the building, firefighters sprayed special foam to counteract and are now waiting for the fire to settle before entering. Our reports state nobody was in the building when it caught on fire. At this time, firefighters do not have any reason to suspect the fire was arson, but we'll keep you updated as we get more information." He stops. "This happened Monday night."

"It has to be her," I state softly. "Grayson said she mentioned Dallas, and with Diego in the same location, it's means he tracked her there. If that happened Monday night, she should be here by now, right? Or close?" I refuse to believe she didn't make it out alive.

Pieces of the puzzle shift and align themselves in new positions in my mind, and I barely hold back the roar when the two revelations hit me in the gut like a sucker punch. Reeling from the knowledge, I shudder and take a deep breath. I need to focus on the enemy first. "Diego's more than just a traitor. He either killed Marcos or he was there when it happened. But why? For money? Grayson, review his finances and see if we can find how far back this goes. Mateo, send Zane and Sterling the information. If she saw him shoot Marcos on the video, it's no wonder we were number one on her list of suspects. It also means he likely took down Agent Antonio too, but don't alert the ATF."

"He's a traitor, mole, killer…" Mateo trails off. "But he's not smart enough for the rest of it, which means he's only a pawn but probably a useful one. We need to capture him alive so we can interrogate him." He eyes Grayson when he says the last part because he would be doing the interrogation.

I contemplate his suggestion and jerk my chin in agreement. We need to know who the hell is gunning for us. If Diego has any information, Grayson will pull it out of him. He's got a particular skill for interrogation. Zane's even used him on a few missions.

"He's not standing trial," I state unequivocally.

Grayson and Mateo simultaneously reply, "Agreed."

CHAPTER 37

HENLEY

P eyton arrives at six to help me get ready. He styles my hair in big cascading curls of pink, making them look soft and luxurious. I sip champagne and let him mess with my hair. The bubbles tickle my nose and I laugh. He grabs the glass and downs the rest of the champagne.

"Hey, that was my glass," I protest with a pout for good measure.

"You can have more later," he promises. "You're such a lightweight. Pink cheeks, glittery, smiley eyes, and giggling—all signs of being tipsy. Although, I won't need to use any blush on you now." He admires the tint on my cheek, then waves his hands in frustration. "The point is, we need to walk steadily into the party, not get thrown out before we've even gotten a chance to get a glass of champagne or show off your dress to the press. Hold off, you lush."

He adds the finishing touches to cover the bruises on my body, then motions me over to the screen in the corner, where the dress waits for me.

I step into the dress and pull it up. The top portion of the dress is a bustier with satin straps. It's a royal blue color and slightly sheer, with a tan underlay. The bottom of the dress is split, with the royal blue front skirt very, very short and the multi-colored back skirt long, flowy, and voluminous. I smooth down the slightly poufy skirt and eye the almost indecent amount of leg I'm showing. Another inch, and I think you'd probably be able to see my hoo-ha.

The skirt sways and I bite my lip, waiting to see if I flash anything, but somehow, the skirt falls long enough to keep it covered. Turning to the side, the voluminous skirt flows around me. You can't even see the short skirt in the front.

I slip my hands into the sides of the full skirt and find the pockets. They're perfect. Deep, but completely hidden by the folds of the skirt.

Moving out from behind the screen, I twirl in front of Peyton. He studies every inch of his creation. Finally, he nods. He reaches behind me and pulls out my mask. I gasp at the sight of the beautiful creation. He secures it to the front of my face.

Dragging me in front of the mirror, he steps over and flicks the lights off. Special glowing threads sewn into the back skirt and in the peacock feathers attached to the mask light up with various colors.

"It's a masterpiece," I murmur, unable to take my eyes off the beautiful creature in front of the mirror. I'm the epitome of a peacock with glowing iridescent colors. The only thing I recognize about myself is the pink hair. "They're going to be talking about this dress for a long time."

He beams and waves his hand nonchalantly, but I see the sheen of tears in his eyes. "Girl, they're going to be talking about those legs of yours for a long time to come. I'm even jealous."

I blush. "Go change. We've got to get going."

When he steps behind the screen, I head into the bathroom and close the door. Reaching under the sink, I grab my backpack and pull out the three pairs of glasses and a couple of notes and slide them into each pocket. I add my phone, and that's it. I don't need anything else tonight.

When I come out, Peyton's standing in front of the mirror. He dyed his hair royal blue for this evening, and his suit is all gold, which matches the delicate shoes on my feet. His mask is royal blue with gold thread that glows.

"We're gorgeous," I drawl. "You're going to have women clamoring at your door wanting you to dress them after tonight."

CHAPTER 38

<u>THIAGO</u>

The rich and famous pour into the ball, their costumes a veritable feast for the cameras and fans waiting to catch a glimpse, a pic, or a video for their social media posts. Over the years, we've carefully crafted an air of secrecy and glamor around our highly exclusive event. The theme is the biggest secret.

One month before the event, each guest receives an elaborate announcement revealing the theme to them, which they're allowed to share with their fans on social media, and it kicks off an entire month of buzz and press for the event as everyone tries to guess their costume. More importantly, it generates donations from the fans who want to support the same charity as their idol.

This year's theme was chosen by Mateo, of course. He's been wanting to do something with technology for a while, and he's currently fascinated with the use of it in nature. We've seen the gamut of costumes tonight, from dresses made entirely of flowers, to a ballgown crafted of grass with electronic bees flying around. One basketball player came as a tree with LED leaves, and another as a giraffe. There's a lot of variance in nature, and it's interesting to watch how the guests and their stylists interpret the theme. Social media is blowing up with vivid images, videos, and voting polls.

Zane, Grayson, Mateo, and I stand inside the entrance for the first hour to greet the guests. Many stop to speak to Zane and ask about his lively friend Marcos, and it's all we can do to keep stoic expressions on our faces.

The crowd slows for a minute, and Mateo glances at his watch. "It's eight-thirty," he murmurs. Running a finger under his collar, he flashes Grayson an irritated look.

Grayson ignores him. Every year, Mateo begs us to go in costume, but neither I nor Grayson ever agree, so he's stuck wearing his least favorite uniform—his tuxedo.

A group of women enter and make a beeline toward us.

"Your bevy of beauties is headed this way," I inform Grayson, expecting to see him break out the smile he reserves just for them. Instead, I'm astonished when he scowls at me like I've said something offensive.

"Ladies," he exclaims, pasting a quick smile on his face. He greets each one and smoothly maneuvers them into the ballroom, promising them a dance later.

Honestly, none of us want to be here tonight. I can't stop picturing the fire in Dallas and wondering where the hell Henley is or why she hasn't called.

Sterling and Cruz arrive moments later. Sterling is impeccably British in a tailored tuxedo from Savile Row, if I'm not mistaken. Cruz is dressed all in black, but he's sporting green garland and lights across his wheelchair.

Surprised, I glance at Zane, and he shrugs.

Grayson is eyeing Sterling's attire and muttering something about updating our tuxedos, and I smother a groan.

Mateo's gaze is fixated on the entrance.

Tensing, I turn and see a woman's dress light up with different color threads. The crowd oohs and ahhs at the couple. The press goes wild. Tilting my head, I try to see what has Mateo so fascinated, and that's when I notice. Her hair is pink. I step forward, and Mateo yanks me back.

"If we go to her, we might as well paint a target on her back. Let her lead the way tonight. She's obviously got a plan, or she wouldn't be dressed in costume," he murmurs.

Grayson leans in and asks, "What is it?"

Mateo whispers in his ear, and he jerks around to the entrance.

He inhales sharply. "Where the hell did she get that dress? And where's the rest of it?"

Puzzled, I swivel back to reexamine the dress, but this time, she's walking toward us. With the back of the colorful dress flowing out behind her and the mask garnished with feathers, she almost looks like a peacock strutting toward us on the best damn legs I've ever seen. Long and lean, but with beautifully defined muscles, and all I want to do is cover them up.

Zane leans forward. "Is that who I think it is?"

"Yes," we all three answer in chorus.

He whistles, and I snarl at him.

Sterling and Cruz roll up next to us and watch Henley walk the long red carpet, and I start to lose my cool. "Don't you two need to be somewhere? This is the receiving line for the guests."

Zane jumps in before it can escalate between us. "Move, Slick, now. Take Cruz with you. There are a lot of guests coming down the carpet, and you need to get out of the way. Do not speak to her unless she comes to you, or you'll blow her cover."

They take one last look at Henley, then discreetly flip us off as they move farther into the ballroom.

Before the next guest gets to us, Zane leans over and spits out, "I blame you for the dissension in my ranks."

"They can't have her. End of discussion," I state crossly before turning a wide charming smile on the older lady standing in front of me.

Anticipation thrums in my veins. She returned to us.

CHAPTER 39

<u>HENLEY</u>

Given the theme of technology and nature, the costumes have been utterly fantastic to gawk at while we wait for our turn to walk the red carpet into the ball. Flower dresses with LED lights cleverly hidden in the center, abstract 3D-looking concoctions which remind me of the metaverse, and animals galore with feathers and fur. Peyton's whispered commentary on each outfit, from the difficulty of the design to the fabric used to create it, has given me an entirely new insight into the world of fashion. He's in absolute designer heaven right now.

I like clothes, but I can't help but think this is what I sound like to people who only want the barest of explanations when I'm talking about technology.

"Henley Night, and clothing designer extraordinaire, Peyton Wyatt," I tell the lady checking the invitations. From the corner of my eye, I catch Peyton's grin at the illustrious title I gave him.

"Oh, you're one of the hotel's auction winners. Your donation was extremely generous, and we can't thank you enough," she gushes.

Motioning over to the press, she explains who I am, and they come over to congratulate me and exclaim over my beautiful dress.

When they move to take our picture, I hold up a hand and move backward into the hotel where the light is dimmer. The dress glows brightly, along with the feathers in the mask, and I hear them snapping pictures and exclaiming over the dress.

The reporter thrusts the microphone in my face. "Who's the designer?"

"Peyton Wyatt." I pull him over and introduce him so he can get some press time.

She asks Peyton about his inspiration, and he explains that a woman should showcase her best assets and since mine were my legs, he felt a high-low dress would be perfect. Add in the wondrous nature and technology theme, and bam—peacock.

We move away from the first entrance and step into the receiving line.

"Fantastic answer," I whisper to him with an excited grin. "Women love to know the designer's going to showcase them." I lift my fist, and he tilts his head in disbelief but gives it a bump. "You do have a website and stuff, right?"

He rolls his eyes. "Of course."

I peek around the shoulders of the man in front of me to see how much farther we must go to get into the actual ballroom, and my eyes lock with Thiago's, whose dark eyes are glittering with emotion behind his rather plain black mask. Returning his attention to the line, he absentmindedly shakes the hand of the person in front of him. Whatever the person says makes him laugh. I shiver. Even his laugh is larger than life.

A man in a black tux shifts next to him, and Mateo's warm brown eyes sweep me from head to toe. Instead of the admiration I thought I'd see, he's frowning. I examine the dress to make sure it isn't ripped or anything, but I don't see anything. Maybe something else is going on.

I look beyond Mateo to the man next to him and see Grayson. He's entirely focused on the people in front of him.

Not expecting anyone else, I'm surprised to see Zane standing with them, greeting the guests. It takes a minute to remember his role with the rescue missions and the charity.

Peyton peeks his head out to look with me, and Mateo zooms in on him like a bug under a microscope. His lips quirk upward in a smile. I'm kind of jealous Peyton got a smile when all he offered me was a frown. I wonder what that's all about?

We're the next ones through the receiving line, and I use the advantage to stare at Thiago without him noticing. All the emotion I locked inside the last few days starts to build until I just want him to hold me like he did that one night and tell me it's going to be all right. My eyes start to water, and I panic.

Glancing at Peyton, I notice a bright pink strand peeking out. "Is that a wig?"

"Of course," he replies with a sarcastic tilt to his head. "I don't want to be bald because I dyed my hair too much. I want to be suave and debonair, with a full head of hair until I'm dead. We're up."

I slowly turn my head to meet Thiago's dark eyes, my hand automatically reaching for his. He gives mine a tight squeeze, then uses the leverage to pull us closer together. His lips kiss one cheek and slide within a hairsbreadth of my lips to the other cheek to place a similar kiss. My breath hitches at the closeness of his mouth. I lower my lashes to prevent him from seeing everything I'm feeling.

"Hello, Henley. You look beautiful. I was worried you wouldn't come," he informs me huskily, keeping his remarks purposely vague. The tightness around his eyes evidence of his real concern. "Is this the designer?" He releases my hand to shake Peyton's.

"Yes, Peyton Wyatt," he says, introducing himself.

"The design is remarkable and fits the theme perfectly. I look forward to seeing more of your designs on our guests in the future." After one long glance in my direction, he turns to the next person in line.

We move along as well. "Mateo," I murmur, needing to say his name to reassure myself he's real and in front of me. My eyes automatically glance at his wound and find it's mostly been covered by his hair. Not a bandage in sight.

His brown eyes are a burning ember of warmth behind his mask. When I reach out with my hand, he clasps it and rubs his thumb along the inside of my palm, reminding me of the kiss he gave me when I left. Letting go, he reaches for Peyton and introduces himself, since I seem incapable of speaking right now.

Stepping up to Grayson, I see him frown at my dress, and I narrow my eyes at him in warning. "Grayson, this is Peyton Wyatt, the designer of this beautiful dress." I emphasize designer and dress.

He immediately reaches out to shake Peyton's hand. "She looks exquisite. How did you get her out of those baggy clothes?"

"By giving her lots of champagne and no other options," Peyton replies with a smirk toward me.

"True, but it doesn't mean those tactics will always work," I retort, with a pointed look at Grayson. "Although the champagne was truly lovely. We should go get some now, Peyton."

"Zane." I greet him with a small smile and introduce him to Peyton.

They shake hands, and we start to move along.

"Please, save me a dance later," I toss over my shoulder. "I'd love to talk more about this charity I just donated two hundred and fifty thousand dollars toward."

He coughs and dips his head before moving on to the next person in line.

"Did you really donate that much money?" Peyton asks curiously.

"I did," I confirm, hesitating only for a second before I continue, "They rescued me a long time ago, and I support everything they stand for and do."

When we enter the ballroom, we both stop and stare in awe at the scene before us. The entire ballroom has been transformed into a fantasy garden. Life-sized trees in various shades of muted pastel colors stand tall, with boughs of flowers and lights dripping from them. The ceiling has been completely obscured by the canopy of their branches, while their roots wind around tables and chairs, lending a touch of whimsy to the seating. Directly below our feet is a river flowing under transparent glass, the water changing color every few minutes, thanks to the row of LED lights hidden on the sides. Along its banks, a plethora of grass, plants, and little mechanical animals guide you along the way. It's utterly fantastical.

Peyton squeezes my hand, his eyes lit up with the magic of the scene in front of us. "This is incredible. I've waited years to come to this event, dreaming of some beautiful creature wearing my design, and here I am."

He plucks a couple of champagne flutes off a tray and hands one to me. "Cheers, Henley Night, and thank you for helping to make one of my dreams come true."

"One, huh? I can't wait to hear more. Cheers, Peyton, and thank you for designing this fabulous dress and coming with me," I reply, clinking my glass with his.

He drinks the entire glass, and I laugh. Setting down the empty flute on a tray, he points to the restroom and leaves me standing in the middle of the room by myself.

Staring into the glass of champagne, I reflect on how lucky I was to meet Peyton. Having someone, even a new friend, by my side tonight eases the massive anxiety I was having about attending such a huge public event by myself.

"Penny for your thoughts," a deep *familiar* voice murmurs next to me.

I twirl around and find Cruz in a garland and lights bedecked wheelchair behind me. My eyes water, but I don't dare cry with this mask on, so I suck in a deep breath and blink a few times.

"When I left you at the hospital, I didn't know if you'd make it," I admit hesitantly, still feeling guilty about dropping him off without checking.

"If I'd have had to wait for an ambulance, I likely wouldn't be here. I was bleeding internally. You saved my life… twice," he states with a serious expression on his face.

"I'd say we're even," I counter. "Nice costume." I point to the decorations. Then I look at the man beside him. "You're looking exceptionally sharp, Sterling. Very British." He preens at my comment, and I smirk.

"Who's British?" Peyton comes over to stand next to me with a glass of champagne in his hand. He looks at Cruz and Sterling, then at me. "Is everything okay?"

"Yes, everything's good," I assure him, then introduce him to the two men. "I'm surprised they let you out of the hospital so soon." I glance at Peyton. "He was in a horrible accident last weekend."

Sterling snorts. "He didn't ask their permission, nor did he tell them he was leaving. He called and ordered me to give him a ride. I couldn't let him just go alone. He's returning immediately after this event."

"We should call you Snitch instead of Slick," Cruz says snidely.

Explains why they're not wearing a mask, although I find it interesting that Sterling has such a beautiful tux just hanging in his closet.

"Sterling, thank you for being such a good friend to grumpy here. Cruz, go back to the hospital, please. I'll call on you tomorrow, okay? We're going to make some rounds," I tell them. Tugging on Peyton's arm, I walk away.

"It's a good thing I'm gay, or I'd probably be laid out on the floor by now. You didn't tell me you had so many delicious men interested in you," he murmurs.

I slip him a confused glance. "They're just friends," I remark. Craning my neck, I search for the dance floor, but I don't see it.

A lady comes over to gush about my dress, and I quickly introduce her to Peyton. Giving him a thumbs-up, I leave him with his potential client and continue my search.

I'm walking toward the outside when someone grabs me and pulls me deep into the shadows. I open my mouth to scream, and a hand swiftly covers it.

"It's me, Thiago," he whispers into my ear.

As soon as his name registers, I turn and burrow into his arms. After the last few days, I need his strength—to feel safe and protected for just a second.

"Diego," I say, then stop. This isn't the place to tell him.

"I know," he returns in a harsh whisper. His arms tighten around me. "Mateo found the article on the fire. It was your home, wasn't it?"

I lift my head to stare into his angry, dark eyes and nod. If I start talking about it, I'm going to cry.

He darts a quick look behind me before dropping his arms. "What's your plan?"

I straighten and dip a hand into my pocket, then give him a pair of the glasses. "Tell Grayson and Mateo to ask me for a dance."

"Wait, you mean by dragging you in here, I missed my chance to dance with you in that dress? I don't think so," he muses. "Once I finish greeting the guests, I'll find you."

A heel striking the concrete startles me, and I swing around to see a woman stumble by the opening. When I turn around, Thiago's gone.

Heading in the same direction as the woman, I'm about to step outside when a hand grabs my elbow. Tensing, I swivel around and see Peyton's blinding white smile.

"There you are. I've been looking for you," Peyton says excitedly. "I have my first client from the ball!" He clasps my hand and yanks me forward. "Come on, let's dance."

The dance floor is open to the night sky, and my dress shines like a beacon against its dark backdrop. I run a finger across the beautiful silky fabric.

"This is truly an amazing dress." I give a carefree laugh, then twirl around to make the dress billow out behind me in a riot of color and light, like a peacock fanning his train to attract a mate.

I reach for Peyton, but he holds his hands up like he's surrendering. A strong, lean hand comes around the small of my back and pulls me in close, just as the music changes to something slower.

"Mateo," I greet him softly, placing my left hand on his shoulder and my right in the hand he's holding out to the side. My breath comes out unsteadily when I look at him. "You look very dashing in your black mask. Like Antonio Banderas in the movie *Zorro*."

The tense expression on his face eases, and he laughs loudly. "You never say what I expect you to say," he remarks with a shake of his head. "I've never seen the movie. Does he save the fair maiden?"

It's been so long since I've seen it, the details are a tad fuzzy. "If I remember correctly, they save each other, and a lot of the towns-people," I inform him. "I'll watch it again with you."

His warm brown eyes twinkle behind the mask. "A hero, huh? It's a date. Maybe you could wear the blue blouse Grayson bought you?"

Surprised to hear the word date, I slowly nod. "It's a date."

"Você está linda. You look beautiful," he says fervently, his blazing eyes trailing over my body to my feet. "The dress is incredible and exactly the kind of idea I had in mind when I dreamed up the theme." He pulls me in tighter.

"I would have never guessed you were behind this theme," I tease him. "And thank you. Peyton did an outstanding job."

"He had a beautiful woman to design for," he smoothly interjects.

"Where are your glasses?"

"Contacts," he replies with a grimace.

The song slowly comes to an end. I lean forward and kiss one cheek. "Don't forget to check your pocket," I whisper, then follow with a kiss on the other cheek. I slip the glasses and a note into his pocket. "Thank you for the dance."

Walking away, I find Peyton waiting for me on the side of the dance floor with a fresh, cold champagne glass in his hand. "You're the best."

"I'm the best," he smugly agrees. "Girl, that dress has power. Serious pulling power. It's like a magnet."

 CHAPTER 40

<u>HENLEY</u>

I 'm not on the sidelines long when a good-looking guy dressed in a green suit and mask comes over and asks me to dance. Peyton chokes on his champagne. The guy stands there with an amused smile on his face. With a strangled groan, Peyton takes my glass and shoos me onto the dance floor. I raise an eyebrow, wondering what's got into him.

When I look at the guy, I'm puzzled for a second, but shrug it off. He looks at me warily, but I slap a smile on my face and motion to the dance floor. While we dance, he talks about his latest trip to Paris, and I can't help but be jealous.

"It sounds fabulous," I respond. "What's your favorite thing to do there?"

He considers the question, and with a sheepish smile, he replies, "I like to walk at night when there are fewer people out, and I can breathe without everyone stalking me. Plus, I can stand and gawk at a piece of history or architecture without seeing a picture of myself staring at it on social media."

Social media? I look closer at him, but he doesn't look familiar.

"I love the night too," I reply. "Although I'm usually working, not playing tourist."

When we turn, I see Grayson standing on the side of the dance floor, surrounded by his usual bevy of beauties. He's wearing his charming persona, laughing and twirling the women around him. As I dance by, his eyes flick to mine and narrow. What's wrong with him?

"What do you do?"

"I design tech products." His eyes light up with interest, but I laugh. "It's nothing flashy, like the next gadget or anything. The stuff I design is more necessary, even utilitarian." He looks kind of bored, but I'm not surprised. It's the usual reaction when I tell people about my work. "What do you do?"

"I'm an actor," he says with a frown. "Do you really not know who I am?"

I peer closely at him, but I don't see anything familiar. "Maybe I just don't realize I know you. What movies have you been in?"

"Jared Lawson. I'm on the show *Brainiac University*," he says slowly. "For the last five years, it's been the most popular show on network TV."

"TV?" I ask with a grimace. When he nods, I give him an apologetic look. "Sorry, I don't watch TV."

"Ever?"

"No, sorry, I—" I stop when the suit he's wearing changes colors. "I knew it! You were wearing a green suit when you walked up, but when we walked on the dance floor, it was blue. I thought I was losing my mind. What kind of fabric is this?"

He shrugs. "Look, you're a nice..." He pauses for a brief second and looks at my chest. "Girl and everything, but I only asked you to dance because I saw you with Mateo Santos earlier, and I was hoping you could introduce me to him."

I blink. "Why do you want to meet Mateo Santos?"

"I'm looking to secure backing for a new TV show based on a tech genius," he says dismissively, looking around the dance floor.

"Why not Thiago or Grayson?" I ask, curious to hear his answer.

"Thiago lacks the vision I'm looking for in a new partner," he drawls. "And I need someone who's going to understand the intellectual aspects of my project, not a playboy."

I jerk to a stop. "Let me see if I've got this straight. You want to use Mateo to fund your TV show and feed you tech ideas for the script. Thiago isn't a fit because he'd see right through your bullshit," I respond with a sneer. "And Grayson? You didn't do an ounce of research on him, or you'd know he's tech savvy and creative, even designs the financial software SEI installs in Fortune 500 companies. He's got an MBA from Wharton too, which means he's a hell of a lot smarter than you," I scoff and turn to storm off.

All three Santos men are standing behind me. Mateo's amused. Thiago's face is inscrutable, but his eyes are sharp with fury. Following his gaze, I'm incredibly glad to see it's directed at the idiot behind me. Grayson's wearing a placid expression on his face, but his deep blue eyes are filled with anger... at me. My breath catches.

Thiago raises a hand, and the band stops playing.

"Mr. Lawson, I'm going to have to ask you to leave. Be sure to let your agent know that in one night, you managed to piss off all three of the Santos men, and you'll not be invited to future balls," Thiago states clearly.

The guy gives a nervous laugh. "She completely misunderstood what I said. Obviously, she lacks an understanding of the entertainment business and how critical it is to find the right partner to make a show a success."

Surprisingly, Mateo laughs.

The guy looks at him in relief.

Mateo steps closer, and in a loud voice, he says, "You really are an idiot. This whole time, you've been dancing with a tech genius, and you didn't even realize it." He points to me, then shakes his head. "Sorry, I have little tolerance for those who have the IQ of a gnat."

Thiago signals to side of the dance floor, and security comes forward. "These gentlemen will escort you out."

When he looks around at the other celebrity guests, Jared Lawson makes the wise choice to leave without another word.

Grayson scowls at me, then walks over to his "beauties."

My face reddens.

Mateo comes up and shakes his head. "He has his reasons for living the life he does," he states with a heartfelt sigh. "Don't judge him too harshly until you know his story."

With a nod, I pull out the last pair of glasses and slip them in Mateo's pocket. "Would you mind giving him the last pair?"

He squeezes my hand, and I whisper a thank you toward Thiago when I pass by.

Peyton's gawking at me from the sidelines. "Anytime you want me to be your plus one, I'm in. This is the most entertainment I've had in a long while," he says fervently.

"Maybe you need to get out more," the man beside him interjects.

Peyton gives him a flirty smile. "You'll have to do more than look good to get my attention."

I clear my throat. "I'm exhausted, so I'm going to my room. You should stay and get some more lovely clients."

He pulls me into a hug. "That was amazing, and I'll be fine," he says, flashing another glance at the man beside him. "Call me soon and we'll grab lunch."

"Peyton, this dress was truly a dream to wear. I can't wait to see what you come up with for next year." I wish them both a good night, then head down a side hall shortcut to get to the elevators.

"For the record, I don't care what some overblown actor thinks or says about me," Grayson snarls.

Whirling around, I watch him stalk angrily toward me, and I take a couple of steps back.

A hand lands on the wall beside my head, and he leans down to bring his mouth close to my ear. "The next time you feel the need to defend my honor, don't. I told you I'm not the good guy. You almost ruined the reputation I've so carefully cultivated. I've worked very hard to achieve every bit of my success, and if I want to spend it with my 'beauties.' it's my business. Got it?"

I match his furious stare with one of my own. "I couldn't care less how you spend your time, and you've made it abundantly clear you're neither nice nor the good guy," I reply angrily. "However, if I want to set someone straight, I don't need your permission. May I go now?"

For some reason, my dismissal seems to piss him off further.

He raises his head and glares at me. Leaning back a little, his eyes walk the length of me and back up, and his expression shifts. "This dress should be illegal. I've waited all night for you to flash the tiniest hint of what you're wearing underneath, but it's as if the dress was designed to tantalize and tease but never satisfy. It's all I've been able to think about, and it's been driving me crazy."

A large knee slides in between my legs, and I gasp.

"We're in public," I remind him, raising my chin to meet his challenge.

"It's late, the hallway is dark," he retorts. A large hand lands on one of my thighs and I watch him swallow. Fingers grasp the hem of my short skirt and lift it an inch.

He stops and looks at me, an eyebrow raised, waiting for me to stop him.

I lick my lips but say nothing.

His knee presses into me, and my body shifts to accommodate more of him between my legs.

His thumb slides up the inside of my thigh as he raises the skirt another two inches, and I gasp at how close it is to sliding right into me. The cool air caresses my damp underwear making me suck in my lower lip, and a devilish look appears in his eyes as he slowly squats down to peek at the treasure he's uncovered.

His eyes slide from mine to my body, and he groans when he sees the semi-sheer flesh-colored underwear I'm wearing.

"It's as if you're wearing nothing at all," he rasps. "Fuck, you tempt me until I just want to throw the rules out the window."

A finger trails along the edge, and my hips involuntarily shift toward him, needing more than he can discreetly give me in this public hallway.

"Stop." I slide my fingers through his hair and pull up until he stands.

Grasping my hips, he leans his full body into mine until I feel every bit of his hardness against the thin fabric of my underwear.

Needing to release some of the tension and emotion he's built inside me, I pull him down for a scorching kiss, pouring pure gasoline on the fire, until we're both nothing but flame and need. Breathing heavily, I drag my lips away from his and look into eyes almost navy with desire.

"Darling, Grayson, is that you?" a melodic voice calls from the nearby main hall, dousing me with ice-cold reality. "We're heading to the bar. Do you want anything?"

Gripping his hips, I push him away and adjust my dress. "Goodnight, Grayson." I straighten from the wall and brush past, leaving him standing there alone. Free to rejoin his harem.

 # CHAPTER 41

<u>MATEO</u>

After my dance with Henley, I slip my hand in my pocket and pull out a familiar pair of glasses and a note. I caress the curved edge of the frame with my finger. Closing my eyes for a second, I reconcile the two conflicting views I have in my head until I'm able to see my way forward. Thiago strides over and looks at the dawning comprehension on my face and nods. I wonder how long he's known.

"What does the note say?" he murmurs, not wanting anyone nearby to hear our conversation.

I unfold the note and read the first few lines. "It's a list of instructions on how to get to a virtual reality space, what to do to prepare, and how to connect the three pairs into one unit so we can all 'travel' together," I reply, then blink. "The last time I saw these glasses, they weren't working properly. I guess they are now. At two a.m., we'll need to pull Grayson aside and let him know so he doesn't go home with one of his entourage."

"He won't," Thiago states confidently. "Does it say anything else?" His eyes flick to the note in my hand as he takes a sip of bourbon and looks around.

"She couldn't get into the server to get our new cell numbers. Says neither of our credentials worked, and she was redirected to another IP." Disbelief and anger eclipse my voice for a second, until I get it under control. "Philip Carlton. He's in on it."

"I'll speak with Zane," Thiago spits out, his face thunderous with anger. "Another one who's been with us since the beginning. We're going to need to clean house from top to bottom." He stretches his neck to ease the tension building within him. "Anything else?"

"A number. Hers, I'm guessing," I reply. Copying it directly into my phone, I send it to Thiago, Grayson, and Zane. I glance at the time. "It's almost one a.m. now. The party's moving to the after-party location and winding down here. Do you want to meet at our table in an hour?"

"Where are you going?"

"To get another glimpse of her in that dress," I reply, with a side-glance.

"I'll go with you."

———

AT PRECISELY TWO A.M., we're standing in our hotel suite beside a table with a bottle of tequila and three shot glasses filled to the brim beside it, with three chairs a few steps behind us. The three pairs of glasses are connected, and I've given Grayson and Thiago pointers on how to walk, talk, and move in the metaverse, so I click on the app. Seconds later, we're inside. I look at Grayson and Thiago, and I'm amazed at how close she got their avatars. I'm assuming mine is close as well, since neither of them are looking at me oddly.

Glancing around, I see avatars standing or hanging around chatting with each other, and I slowly turn in a circle until I find the two street signs. One street says "Hell" and the other, "Good Intentions." This is it—the Crossroads.

"The instructions said to go directly to hell." I relay the information to Thiago and Grayson, and we take the road on the left. "Walk until you see the pink phone booth."

This is Thiago and Grayson's first time in the metaverse, and their heads are swiveling from side to side in fascination.

"It's literally like a different dimension," Thiago states, his voice hesitant and unsure in this reality. "Why would anyone want to meet here?"

"I'm guessing it's the only place they could safely meet. The real world offered no options. Here, they can make their avatars look like anything or anyone. She made ours similar to our real faces tonight to make us more comfortable," I muse. This evolution is fascinating to me, but Thiago's never going to be comfortable with anything he thinks isn't "real."

"Why are most of the people cut in half?" Grayson asks, bewildered to see half bodies floating around everywhere.

"Most of the current headsets aren't designed to pick up on the entire body yet, but like these glasses, there are new products hitting the market every day. The avatars will become more sophisticated over time. You won't have to even choose a human form, but we'll leave that for another discussion," I explain, chuckling at the expressions on both of their faces.

We pass a few bars and stores, but not many. It's growing, though. I spot a glowing pink booth and point them to it. Sliding open the accordion door, I motion for them to get in, and we crowd together. I punch in the code, and the booth blurs for a second. When it resolves itself, there's a door in front of us with a neon sign on it.

"Nacho Tequila"

All three of us start laughing. When we were kids, Marcos would catch us sneaking a sip of his tequila, and he'd yank it away and jokingly say nacho tequila, meus pequenos selvagens, before cracking up at his own punny humor.

We open the door and walk into a neon filled virtual bar. To the right is a black bar top edged with a neon chartreuse LED light. Barstools line the bar top, each seat a different neon color—hot pink, lime green, cosmic orange, and electric blue. The shelves behind the bar are edged with the same neon chartreuse as the bar top, and behind them is a mirror reflecting the rest of the bar. The shelves are lined with about a hundred different tequilas.

Two purple booths with chartreuse tables line the left wall. At one of these booths sits Henley, with a shot of tequila sitting in front of her and one in front of the seat next to her. She's staring wistfully around the bar, lost in the memories of the past, I'm guessing.

We walk over, and she slides out of the booth. I quirk my lips to see the maneuver.

"Marcos had a rule. When you were in his bar, you embraced the experience. If you're sitting in a booth, you slide out as if you were sliding out of a real one," she explains with a shrug. Tapping the air in front of her, the booth changes to five chairs. "Have a seat."

In the real world, I hand Grayson and Thiago their shots, and help them sit in their seats before doing the same.

"To Marcos," she toasts the empty seat beside her where the second shot of tequila sits. "Saúde!"

We three pause, remembering the memorial service not too long ago, then smile. "Saúde!"

"This doesn't even look like Marcos," Thiago muses. "Are you sure he designed this bar?"

"Every inch of it," Henley replies, her voice filled with laughter. "It's atrocious, but he'd get a kick out of it every time we walked through the door. After working on a project together at the lab, we'd come here for 'happy hour.' It made us feel like normal colleagues getting a drink at the local bar after working together all day. He had a few rules, though. I've already mentioned the first one. The second—we could only drink tequila. Third, no current project talk, only ideas and dreams could be discussed here. Last, it had to remain a secret."

Grayson leans forward, and I watch as Henley blushes.

Hmm, I wonder what's occurred between those two?

"Do you like tequila?" he asks her nonchalantly, but the yearning in his voice is an indication of how much he misses talking about it now that Marcos is gone.

She laughs and wrinkles her nose. "Some of it, more the silver or blanco than the others. Marcos used to say I had the heart for it, but maybe not the taste."

Grayson sits back with a small, sad smile on his face.

"You said you worked on projects, then came here." Thiago recaps her earlier statement. "You're CJ Tech?"

"I am." She tenses, expecting him to explode, but when he doesn't, she glances at Grayson and me. "You all know? Since when?"

"I knew when you told us you won a scholarship for an algorithm you'd developed," Grayson reveals, to my surprise. "One of the first big projects JF Technologies brokered through SEI was an insurance algorithm. When I pulled Marcos' bank statements, he'd paid most of the money out to CJ Tech. It was a bet on my part, but a pretty solid one."

She looks impressed with his reasoning. Looking over at me, she waits for me to answer.

I groan and give her a wry smile. "I knew tonight when I pulled the glasses out of my pocket. I helped Marcos craft the design because he wanted something younger people would wear," I admit, hating I didn't catch on sooner. "I resented CJ Tech, but I liked you, so the two never existed as one in my mind." It's the only way I can explain the huge miss on my part.

She looks at Thiago with a hesitant expression.

He heaves a sigh. "I knew when I saw the picture of Diego standing in front of the fire in Dallas. There's only one reason he would go that far to get you—the video. And it suddenly clicked, as if the pieces had been there all along but I couldn't see them. Marcos would only have sent that video to someone he trusted and to a location not easily found in his everyday life. To CJ Tech, to you." He tilts his head. "I'm so sorry, Henley, for not giving Marcos and you the benefit of the doubt. It shocked me to hear about this secret long-term partnership, and to know he didn't trust us or me with the information." His eyes are filled with sadness and doubt. Marcos' secrets have shaken his foundation.

"He wanted to put CJ Tech on the products since the beginning, but I repeatedly refused. I didn't want a single part of my life exposed. When we finished the AR project, though, I knew it was going to be truly breakthrough technology and if I didn't add a piece of me, I would regret it." She bites her lip, then shrugs.

"There's one thing we don't understand. If they have the software, why haven't they left us alone?" Thiago asks, a glint in his eye.

"Are you ready to watch the video?" she asks with a catch in her voice. A filled tequila shot suddenly appears in front of her avatar. When he nods, she downs the shot and taps the air. The TV above the bar displays a play button. She taps it.

Thiago and Grayson forget they're in a virtual world, so when they jump up, I grab them in the real world to prevent them from pacing. We don't have enough room to allow for the movement.

Instead, they stand there shouting and cursing while they stare at the last image of Marcos.

Tears run down my face, and I lift the VR glasses to wipe them away. It's wrong, so wrong. Marcos had been betrayed so many times in his life, and to die by betrayal seems the cruelest thing of all. I'd rather he'd died rescuing someone or in an accident. No wonder Henley felt strongly about getting the files.

Henley's hand raises to her face and swipes. She blips out for a second, then returns with a white paper. When she wipes her face, I realize it's a tissue.

"I have an untampered copy of it on a drive in Miami," she says. "When I get a chance, I'll—What are you doing? Diego?" She jerks violently to the side, then rises off her seat and goes flying to the ground. "Four thirteen!" she screams. Her avatar shakes, and I close the connection and tear off my headset.

Thiago and Grayson are still sitting there, stunned, probably unsure what's real or not. I pull off their headsets and start running toward the bedroom.

"She's in the hotel. Room 413!" I yell, racing to the lockbox in the bedroom. We never travel anywhere without our guns. Entering the combination, I pull out the magazines and guns and hand them off, then I'm running for the door.

Grayson's right behind me, and Thiago's in the rear, yelling into the phone. I assume he called Zane. I hit the elevator button, and it swiftly glides up to the presidential suite. Grayson disappears.

Thiago and I pile in and take it to the fourth floor. When the doors open, a shot hits the elevator, and we duck down. Thiago nods, and I fire a couple of random high shots, while Thiago takes the shooter out from down low.

Someone comes out of their hotel room, yelling about noise, and the remaining guy grabs him and holds the gun to his head. Behind the guy, we see a third body on the ground. No Henley.

"Put it down, Thiago," the guy orders. He steps toward the stairway, dragging the guy with him.

Furious to know it's another fucking traitor, Thiago reluctantly lowers his gun. The guy motions to me, and I lower mine. He peers behind me, but there's nobody there.

He takes aim at Thiago, who immediately jumps into the open doorway to his right.

The remaining gunman pushes the hostage away to aim at me, but I just stand there and watch Grayson take the shot. He'd come down the stairway and entered the hall behind the gunman.

When he crumples dead to the floor, we dash to Henley's room, and it's a disaster. Glass and blood everywhere. I grab the AR/VR glasses from the floor and put them in my pocket. Looking around, I grab her cell phone, laptop, car keys, and… My eyes dart around, trying to figure out what else to take, and land on the dress. I snatch it up. The police can have everything else.

CHAPTER 42

HENLEY

The floor is cold and hard beneath my cheek. Little bits of dirt and gravel scrape my skin when I move my head to look around, but all I see is grey concrete for days. I lift my head and finally see windows near the ceiling. Confused, I stare at them, trying to figure out what kind of building has windows that high.

My shoulders burn, and I try to ease the pain by sitting up, but my hands are caught on something behind me. I twist around to figure it out, but all I see are my feet. Maybe I can straighten my legs, then roll over onto my stomach and get to my knees that way. I start to uncurl my legs, and pain shoots across my shoulders, and I rock back and forth in agony. It dawns on me what my hands are caught on—my feet. I'm hog-tied.

A metal chair scrapes across the floor, and I hear heavy boots walking toward me. Meaty hands jerk me up by my shirt, and Diego's beady black eyes stare down at me. Without saying a word, he punches me in the face.

"Fuck," I scream as my face explodes with the initial impact. Blood fills my mouth, and I spit it out.

He laughs, then does it again. This time, everything goes black.

———

IT'S pitch dark when I wake this time, and the floor is even colder, or maybe it just feels that way because I've been lying on it for an entire day. It's seeped through my clothes and into the heart of me, causing tiny shivers to race up and down my body. I guess it's good I'm in Miami and it's spring, or I'd be screwed.

Well, I guess I am anyway, but dying of hypothermia sounds like a bad way to die. I hate the cold. I look toward the window and finally see a faint light, but that's it. I must be somewhere where there are very few streetlights, if any.

Not wanting a repeat of the last time, I move in tiny increments, desperately anxious to avoid Diego's fist. I rotate my jaw a few times, and while it's painful, I don't think it's broken. My left eye is almost swollen shut, and it hurts like a mother trucker.

I tug on my hands, but they're still tied behind me. Shifting my legs an inch doesn't tell me anything. I listen for any movement, then shift them another inch. This time, I feel a tug on my wrists. It's not the agony I felt before, which kind of concerns me. If my hands are numb, does that mean blood isn't flowing to my arms?

Focus on something productive, Henley.

To roll onto my stomach would require momentum, so that's out. If he leaves, I can try it, so I leave the possibility in the option column. Besides rocking, the only movement I can make is a shuffle. If I use my knee to push off the floor, I can scoot, but it's not enough.

I slide my fingers inside the pockets of my jeans, but except for a piece of lint, they're empty. Tears slide down my face, but I don't let one whimper or sob escape.

I knew I should have bought one of those paracord survival bracelet things when I saw the ad online. To keep my mind busy, I focus on remembering what it had in it. A fire starter. It could be used to melt the rope or zip ties or whatever is around my wrist. A whistle. Nope. Not helpful in this scenario. Compass, yes, when I'm free. A scraper for ice. Maybe, as a weapon. A twine knife. Yep, I could use it to cut the ties from my hands and feet.

My mind wanders until the familiar sound of scraping metal pierces the air. I close my eyes, pretending to be asleep, but it doesn't matter. He picks me up and shakes me until I open my functioning right eye. The room's partially lit by some light he turned on in the corner. When I see Diego's face so close to mine, I wish for the darkness again. The stench of alcohol makes me gag, and I see something certifiably crazy in his eyes. I stare at him, waiting for him to hurt me. He doesn't disappoint.

He rears back and punches me in the gut. All the breath whooshes out of me. Pain radiates from the center of my body outward. I can't even cry out because I can't take in any air. Finally, after several excruciating minutes of pain and sheer panic, something starts working again and I take a deep breath. Coughing racks my body, but I do it again and again.

"How many is that so far?" he asks me, shaking me like a rag doll until I answer.

"How many what?" I say hoarsely.

"How many times have I hit you? What, are you stupid?" he slurs and spits when he gets in my face.

"Three," I say wearily, wondering why he's counting.

"Good, three hits for the three men you killed in Dallas with your fire." Satisfaction fills his voice. "I would have been number four if that asshole hadn't called me, much as I hate to admit it."

"Who, Thiago?"

"No, stupid genius hired by my boss to get the software," he laughs. "Marcos showed him old dogs are smarter than young geniuses. He couldn't break Marcos' key in time. When he finally got it open, the data was unrecogni—no, unreco… it was useless."

He is really, really good if he broke the key in only a few weeks. Marcos' time limit saved the day. I hear the anger in Diego's voice. Mix of loyalty? Dissension in the ranks? It might be the only survival option I get. Maybe I can find out more about this "young genius."

"Marcos survived a lot in his life. Hard to get that experience from a computer or a book," I murmur.

"Street smarts," Diego says, tapping his head. "Some got them, some don't. Thiago has them, Grayson too. Mateo couldn't survive without his computer." He laughs, then something changes, and the anger returns.

"You saved him that night in the car," he seethes. He slaps my cheek. "Pay attention. Why did you save him?"

"I didn't." I shake my head in denial. "I saved myself. He happened to be in the car." It's the truth. Kind of.

"You're a terrible liar," he says. "But I'll give you that one." He sways back a step and burps. "Tomorrow, we get the video and destroy it. Can't go to prison if there's no evidence. Get some sleep." He releases his hand, and with nothing to stop my fall, I hit the floor, and my head bounces on the concrete.

Pain stabs my head like an ice pick, and I suddenly feel like I'm going to throw up. Rocking side to side, I pull my knees under me, and using those legs Grayson seems to be so fond of, I push off hard, briefly rolling on to my arms, and over to the other side. The world's spinning like the worst drunk night of my life, and I don't dare close my eyes. Placing my cheek on the concrete, I'm thankful for the cold now. I drift off into some half awake, half asleep state.

———

"WAKE UP." A hand roughly slaps my cheek. When I don't move, he picks me up and shakes me.

I let my head roll listlessly. It's one giant ball of pain, and when I open my good eye, the light hurts.

"I brought you a laptop. You'll sign in to wherever it is and destroy the video. Now, get up," he orders me.

I snort. "Can't feel my hands. How am I supposed to type? Besides, you got the other videos, so you must know how," I throw out there in a belligerent tone. Will it work?

He lays me down on my stomach and proceeds to cut something behind me. Then he cuts another. Reaching down, he straightens my legs, and I cry out in relief. Turning me over, he sits me up, but my head's hurting too badly and I slump down toward the floor.

"I need a wall or something to help me sit up," I inform him, already starting to list to the side.

He sighs and drags me over to the wall. "You're way too much trouble. I should shoot you now."

As opposed to later or never? My personal preference is never, but I'm not sure he's going to give me a vote.

He takes my skinny arms into his meaty paws and starts rubbing vigorously and hard. It hurts, but it hurts worse when the blood starts flowing again. Thousands of needles prick my arms and hands, and I can't prevent the tears from falling.

"Try now," he demands.

I curl my stiff fingers toward my palm, but I can't form a fist yet. "Too soon," I whisper.

"Fuck!" He gets up and starts pacing. Stalking toward me with a murderous look in his eyes, he's stopped by the ring of his phone.

"What?!" he screams into the phone. "Yes, I took the damn computer." He pauses. "To get the fucking video, because you wouldn't do it. Why do you think?"

Whoever it is, they're not Diego's favorite person. I wonder if it's *the* invisible tech guy or just a tech guy.

"I don't need you to do it. She's going to do it," he says snidely. "Now fuck off!" He hangs up the phone, then flips it off.

A loud noise fills the building, and I hold my hands over my ears. Once it stops, I look at Diego.

"What the hell was that noise?"

"Ship, cruise ship, they go in and out of port all the time, and they blow the horn to comply with regulations. How's your hand?" he asks impatiently.

I'd been squeezing them into fists for the last several minutes. "Probably slow typing, but they work," I assure him. Now, if I can think of a way to get a message out to Mateo.

He hauls me up and over to the chair he placed in front of the laptop. My head spins making the nausea rise again, and I breathe deeply in and out until it subsides.

Opening the laptop, I see he's hooked up his phone to the computer so I can get Wi-Fi, which is great because it will be slower. I take a quick look in the applications folder to see what he's got available. Clicking on a messenger app, I open it, then quickly minimize it.

The blue light comes on at the top of the screen, indicating someone has remotely accessed the webcam. Maybe the owner of the laptop? Diego's phone rings again.

"WHAT?!" he screams into the phone.

While he's busy exchanging nasty words with the person on the phone, I flip open the messenger app and shoot a text to Mateo.

Grey concrete building, like a warehouse, rectangle windows up high, not low, ship horn. Trace back.

I minimize the window and download the app for the metaverse.

He hangs up and slams the phone down beside me. "What are you doing?"

I show him the app that's downloading. "It's an app so I can enter the metaverse. It's where I hid the last file." I pretend to look around. "Where's the virtual reality headset or those glasses I was wearing when you kidnapped me?"

"What?" He throws his hands in the air.

"If I don't get the video, it's set to go to the ATF in two days," I inform him. "I need the headset to get into the metaverse."

Unexpectedly, he laughs. "Agent Antonio is dead. He won't be receiving any more videos. The other agent is a friend," he states with a smug grin.

He draws his gun. "Forget it. That asshole on the phone will get my video, or I'll kill him too. I don't need you anymore."

I inhale sharply. "You know they've already seen the video, right? Thiago, Grayson, and Mateo," I tell him.

"So? They can't prove it if they don't have a copy." He lifts a shoulder.

"Well, there are two copies out there, so they could get to one pretty easily," I muse. "But I don't think they're going to follow the route I chose. See, I wanted to send you to prison for a long, long time. But do you really think Thiago's going to send you to prison? Let you live when Marcos is dead?" I start laughing.

He stops and looks at me. "Shut up! You don't know what you're saying. You don't know Thiago." He sneers. "I know Thiago. I've been his friend for over twenty years. He wouldn't kill me."

"Really? When I showed him the video last night, I'd say with a fair amount of certainty, he's not going to let you live after you killed his beloved tio, the uncle who saved him from his father, at point-blank range." I push the point home. "He knows this isn't the first time you've betrayed him. Tell me, why did you do it? He gave you everything, didn't he?"

A wild laugh rings out. "He gave me nothing," he spits out. "His uncle Marcos started Angel Consultancy, and when Thiago came of age, Marcos gave him the money, out of his own pocket, to buy Angel Consultancy and turn it into SEI. He gave Thiago his company. I begged Thiago to give me a share of the company, but he refused. Said it was only for family. Instead, he offered me a job in security."

He shrugs. "I took it because I thought he'd change his mind. Over the years, I started to resent my role. I'm not the only one, either. Several people who started with SEI when it was formed wanted to buy stock, but Thiago refused to make it public. We worked hard for years and years, and all we made is the salary we earned or the bonuses they gave us. Nothing more. While they got richer and richer.

"It wasn't fair," he roars. "We helped build that company. It was ours."

"What did he say when you asked him?"

"He told me the only way to fairly give everyone shares was to take the company public, which means they would no longer have control of it," he mutters. "If he did that, they wouldn't be able to support their foundation, because the shareholders would insist on profit first."

"I'm sure you know the foundation saves people."

He rolls his eyes.

Switching gears. "Why didn't you leave? Start your own company?" I question him.

He sneers. "I didn't want my own company. A big fish in a tiny pond. I wanted a piece of SEI," he states slowly, as if I'm stupid. "That's okay. Somebody else saw my value. Now I have the money I always wanted, and I got out from Thiago's shadow."

"So, you—"

A man in a suit rushes in, and I'm startled to see it's the same man who was with Diego that night at the safe house. "She sent them a message, and they're headed this way. Kill her and get out. I'll meet you at Carlton's." He glares at me and rushes out.

Diego raises his gun.

I swallow and lift my chin, refusing to cower. "I hope Thiago kills you slowly and painfully like the traitor you are, then feeds your body to the alligators in the Everglades so nobody will ever find you. No grave, no peace. Your family will always wonder if you left them, but they won't be sad. They'll be overjoyed to be rid of such a monster."

With a roar, he snaps. I brace myself for the shot, hoping it will be over fast.

When I hear boots pounding on the concrete, I realize he's not going to shoot me. Jerking me up by my hair, he drags me to the middle of the room, and punches me. My head snaps back. A starburst of pain explodes over my already battered face. He sure does love to use his fists.

What was it I thought when I first met him? Face like a prizefighter? I laugh. He punches me in the side, and I hear something snap. Pain washes over me like a river and I let it take me partially under. He hits me again, but I don't feel this one as much.

Despair clogs my throat as I stare at him. How can he be the last face I see? I can't help thinking about Marcos' video. Maybe that's what he thought too. He wasn't looking at the camera when he died. He was looking at his beloved Juliana, Thiago's mom, and his little savages. The photos he kept taped to the shelves. I close my eyes and picture the three Santos men standing on the dance floor last night, then bring up an old picture of my mom laughing.

A shot rings out echoing loudly in the room. Everything dims.

THANK YOU!

Thank you for reading. I hope you enjoyed this RH tech thriller series. It was a passion project for me and while it may not appeal to everyone, I loved it. My brain needed a break from paranormal and with all the reading I've been doing on the metaverse, AR, and other technology, the idea sparked. I'd love to hear your thoughts. Whether it's "give me more," or "I think this character needs more love," reviews help me write the next story. Please consider leaving one for this book.

Continue with book 2 - Savage Ruin.

*If you find an error, feel free to email me at Stellabrie@stellabrie.com.

>>To get a free eBook copy of my first book, My Salvation, just subscribe to my newsletter.

Website: https://www.stellabrie.com/my-salvation

BRAZILIAN PORTUGUESE

Special thanks to the beautiful and wonderful Vanessa Santos—
from Natal, Brazil—who helped me translate phrases, sent me
musical inspiration, and helped me decide the city where my
characters were originally from. Thank you!
*Phrases you might see in this book and the series along with their
translations.*

Meu anjo – My angel
Meu amigo – My friend
Você é meu - you are mine
Desgraçado - Bastard
Querida – Sweetheart
Foda / Caralho - Fuck
Meus pequenos selvagens – My little savages
Você está linda – You look beautiful
Que porra é essa? - What the fuck?
Olá, Bom Dia - Hello, Good Morning
Meu Deus – My God
Merda - Shit
Obrigado / Obrigada – Thanks
Saúde! – Cheers!

Meu Filho - My Son
Minha Linda - My Beautiful
Filho da Puta - Son of a Bitch
A Morte Não Me Quis - Death didn't want me

276

AWESOME PEOPLE

Huge thanks to everyone who make my books possible!

To my readers, friends, and fans! Thanks for all the wonderful words of encouragement, friendship, and love for my books! And for participating in my shenanigans and all the other weird things I post. You guys rock! I couldn't do it without you!!!

My beta readers, who catch so many big and little things, help me with names, show me such amazing friendship, encouragement, and excitement, even when you can't share it with anyone! I know my books are a thousand times better because of your feedback. Thank you, Nia, Bianca, Iliana, Melissa, Rachel, Sandi, and Debbie for all your feedback on this book!

My ARC team who gives me so much support and enthusiasm even though I drop things on them at the last minute. Ooh, look, cover reveal! Book's launching in a week! Seriously, I appreciate all of you!!

My biggest supporters—my husband and mom. I'm so lucky to have you both! Love you!

And always… a special thanks to all the wonderful authors in the reverse harem community who support each other day in and out. Writing would be a lonely and weird world without you. It would be me and my characters sitting around chatting (drinking) while we plot the next book. Your friendship and support mean a lot to me!

ABOUT THE AUTHOR

Stella Brie lives outside of Nashville, TN, with her husband. After mentioning her desire to write a book a million times to her husband, he challenged her to sit down one day and write a paragraph. Instead, she wrote her first book, *My Salvation*.

She traded in her career in digital marketing, working on big brands, for this wildly creative one. Armed with a notebook crammed full of ideas, she's constantly thinking about bold heroines, sexy men, and HEAs. Whether it's a paranormal book full of creatures and magic or a contemporary romance full of heat and drama, she's always thinking about how she can bring her books to life.

Latest News and Updates:

Facebook Group: Stella's Stalkers

Instagram: @stellabrie_author

TikTok: @stellabrie_author

Website: Stellabrie.com - Exclusive sneak peeks, cover reveals, giveaways, and more!

BOOKS BY STELLA BRIE

PARANORMAL WHY CHOOSE

KILLIAN BLADE SERIES

The Rowan (1)

The Rowan's Stone (2)

The Rowan's Destiny (3)

The Light Falls (4) - Meri's story

The Dark Rises (5) - Meri's story

Spin-offs:

Wicked Savior - Lucifer's story (MF Romance) - Book 3.5

CONTEMPORARY WHY CHOOSE

THE SAVAGES SERIES

Savage Traitor (1)

Savage Ruin (2)

Spin-off:

Lethal Vengeance (Standalone)

My Salvation (Standalone)

To get a free eBook copy of my first book, My Salvation, just subscribe to my newsletter.

Website: https://www.stellabrie.com/my-salvation

www.ingramcontent.com/pod-product-compliance
Lightning Source LLC
Chambersburg PA
CBHW021303190726
48288CB00003B/665